Britta Bolt

Britta Bolt is the pseudonym of the South African-born novelist and travel writer Rodney Bolt, and the German former lawyer Britta Böhler, who has worked on high-profile terrorism and security cases. Their collaboration began in 2010, when Britta Böhler, on holiday and reading her favourite crime fiction, felt the urge to turn her past experiences into a novel. Rodney Bolt was at home, writing biographies and travel stories, and dreaming of doing the same. Soon afterwards, they had teamed up to write a crime series set in their beloved adopted city Amsterdam.

Also by Britta Bolt

Lonely Graves

BRITTA BOLT

Lives Lost

MULHOLLAND
BOOKS
HODDER

First published as *Vastberaden* in the Netherlands in 2014 by De Arbeiderspers

First published in Great Britain in 2015 by Mulholland Books
An imprint of Hodder & Stoughton
An Hachette UK company

First published in paperback in 2016

1

A CIP catalogue record for this title is available from the British Library

Paperback ISBN 978 1 444 78730 6
eBook ISBN 978 1 444 78732 0

Printed and bound by Clays Ltd, St Ives plc

Hodder & Stoughton policy is to use papers that are natural, renewable
and recyclable products and made from wood grown in sustainable
forests. The logging and manufacturing processes are expected to
conform to the environmental regulations of the country of origin.

Hodder & Stoughton Ltd
Carmelite House
50 Victoria Embankment
London EC4Y 0DZ

www.hodder.co.uk

Innocence is lucky if it finds the same protection as guilt.

François de La Rochefoucauld

JULY 2011

I

Pieter Posthumus had never seen so much blood.

'*Jesus*,' said someone behind him. He felt a hand nudge him in the back, pushing him into the room.

'You're used to it.'

'We don't usually see the bodies,' said Posthumus. 'Not like this.'

The night that Zig Zagorodnii was killed had begun quietly enough. June just over. The smell of linden blossom still hanging in heavy pockets in the air, catching you unawares as you rounded a corner. Muggy. It had been unseasonably rainy. Posthumus had cooked something Moroccan, a new direction for him – chicken and orange tagine. Then a glass or two of wine, sitting in his front window, looking out over the canal.

At nine he'd decided to go down to De Dolle Hond. The weather seemed to be holding, or at least it would for the ten minutes the walk would take him. There was always a lull between the after-work and post-dinner crowds, even on a Friday. The café would be quiet. He could sit at the bar and chat with Anna before things got too busy. They hadn't seen each other for a couple of days, had some catching up to do.

The Kesters, from the tobacconist's around the corner were there. (When not? thought Posthumus.) He nodded a greeting as he came through the door. A few other regulars. The English couple who ran the snack bar near the Dam. The woman from the new boutique down the alley, at the fireplace with a friend. Paul de Vos at the bar, saying something that made Anna laugh. Posthumus gave a sour smile. The Fox Trio didn't start till ten. He hoped that little fling of a few weeks back wasn't flickering into life again. What Anna could see in a man whose chief reading was vintage X-Men comics perplexed him.

'Howdy pardner,' said Paul.

His urban cowboy image extended from the tip of his tongue to the toes of his embossed leather boots. Posthumus gave a dry nod and joined them, taking his usual stool, where the bar counter met the wall.

Paul hung on talking until the rest of the trio arrived, then sidled over to set up at the far end of the café. A couple of tourists came in, surprised at finding a place like De Dolle Hond on the edge of the red-light district. They sat silent over their drinks, bright-eyed, the girl taking photos with her phone – the Delft vases, the carved heads along the wainscot, bric-a-brac that was a legacy of three generations of Anna's family. Leaning back against the wall, Posthumus settled into the cosy familiarity of it all. Anna poured him another drink, then went to serve a clutch of newcomers. Irene Kester nodded drowsily, almost in a doze. Paul began with a little riff on the piano, then turned on his stool to announce the first set.

'Hey there, dudes and dudesses, good evening. For those of you who don't know us yet, we are The Fox Trio . . .'

It was then that they heard it. Not so much a scream, as a wail.

'Anna! Anna! *Anna!*'

Seconds later, Marloes from the guest-house next door was outside, banging so hard on the window that she cracked the glass.

★ ★ ★

Posthumus was first out of the café. Marloes stared at him, as if he were a stranger.

'Zig. Zig,' was all she said.

There was blood on her cheek, down one side of her dress.

Posthumus ran. Past Marloes, past the painted-out street windows of the guest-house, and in the door. Straight up to the first floor, where the rooms were. He shot a glance around the small landing. One door open. On the right, at the back. He stepped over to it, and stopped dead in the doorway. A salvo of soles on wood, as others from De Dolle Hond followed him up the narrow stairs.

There was blood everywhere. A dark pool beneath Zig's head, where he lay half-on half-off the bed. A lopsided halo with a sticky sheen. More on the radiator at the back of the room, running down in dried dribbles to the floor. Splashes. Crimson smears on the walls, thinning into pale smudges. Scarlet sock-prints on the lino. Blood drenching Zig's T-shirt, soaked into the bedding. Posthumus reached for his phone. An odd sensation welled through him, a wave of weakenings, of internal stays giving way, as if he had been holding back tears and was about to break down. Someone behind him was gagging. Someone ran back down the stairs.

'He's got to be dead,' a voice was saying. '*Jesus!*'

'Shouldn't we check?'

'Maybe we can do something?' A nudge in his back. 'You're used to it.'

'We don't usually see the bodies,' said Posthumus. 'Not like this. I'll phone an ambulance.'

'I already have, and the police.'

It was Anna. She was standing behind the others, her arm around Marloes, who was making odd, strangled whimpering noises, still staring blankly. The little group crowded on the

5

landing was hushed, and stood looking at the scene framed by the doorway as if it were unreal, on a screen.

'But maybe you should check . . .' Anna went on.

Posthumus nodded to her, paused, then turned and took a step into the room.

'We shouldn't touch anything. Don't they always say that?' came one of the voices from the landing.

Posthumus trod carefully across the lino, avoiding patches of blood. He had no real idea what to do, but if there was still a chance . . . The bed was against the left-hand wall, pushed up into the far corner of the room. Zig lay on his side on the floor, his head on the bed, facing out to the landing. With his marble skin and soft curls he looked like the broken figure of a cherub, crashed to earth from a church ceiling. He'd pulled off the bedding, maybe trying to use it to staunch the blood. Posthumus could not see a wound. It must be on the right side of his face or head, he thought, from the way the blood had pooled on the mattress, run in threadlike lines along its seams. He reached over to place two fingers on Zig's neck. But even before he touched the youth, Posthumus knew – the eyelids half-lowered, the mouth slightly open, jaw slack to one side. The sense of an absence, of something departed. He returned to the landing.

'I think it would be best if everyone went back next door,' he said.

'Come on, you lot,' said Anna. 'Let's do what the man says.'

They needed no encouragement.

Anna exchanged a glance with Posthumus, and said quietly to Marloes, 'Come with us. I'll make you a drink. PP will sort things here. There's nothing we can do. The police are on their way.'

'Police, yes.' Marloes was quieter now – glancing about her, but still not seeming to take everything in. There were tears on her cheeks. Her hair hung loose, grey at the roots. She moved to follow the others down the stairs, heavy, unsteady, hands gripping at the fabric of the baggy, home-sewn dress she wore.

'Zig, Zig, little Ziggy,' she said.

Anna followed her down, touching Posthumus lightly on his forearm as she passed.

Across the landing, the only other resident who seemed to be in remained swaying slightly at her room door. A skinny blonde girl, very stoned, the music in her earphones so loud that Posthumus could hear its sharp tsikka-tsikka from where he stood.

'It's OK, I'll deal with this,' he said.

The girl looked at him with glazed eyes, not a flicker of curiosity. One of Marloes's strange brood. It wasn't a guest-house, really, more of an informal refuge. A shelter for the lost and broken young souls Marloes took under her wing. And God knows there were enough of them around here. Zig had been one, some time back. He'd been a rent boy, Posthumus thought, from eastern Europe somewhere. He wasn't sure exactly.

'Go back inside.' Posthumus mouthed the words exaggeratedly as he spoke, pointing into the bedroom.

The girl shrugged, stepped back and closed the door behind her.

Posthumus heard a police siren, but it stayed distant. He checked his watch. Four, five minutes since Anna phoned? They should be here by now. He stood outside Zig's doorway, facing the landing as if on guard. Who the hell would do something like this? Zig was such a pleasant young guy, hadn't been on the game for years, as far as Posthumus knew – had some sort of bar job somewhere, and helped Marloes out in the guest-house. He was really kind to her, came in to De Dolle Hond with her quite often for a drink. Posthumus shuddered away the feeling that Zig was staring at the back of his neck. He turned and looked again at the young man, crossing his arms tightly over his chest as he did so, as if trying to hold himself together, prevent his own life-force from flowing away so freely.

Zig's room was in complete disarray. Now that was something Posthumus *was* familiar with. Every week, he surveyed apartments of the dead, of the anonymous and abandoned, of the friendless and depressed, of people disowned by their families, sloughed off when they died to the care (and expense) of the city burials department. And far too frequently came the flotsam and jetsam of the underworld, leaving just such scenes of tumult. Posthumus's eyes darted about the room. Bedside table awry, broken reading-lamp, half-open sports bag with a pair of trainers poking out. An easel, knocked off balance against the right-hand wall, paint-tubes scattered on the floor. Posthumus glanced at the painting. A copy of a Vermeer, and not too bad at that. So the lad was an artist of sorts. More Old Masters on the wall – postcards, mini posters, pages torn from art books.

Sirens again. This time clearly converging at the end of the street. Posthumus took a step away from the doorway, with a glance back at Zig. This would probably end up being one for the Funeral Team. The call from the police in a week or two, even if they had traced family, handing his department the responsibility of finding someone to pay for the funeral, or of sorting it themselves. He gave Zig's corpse a sad little smile. Marloes might adore the lad, but Posthumus doubted she'd have five grand to spare. He would make sure the case landed on his desk. The others didn't care. Posthumus alone checked bookshelves, went through music collections, rifled among private letters to build up a picture of his 'clients', to give them a more personal send-off. His colleague Maya called him a macabre snoop.

Blue lights were flashing outside, flicking through the fanlight above the door on to the stairwell. Car doors banging. The doorbell rang. Posthumus went down to let them in, closing the door on the ground floor that led to Marloes's apartment as he passed.

Within minutes, police tape stretched across the road from either side of Marloes's house. Posthumus ducked under it and elbowed his way through the gaggle of gawpers standing on the other side. Anna had closed De Dolle Hond and pulled down the blinds. He tapped on the door. Anna opened it herself, just enough to let him in.

'What's happening back there?' she said. 'I've asked those who went next door to wait around a bit. I thought they should, until the police got here.'

Posthumus slipped inside. People pressed behind him, trying to peer over his shoulder into the café. He pushed the outer door shut, but stayed with his back to it, in the entrance area.

'They've called in forensics,' he said. 'I told the guy in charge we'd be here when they wanted us.'

He did not mention Marloes directly, but glanced around the café, recognising faces that had been on the landing, and a couple of stalwarts who had stayed behind anyway: Irene Kester comforting Marloes at a table near the fireplace, Paul and one of the other musicians from the trio dispensing coffee behind the bar.

'Someone will be over any minute,' he went on. 'Good that you got them to stay.'

'Those tourists left, said they didn't want to get involved,' said Anna, turning to rejoin Marloes. 'They didn't want their weekend messed up, and I couldn't do anything to stop them really.'

Posthumus remembered the young man had been on the landing. 'Can't force them to, I guess,' he said.

He walked up to the bar.

'No, no . . . I need a drink, some wine,' he said, as Paul slid a cup of coffee across the counter.

But he took a biscuit from the plate that had been laid out. It was bizarre, but the sight of Zig had made him feel hungry. Ravenous. For something homey, substantial – *hutspot*, the sort of food from his childhood he almost never ate now. What was *that* about? Some weird sort of affirmation that he was alive? Instinctive preparation to fight, to strike out against whatever was responsible for that broken young body lying next door? Poor, cheery, laid-back little Zig. *Why?* He looked over to the table near the fireplace. Marloes seemed emptied, completely bewildered.

Posthumus picked up his wine, and another biscuit, and after a glance to Anna to see whether he should, went to join them at the table.

'What's for him in Berlin?' Marloes was saying. 'As soon as he's real, he wants Berlin. And now I have to clean. We can't stay long.'

She wasn't making a lot of sense. But then Marloes was a bit of an oddball at the best of times.

'Good, good,' said Marloes, looking up at Posthumus as he came closer. 'He doesn't like coffee. But not wine, beer. Beer.'

'Marloes and Zig were going to come across for a drink together,' Anna explained. 'That's why she went up to his room. When he didn't come down . . .'

Anna noticed Posthumus's glance. There was no longer blood on Marloes's face and hands.

'We helped her clean up a bit,' said Anna to him quietly. 'She was in such a state about having it on her. I think she went in there and cradled him when she saw.'

'Zig, my baby,' said Marloes. She was rocking slightly, backward and forward in her chair. 'We must help him. Are they helping him?'

Anna's face was creased with concern. She looked a little panicked, out of her depth. After nearly three decades behind the bar, she was adroit at dealing with heartbreak and disaster. But with Marloes, she seemed at a loss.

'Marloes,' said Posthumus, sitting down at the table. 'Something terrible has happened. To Zig. You know that, don't you? What you saw . . . Zig is dead.'

'He wants to go to Berlin. To leave. What's in Berlin for a boy like him?'

'Marloes . . .'

Posthumus waited until she made eye contact, then continued.

'Zig is dead, he is not going to Berlin. I know this is difficult for you, and seeing him like that was a terrible shock, but Zig is dead. I am sorry that this has happened to you.'

He realised that he was falling back on phrases from the training course he'd gone on before joining the Funeral Team, and that they were failing him.

'The police are next door, and they will be coming here to ask people questions,' he said. 'They will want you to remember everything you saw.'

'No, not now, I am too tired. So tired. I want to sleep,' said Marloes.

Anna looked across at Posthumus. She had clearly been through all this already. She took Marloes's hand. She must have known Marloes all her life, Posthumus thought. What was Marloes? Mid-fifties? Not that much older than him or Anna, he suspected, though she looked more. And her family had owned the building next door almost as long as the generations of de Vrieses had been at De Dolle Hond. For a moment

Posthumus pictured Marloes and Anna as children, playing together in the street. He wondered whether she had always been so odd. Certainly, as long as he'd known her – a local institution, in her gaudy home-made dresses and beads. Scatty. Her conversation always a bit all over the place. And the guest-house. Taking those people under her wing, like a giant neighbourhood Mother Hen.

Marloes had fallen silent, just sat there shaking her head. Irene Kester patted her on the thigh, with a: 'There, there. He's in a better place now.'

Posthumus sighed.

The others who had been up on the landing sat talking quietly round a table in the front corner of the café. Paul was tidying up behind the bar while his fellow musician packed up on the podium. The old clock on the back wall ticked heavily. There was a rap at the window. Posthumus got up to let in the police.

2

'You *don't* say. They didn't!' Pia Jacobs put down her knife and flopped the thick, glistening wad of steak on to a sheet of waxed paper.

Marty Jacobs turned his back on his mother, and screeched a piece of shinbone through the band saw. 'Gossiping old cows,' he muttered to himself, and again drowned out their voices as blade bit into bone. Irene Kester had been in a full ten minutes, leaning over the counter with news of a gory murder on the Nieuwebrugsteeg, the customers backed up behind her all listening in. On a Saturday morning, too. It was going to be hell later on, with a backlog like this already. Still, he was buggered if he was going to serve anyone, not while he had this to finish. He wiped a puffy, damp palm down the front of his apron. *And* he'd been up since five . . . well, six, a bit late, while his mother came swanning down as usual, well after eight, expecting everything to run like clockwork.

'Can you believe it!' Irene was saying. She pursed her lips in indignation. 'Poor Marloes. A "formal statement" they called it, down to the station right away. Pieter Posthumus, too, because he'd also gone into the room. Fine for him, he's used to that sort of thing, I'm sure, but not Marloes. I was furious. Felt like giving them a piece of my mind, I did, after all I'd been doing to comfort her. She was in such a state, poor thing, not making any sense at all.'

'Never does,' said Pia. 'Completely batty, if you ask me.'

'*And*,' said Irene. She lowered her voice. The other customers craned forward. Even Marty found himself pausing at the machine. '*And*, they took all her clothes. Shoes, the lot. There was blood down the front of her dress.'

'Not that you'd notice it much, those colours she wears,' said Pia, dropping the wrapped steak into a plastic bag.

There was a titter from someone near the door.

'Probably popped the little scally herself,' Pia went on.

Marty gave his mother a sullen stare. Typical of her, he thought. Saw herself as laugh-a-minute.

'Pia, you are *terrible*!' said Irene. 'The poor woman went in and held the boy when she found him. You know what she was like with him.'

'With the lot of them,' said Pia. 'Mad as a hatter. The place should be shut down.'

Marty's fingers closed over the end of the bone like a bloated pink sea anemone. He thumped it on the cutting plate.

'All that bother. I felt quite sick,' said Irene, turning to the shop, for the benefit of a few newcomers. 'And to think it happened in my own back yard! You can see the boy's window from our kitchen. I didn't go up myself, of course, stayed down in the café, but my Albert told me what he'd seen. *Terrible*. Blood *everywhere*. Anyway, Anna from De Dolle Hond had to go round and find something for Marloes to change into. So there I was, on my own, trying to do my best for her, but you know how it is, what can you do? Not a word of help from the policewoman. And for this we pay our taxes! They took Pieter Posthumus's clothes, too. There was blood on his shoes and trouser leg. So they said. You couldn't hardly *see* anything. He was *not* happy, you know what he's like, always so chic. But *he* had a change of clothes upstairs at De Dolle Hond.'

Irene paused for the significance of this to sink in.

Marty cut off the final piece of shin.

'At least the others didn't have to go in last night, for their "formal statement",' said Irene. She gave the phrase a hollow, officious tone. 'But they have to go in today. Albert, too. I mean, what's the use of that? To say the same thing all over again. And what would Albert have seen that the others didn't see? So I'll be in the shop alone on a Saturday. You *know* how I hate that.'

Marty surreptitiously picked his nose, deposited the result behind the edge of his apron, and wiped his fingers on the side of his shirt. He put the tray of shinbones into the counter cabinet, and turned at last to serve. Stupid bitch, he thought, she really doesn't have a clue. Selling kitsch souvenirs and cigarettes in that poky little place on the Zeedijk was about as far as she went.

'All those drunken Brits,' said Irene, taking her steak from Pia. 'I said we should just close for an hour or two, but Albert's having none of it. So, that's me for the morning. Better get a move on!'

She flashed the customers stacked up behind her sweetest, long-suffering smile, and made for the door.

Posthumus swung from the saddle of his heavy black bicycle, flipped down the stand, and was bending over to slide the back wheel-lock into place, when Irene Kester came out of the butcher's. He felt his shoulders slump. This was all he needed. Last night. His precious Saturday morning disrupted. And now to top it all he was about to be cornered by La Kester. He braced himself. Lack of sleep made him testy, and it had been well after two by the time he'd given his statement, helped Anna with Marloes, and got home to bed. Not for the first time that morning, he felt a surge of rage, as an image of Zig's dead body pierced his other thoughts.

'Pieter, Pieter, how are you, my dear?'

For a moment he thought she was about to embrace him, but she didn't wait for an answer.

'Terrible, isn't it?' she said. 'I'm quite done in by it all. To think, it could have been Bert and me murdered. Or Anna. You know how easy it is to get around those yards at the back! And now I've got to be alone in the shop while Albert goes off to give his "formal statement". Honestly, such a to-do. *And* I'm late.'

With that she set off, under full sail, for the Zeedijk.

Posthumus looked in at the butcher's window. The shop was crammed with customers. He thought he might have escaped that, coming by nine thirty, but no. Pia Jacobs gave him a wave from behind the counter. Marty was serving morosely beside her. Posthumus made a circling motion with a raised forefinger, indicating he'd do his other shopping, then come back. But he couldn't face it, especially if Irene had just been in there. She'd have been going on about last night, for sure. He'd have to cook something else for Merel. His chicken and fennel standby, maybe? He scowled. He had planned the menu for dinner with his niece days ago, made his lists. She was so full of some big news she had to tell him. And, what with everything that had happened over the past few weeks, it was important that he saw her. He didn't want to cancel. So, antipasti then fennel chicken? Could work. And at least it would be quick and easy, given the morning that he had ahead of him. He flipped the stand back up and bumped his bicycle off the pavement.

The street was empty, save for a couple of window-girls, each with a big bag slung over her shoulder, one in impossibly high heels. On their way home probably, but who knew – some started this early. A street-sweeping machine chugged towards the far end. There were few other shoppers about.

Jacobs Butcher's stood alone among coffee shops and porn stores, tacky souvenir vendors and cheap fast-food joints, in the heart of the red-light district. It was a part of the life of the quarter that belonged neither to the tourists' rosy view of the place, nor to the hard world of those girls up ahead, but to a smaller milieu, of the people who lived and worked there – a few, like Anna and Marloes, all their lives. For generations, some of them. A handful, now. It was a way of life that had all but disappeared, as shady conglomerates bought up properties, and businesses aimed themselves squarely at the tourist trade. That, or were simply fronts for money laundering. Posthumus thoroughly approved of the city council's recent efforts to inject more variety back into what was one of the oldest parts of town.

He remounted his bike. It had rained heavily during the night. The cobbles and gabled façades in the empty street glistened, saturated, almost unreal. The meat in the butcher's window stood in startling parallel to the flesh of porn mags on display next door. Silence, except for the swish of the street-cleaner brushes, the clip, clip of the window-girl's heels. It was like a Hopper painting, Posthumus thought, or rather a theatre before the audience came in – void, expectant, waiting for the show to begin. He rode off towards the Nieuwmarkt.

Saturday mornings were usually sacrosanct, kept devoid of appointments, taken entirely at his own pace – part gentle routine, part spontaneous. Well, mostly routine, he had to admit, but enjoyably so: relaxed preparation for the week ahead, leisurely food shopping. But there would be no stroll around the Farmers' Market today, only a quick visit for essentials to the Nieuwmarkt, closer to home. Posthumus checked his watch. Just before ten. He had an hour, maybe, then he'd have to be at De Dolle Hond. Anna had taken Marloes back down to the station at eight, for a second go at making a statement. The poor woman had been in no state for anything last night, and the police hadn't been able to get much sense out of her. Anna had promised Marloes that she and Posthumus would help her tidy up, after Marloes had made her statement, and once the crime-scene cleaners they'd called had been in to remove the blood. Marloes had been so distressed about the blood, going on and on about how she had to clean. Posthumus felt another flash of anger against the person who could have done that to Zig. To Marloes.

Anna phoned later than he thought. It was going on for noon by the time he set off for De Dolle Hond. He arrived as Anna and Marloes were walking out of the door, on their way over to the guest-house. Marloes seemed calmer, more together, her hair up in its usual lopsided chignon. Anna was carrying a bag from De Bakkerswinkel.

'I've brought us some *broodjes*,' she said. 'The kind you like. Marloes is going to make us some coffee.'

Marloes came across and took his hand.

'Thank you, Pieter,' she said. 'If you hadn't . . .'

'I meant what I said last night. It must have been a horrible shock for you. I'm really sorry this has happened,' said Posthumus.

'I hardly remember what anyone said last night,' said Marloes. 'Sometimes it seems a hundred years ago, something I saw on TV, and then . . .'

For a moment she looked lost again. Bewildered. Beyond tears.

'I love that boy, *love* him. He always . . . *Why?*'

'Come on,' said Anna. Her voice was very quiet. 'Coffee.'

'We must clean the room. I really ought to clean . . . so much blood.'

'That's been done,' said Anna. 'PP and I will help with the rest. But first, we'd like you to make us some coffee.'

'Yes, coffee, coffee. Of course, then we must start,' said Marloes. She patted vaguely at her hair. 'Let's go inside,' she said. 'I used to sing you know.'

Anna smiled. Now that sounded more familiar. A typical Marloes non sequitur. One of the enigmatic little mind-leaps she made, that so often left people floundering in conversation with her. Anna was used to them.

'Yes. I remember.'

'Every day. Every day. My mother, too. I'll make you some coffee.'

She led the way, past the painted-out windows and in through the guest-house door.

Posthumus glanced up to the room on the first floor, standing behind Marloes as she fumbled with the key to her apartment downstairs. Again, that flash of an image of Zig. And then, uninvited and equally unwelcome, an image of his own brother – bleeding, uncontrollably twitching, mangled with his bicycle on wet tarmac. Not quite as young as Zig, but young. Too young. And, like Zig was now, stuck at that age for ever. Willem hadn't invaded his head quite so much of late. Was that good? A sign that he was finally getting over it, sorting himself out? Meeting Merel again, after all these years, had helped. Maybe he was taking his niece's advice and no longer beating himself up about Willem. About all of it.

Posthumus realised the others had gone in. He was standing alone in the narrow hall. He followed, and took a seat at the kitchen table, as Marloes banged about, making coffee. A pale light filtered in from the street, through the blanked-out glass. Anna looked exhausted. She tore open the Bakkerswinkel bag. Posthumus got up to find some plates. The kitchen was chaotic. Unwashed crockery beside the sink, in the sink. And there was Marloes going on about cleaning the room, seemingly oblivious to the mess downstairs. Gingerly, he selected three plates that seemed clean enough from the drying rack, looked for a cloth to give them a wipe, thought better of it, and carried them back.

Anna improvised a bowl from the torn-open paper bag, and pushed the *broodjes* to the centre of the table. Smoked beef and horseradish on rye, cheese on mustard-bread. Marloes brought over three mugs of coffee on a tray, her chunky necklace clanking against the china. Her dress today was purple, with large red flowers, big and baggy as ever. She wore a thin green cardigan over it, loose, open down the front, and trainers with little white ankle socks.

'I do need to clean,' she said. 'I know I'm bad about it. Mama was always going on at me that I had to clean.'

Posthumus wasn't sure whether she was apologising for the kitchen, or was still stuck on the blood. They each took a bread roll, Posthumus spreading a paper napkin over his plate as he did so. Marloes almost immediately pushed hers away.

'No, I can't.'

'Try something,' said Anna. 'You had nothing at breakfast.'

'He is so good to me,' said Marloes. 'An angel.'

Posthumus wondered whether she had still not taken it on board that Zig was dead, but then it was a common slip, carrying on talking in the present tense.

'He was,' said Anna. 'And *you* were very good to him.'

Marloes turned to her abruptly. 'Oh, they were evil. *Evil.*'

'And if it weren't for you, he would still be mixed up with them,' said Anna. 'Or sent back to Moldova. You gave him back his life. Remember that.'

'They're all my children,' said Marloes. 'But Zig, my little Zig . . .'

Marloes shrank into her chair. There was something of the child about *her*, Posthumus thought, of a timid child – small, submissive, despite her being such a big woman.

'But an angel now,' Marloes went on.

'Is there anyone we should tell?' said Posthumus. 'Any family? Anyone he was close to?'

Marloes shook her head.

That image again. Like a sheet of lightning, but red. Zig's head on the bed.

'Do you have *any* idea—' Posthumus began.

'PP, not now,' said Anna.

Marloes seemed not to be listening. She prodded at her bread roll again, then pushed the plate further away, to the centre of the table.

'Oh, Anna, Anna, I'm so tired.'

'And aren't we all.' Posthumus almost said it, but checked himself. It must be worse for Anna. Marloes had spent the night at De Dolle Hond. That couldn't have been easy.

'Why don't you have a little lie down,' said Anna. 'PP and I can start upstairs. I think that would be best.'

'I should clean.'

'There's no need. You'll feel better after some sleep.'

'I can't. I can't leave it to you.'

'Just a little rest,' said Anna. 'PP and I will make a start, and we'll come and call you when we need help.'

Marloes sat silently for a moment, then rose.

'If you're really sure,' she said.

Anna nodded. Posthumus did not answer.

'Thank you,' said Marloes. 'Pieter, Anna, both. So much.'

She trailed off towards her bedroom at the rear of the apartment.

Anna waited until Marloes had closed the door. Her shoulders slumped. She sighed, and began to clear up the remnants of the *broodjes* and paper bag. Posthumus carried the plates back to the sink, hesitated, then placed them carefully on top of the pile of unwashed dishes.

Then they both went upstairs.

'Don't close the door.'

Anna stepped to one side as Posthumus followed her into Zig's room.

'I'd find it a bit creepy, being shut in here,' she said.

The room was still in disarray. The crime-scene cleaners' visit had been swift and functional. They hadn't tidied up. The bedding and mattress were gone; there were faint smudges on the walls and floor where the blood had been; only the radiator looked completely free of stains. Grey light seeped in from a small skylight and the window above the bed. A sharp, chemical smell gave the air an unpleasant edge.

'What *happened*? I mean, Zig of all people. Who could *do* a thing like that?' said Anna.

Posthumus simply shook his head. Anna leaned back against the doorpost, eyes closed.

'Oh . . . what . . . a . . . night.'

It didn't sound as if she had an ounce of energy left in her.

'You OK?' asked Posthumus.

'Are *you*?' Anna turned to look at him. 'At least I didn't have to come in here.'

'I'm fine,' said Posthumus. He didn't mention the flashbacks, or Willem. Anna had had to listen to enough about Willem over the years. There was a pause. She'd guess, anyway. He didn't need to say anything. Posthumus reached over and brushed one of the more unruly locks of hair off her forehead.

'You don't mind I sent her to bed?' said Anna. 'I thought it would be easier to do this without her.'

'No kidding?' said Posthumus. He leaned a little closer. 'Where *does* she get those dresses?'

'Ssh, PP. Stop it!' Anna's face relaxed, and she gave a conspiratorial giggle. 'She makes them herself.'

'Five minutes a piece, I bet. Fabric from the curtain shop, zzzip up one side, zzzzip down the other, cut a hole for the neck.'

'*PP!*'

Anna pulled herself away from the doorpost. 'C'mon then, we'd better get to it.'

Posthumus glanced back towards the landing. 'Did Marloes say if anybody else is around?' he asked.

'Only a girl called Tina. One of those rooms over there.'

'Yes, I saw her last night. Somehow I don't think she'll be dropping in to help.'

Anna had brought a roll of heavy-duty bin-bags across from De Dolle Hond.

'Where do we start?' she said.

'We can tidy up, first off. I'll check for any papers, and we can pick out whatever looks valuable, or that Marloes might want. Or for family – you never know who might suddenly crawl out of the woodwork. Clothes can go into bags for Humana. Chuck everything else, or at least bin the real rubbish, we can bag other stuff and keep it till after the funeral. Just in case someone does turn up.'

'Mr Professional. And you're sure that's all right? With the police, I mean.'

'They wouldn't have OK'd the cleaners otherwise. Forensics will have removed anything they needed, taken samples all over the place, photographed everything how it was.'

'So that's what the little numbers are all about, that you see on telly?'

'Partly. So they know what sample is from where.'

Posthumus looked briefly about the room, then went to the bedside table, and opened its small drawer. Anna began to straighten up furniture.

'His first name was Stefan, did you know that?' said Posthumus. He was flipping through the small pile of papers he'd taken from the drawer.

'Only ever heard "Zig",' said Anna.

'Brand-new Dutch passport,' Posthumus continued. He held it up. 'All of three weeks old.'

'Marloes sorted that,' said Anna. 'He got his citizenship a couple of months ago. They came in for a drink to celebrate. She sorted his asylum, too, you know, paid for lawyers, all sorts of stuff. Years ago, after she rescued him.'

'Yes . . . what was that "evil, *evil*" all about earlier?'

Anna picked up an upturned box from beneath the easel that had been knocked back against the wall, in Zig's painting corner beneath the skylight, and began to fill it with paint tubes scattered around the floor.

'You know he was a rent boy once?'

Posthumus nodded.

'She got him out of that,' Anna went on. 'There was some horrific background in Moldova, I can't remember now exactly, but he'd been smuggled here by people traffickers, and they had some sort of grip on him, forced him into it. Marloes was really very brave.'

Anna carried the box to a cluttered table near the easel.

'That makes sense of this, then,' said Posthumus. He was holding a sheet of paper that had fallen from the back of a notebook, just the touch of a smile on his lips. 'An odd thing for a lad in his twenties,' he said. '"Last will and testament of Stefan Zagorodnii". It's quite touching, really. "I hereby leave everything I own to Marloes Vermolen, who is my mother, my saviour, my all." Handwritten. He's signed it, no witnesses. Not much legal standing, but nice for her to know he felt like that.'

'Oh, I'm sure she already does,' said Anna.

She was looking at the painting on the easel, a copy of Vermeer's *The Milkmaid*, not quite finished. Posthumus put Zig's passport and the more important documents on the bedside table. He tore off a bin-bag, and dropped the other papers into it.

'This one's for recycling,' he said, holding up the bag, and putting it against the radiator.

'Maybe she'd like this,' said Anna, lifting the painting off the easel.

'We had that up on the wall when I was a kid,' said Posthumus. 'My father loved Vermeer. Even at the very end, Vermeer was one of the few things that got some sort of spark out of him. And could calm him down.'

Anna held the painting at arm's length, and tilted it slightly beneath the skylight.

'I can understand that,' she said.

'It's not badly done, is it?' said Posthumus. 'There's something about it that's not quite right, but yeah, maybe she would like it.'

Anna took the canvas out to the landing.

'No need to play the art critic,' she said. 'She'll like it because Zig did it. Not because there's anything good or bad about it.'

'Of course. I know. Sorry,' said Posthumus. 'Something personal, a nice memento. I didn't even know he painted.'

'Well, he never exactly gave up the day job, but being an artist was his big dream. He wanted to go to Berlin – that's where it's all happening now, apparently – Marloes was really upset.'

She came back into the room, and began clearing the cluttered table near the easel.

'I get to hear it all, behind the bar,' she said. 'Anna of the easy ear.'

'Not that easy,' said Posthumus.

Anna was a good listener, but would cut straight to the core the moment she detected wishful thinking or self-pity. Posthumus walked over to the wardrobe behind the door and started taking out clothes. 'The doyenne of tough love.' It was one of the things he admired about her. He felt lightly through pockets, folding the clothes neatly and putting them in piles on the bed-frame behind him as he finished.

'Oh, PP.'

Anna's voice was shaking. Posthumus leaned back and peered around the door. She was holding a soft toy, an ancient brown dog, rubbed bald in places, spattered with paint.

'Just look at me,' said Anna, wiping her eyes with the back of her free hand. 'Zig's body, Marloes, the police, last night, everything, and I'm fine . . . then I see this and *kerpow*. He must have had it since he was a kid.'

Posthumus walked over and put his arms around her.

'Anna.'

'I'm fine, I'm fine,' said Anna. 'Really.'

She pulled back slightly, patted him on the chest.

'Long time since *you've* seen the waterworks,' she said.

'Look, it's been a long haul for you,' said Posthumus. 'Even more than for me,' he added quickly, before she could object. 'Why don't you call it a day? I can finish this, there's not much to do.'

'Really, I'm OK,' said Anna. She put the stuffed dog back on the table, hesitated a moment, then picked it up and dropped it into a bin-bag. 'See? Tough, no-nonsense Anna after all.'

She frowned slightly, looking over Posthumus's shoulder. He turned. The girl Tina was standing at the door, her skinny body rocking slightly, in time to the thin beat buzzing from her earphones. Not quite as stoned as the night before.

'Zig gone?' she said. She had a high voice, with a touch of a whine.

Posthumus resisted the urge to tear the earphones out of her ears. 'He's dead. Didn't you see last night?' he said.

'So he's gone,' said Tina. She turned, and walked down the stairs to the street door.

Posthumus made as if to call something after her, but Anna touched him lightly on the elbow.

'Where does she *find* them?' he said.

Anna smiled, folded Zig's easel, and propped it sideways against the box she'd put the paint tubes into.

'No, I mean it,' said Posthumus. 'What is it with her? Where do they all come from?'

'All over. Bars around here, people tell her, send them on.'

Posthumus turned back to emptying the wardrobe.

'It's always been like this?' he asked. It had as long as he could remember. He tried to picture Marloes, back when he first knew Anna, when he and Anna were still together. Relationship-together, that was. But he couldn't. For as long as he could recall her, Marloes had simply been the peculiar woman next door. He'd never really taken that much notice of her.

'Her mother ran this as a proper guest-house, but that all stopped when she died,' said Anna.

She walked over to the wall in Zig's painting corner, and began taking down the posters and postcards of Old Masters.

'You don't remember her? Old Mrs V? It was in '86 or '87, I think. You were around.'

Posthumus shrugged, and looked back across the room at Anna.

'Marloes let the place run to seed at first, couldn't really cope,' said Anna. 'Then she started this. All her broken souls.'

She gestured, half out to the landing, half towards the stair-case down which Tina had disappeared. Posthumus slipped the last pile of shirts into a bin-bag, and turned back to the wardrobe.

'But how does she survive?' he said. 'I mean, there can't be any money in it. It must be a real struggle.'

'I guess after all these years she owns the building outright, like I do,' said Anna. 'And I know the kids pay a little for their rooms. Those who can, anyway. And she gets some sort of grant from the council. Got. It was stopped a few months ago, with all the cutbacks. Maybe that's why there're only Tina and Zig here at the moment. *Were* only Tina and Zig. Poor thing.'

Posthumus presumed by that Anna meant Marloes. He closed the wardrobe doors, and pulled open the drawers below.

'Was she always such an oddball?' he asked. 'It's funny, in the middle of everything last night, I was suddenly trying to picture the two of you playing together as kids.'

'And you call Marloes odd?' Anna laughed. 'She was a bit. The big girl next door, but always a bit behind her age. She had a hard time, you know. Her father was at sea a lot. Died very young. Her mother was a complete tyrant, and really mean. I remember grown-ups gossiping about that in the bar. How she dried out coffee grounds, and used them again. That sort of thing. *Über*-thrifty.'

She'd finished with the Old Masters, and slipped the wad into the recycling bag.

'Hence the home-made dresses,' said Posthumus.

'The colours were Marloes's little way of rebellion, I think, and I guess it sort of stuck,' said Anna. 'She was quite put down as a child, you know. Mrs V worked her hard, didn't allow her much time out. She didn't have many friends. Never really hacked it with boyfriends much either, when we grew up.'

Posthumus had pulled a box-file out of one of the drawers below the wardrobe, and was sifting through the contents.

'This must be the lot you were talking about,' he said. 'The ones Marloes rescued Zig from.'

He looked up at Anna.

'Newspaper clippings,' he said. 'About arrests, a trial – 2005, 2006.'

He skimmed headlines.

'Pimps, traffickers, deportations . . . You think this might have something to do with it? Something from the past catching up with him?'

Anna didn't answer.

'I mean, someone could have come back into the country. Or been released from jail. Five years, it's long enough.'

'You're *not* starting all that again,' said Anna. 'PP, come on. No.'

Only weeks before, Posthumus's inability to let things lie had tangled him with a terrorist cell and put his niece in danger. It had begun with just such scratching, at details that bothered him in a case at work, a young Moroccan drowned in a canal.

'Drop it,' said Anna. Her voice was hard. 'You said yourself the police would have taken what they wanted. This has nothing to do with you.'

'Yeah, and the police had it wrong about Amir, didn't they? He was murdered. We proved it.'

'Proved?'

Posthumus was silent. The only real 'proof' was the scenario he had constructed. A few objects lying in his ponder-box at home – alongside bits and pieces from his previous job investigating municipal fraud, mementos of cases that bothered him, which he continued to puzzle over, never quite let go.

'If you're worried about it, give the clippings to the police,' said Anna. 'But *leave it.*'

Posthumus stood a while, then closed the file.

'You're right, you're right,' he said. 'Or maybe Marloes might want to keep these, if she had so much to do with it all.'

Again, Anna didn't answer.

Posthumus went to put the box-file on the landing. But what if Zig's death *was* something to do with this? Did that mean Marloes could be next in line? Posthumus tried to push away the thought. Anna was right. Leave it to the professionals. He went back into the room.

'Sorry,' said Anna. 'Just a bit tetchy. I've had hardly any sleep.'

'No, you're right,' said Posthumus. 'I'll leave it to the police.'

He tried to shake himself free of the image of Zig, now somehow melding with one of Marloes, blood and the colours of her dress mingling. He steadied himself against the door, and looked around the room.

'That's it, pretty much,' he said.

'Just this,' said Anna. She picked up a half-open sports bag, with a pair of trainers poking out of it, upended it and emptied the contents on to the floor: a sweaty knot of gym clothes and underwear, ancient trainers and a mouldy towel. Anna wrinkled her nose.

'Ditch them,' said Posthumus, holding open a bin-bag.

Anna bundled everything in, put the sports bag on the bed-frame alongside the clothes for Humana, and wiped the palms of her hands on her jeans.

'Call it a day?' said Posthumus.

Anna nodded. Posthumus picked up the passport and documents.

'We'd better leave these downstairs,' he said. 'I'll come back early Tuesday to put out the rubbish, and I'll take the clothes to a Humana container then. There's one near me. I'll sort out anything else at the same time.'

'Thanks, I'm completely whacked,' said Anna.

'Can you give Marloes the stuff we've put aside for her? And these,' said Posthumus, handing over the documents.

'I'll go next door and have a nap, then come back,' said Anna.

'We'll have to talk to her about the funeral, too, if no family turns up,' said Posthumus.

He closed Zig's door. There was no key.

'I've a feeling this is going to end up one for us at the department,' he said, 'but if it does I'll make sure I get the case. So we can do something nice. Have Cornelius write a poem. Maybe he even knew him?'

The poet, who Posthumus had recently brought on board to give his funerals a personal touch, was an occasional drinker at De Dolle Hond.

'Perhaps,' said Anna. 'But whatever, that'd be nice for Marloes.'

She adjusted the zipper on the light jumper he was wearing, and brushed a non-existent speck of dust from his shoulder.

'You're a nice guy, PP.'

Posthumus felt he had been forgiven. He led the way back down the narrow stairs.

Downstairs, Marloes's door was closed. A rustling came from behind it.

'Anna? Anna, is that you?'

Posthumus widened his eyes, gave a sharp 'No' shake of his head, and stood stock-still mouthing, 'Not now,' with a pleading look.

Anna sighed, slumped her shoulders, and held out a hand for Zig's passport and documents. But she smiled at

Posthumus, and with her other hand made a shooing motion towards the street door. Silently and quickly, Posthumus slipped out into the street. He closed the door carefully behind him, as Anna let herself in to Marloes's apartment.

3

Out in the street, Posthumus exhaled a long breath, gave his body a shake. Sunlight at last. The sullen grey cover of cloud that had hung low all day was fragmenting, perishing like old rubber and allowing deep blue sky to show through the gaps. He unlocked his bicycle from in front of De Dolle Hond. He needed to get out, to clear his head – to disinfect himself, almost. A cycle though town, along the canals? A museum, maybe? Half an hour or so of looking at something beautiful to wash all this out of him.

Posthumus checked the time. It was well after three, and Merel was coming at seven thirty. The chicken was already marinating, needed only to be cooked. He'd buy the antipasti and dessert. It wasn't like him not to do it all himself, but he really wasn't in the mood. Without thinking, he found himself cycling towards Nieuwmarkt, dodging the tourists wandering gormlessly along the Zeedijk, and the crestfallen old men shuffling out of narrow alleys after encounters with window-girls. Marty, with an impossibly skinny sidekick, clearly finished work for the afternoon and looking very pleased with himself, gave him a wave and disappeared off towards the Damrak. Puccini! For dessert he'd buy chocolates from Puccini. He wasn't that fond of them himself – big, sculpted lumps, with flavours that rather took him aback: tamarind, pepper, poppy seed. But he knew Merel loved them.

Beyond the Nieuwmarkt, the mood changed in an instant. He'd passed through one of those invisible barriers that exist all over Amsterdam – like a glass wall, or as if someone had flicked a switch. What it was that prevented the swill of the red-light district from spilling down the Kloveniersburgwal, Posthumus had no idea, but within seconds of passing the little ice-cream salon on the corner of the Nieuwmarkt, he was back in old Amsterdam, *sans* neon, *sans* titillated throngs. He travelled this route home from work almost every weekday, yet there were still moments when he'd be transported by a detail on a gable, or an elegant façade – the buxom, bare-breasted sphinxes atop the doorway on an impossibly narrow house-front – the houseboats and hump-backed bridges on the Raamgracht, which branched off through a tunnel of trees. He turned into Staalstraat, and cycled over the little white wooden swing-bridge towards Puccini.

It was good to be out, especially with sunshine at last. But something troubled Posthumus. Something to do with Zig's room, and . . . and something else he could not quite place. He flipped down the stand of his bike outside the chocolate-rie, slipped the rear lock shut. He tried to ignore the sensation, a feeling of something gently gnawing at him. This was just what Anna had been warning him about. The first little scratchings of unease that led him who knew where.

Aromas of chocolate warmed the air of the small shop. Posthumus waited patiently while the three customers before him made their choices. If he could only grasp whatever this thought was, then maybe he could take Anna's advice and put an end to it. He tried a few of his memory exercises, in reverse. Visualising Zig's room, placing every element in it and pausing at those that carried some association for him, following associations back, step by step by step. Still, the niggling irritation would not go away. But he was almost there. He could understand where the expression 'that rings a bell' came from. It really was as if a bell were ringing – faintly, on a faraway hill. But persistent. And getting louder.

Posthumus tapped six cellophane-covered boxes of cookies, which had been knocked askew by a careless customer, back into a neat row on the display shelf. The painting. It had to do with Zig's painting. That, and . . . Bingo! He nearly called it out aloud. That distant bell. It was sounding from nearly a year ago, from the first case he'd had to deal with when he joined the Funeral Team.

'Sir?'

He realised the assistant had addressed him twice.

'Oh, I'm sorry. Miles away. A selection, please. Six, make it eight, doesn't matter what, but mainly dark, no white.'

He remembered the case not so much because it was his first, but because of the grisly photo that came with it. Someone who died in a sauna, and had been left there all night. It was quite unnecessary for the team to have the photo, but – he knew now – one of the cops they dealt with got a kick out of sending them the gory ones. Rubbing their soft noses in it. But it wasn't that photo, it was something else. A painting in the young man's apartment. It had struck him as odd at the time, as it didn't fit with the taste of anything else there – a Rembrandt, a copy, but, like Zig's Vermeer, with something not quite right about it. And the young man was – Posthumus was sure he remembered correctly – also from eastern Europe. Another displaced corpse, far from wherever there might have been friends and family, left to the Funeral Team.

By the time Posthumus's chocolates were boxed, he had made a decision. The office was only two minutes' walk away, and he had his key.

* * *

35

Posthumus propped up his bike against the façade of the modest step-gabled building that housed the city council's Department of Emergencies and Internment. Not for the first time since he'd been working there, he was glad that 'Despatches and Disasters', as other municipal workers mockingly called it, led a solitary existence in a canal-house on a forsaken stretch of the Staalkade, and wasn't bundled in with the rest of them under the watchful eye of security guards at City Hall.

Behind him, the voice of a cox bleated as if through a tinny megaphone, as a boat of rowers slipped by on the Amstel. He unlocked the door. A faint trace of Alex's perfume lingered in her realm at Reception. Posthumus took the stairs to the Funeral Team's office on the first floor in easy strides. He caught himself giving a cautionary side glance to Maya's desk – even in her absence expecting some snide remark about time-wasting. Sulung's desk of course a mess, a mound of files and paper. Posthumus went to his own place and switched on the computer. While it was booting up, he checked through the hard-copy files on the shelf across the room. He was sure the name began with V, W, Z, something at the end of the alphabet. Antoni Wojciechowski. No wonder he couldn't remember it.

He flipped open the file. The police photo was on top. Wojciechowski's body: bloated, blackened, blistered, barely recognisable after twelve hours at 110°C. He skimmed his notes. Polish, twenty-six, probable drug-induced hypoventilation and heart failure in the sauna. A few newspaper clippings. There had been a lot of media coverage at the time, Posthumus remembered. A negligent gym worker had locked up for the night without checking, and had left the sauna on. There had been talk of Wojciechowski's criminal connections, too, Posthumus was sure.

He went over to his computer, accessed Wojciechowski's digital file. The photo he wanted would be there, among the others they always took in a client's apartment. To protect themselves, mainly, should any relatives suddenly crop up and start making claims about valuables. Posthumus found the image he'd been looking for. A close-up. He stared at it for a long time. Rembrandt's *The Syndics of the Drapers*. Six soberly dressed men, in severe Protestant black, tall hats, square white collars, gathered around a table, looking outwards at the viewer. But something jarred, clashed with the images Posthumus still carried in his head from long rainy afternoons spent poring over the coffee-table books his father had at home. He made a printout.

A quick visit to the Rijksmuseum. It was just what he felt like, anyway. There wouldn't be much of a queue at this time of day, and he could drop in at that good Italian deli round the corner to buy antipasti. Back on the street, he took out his phone. Anna might already be having a nap, but it was worth a try. It was a brand-new iPhone. He'd finally succumbed to Merel's nagging and given up on his ancient Nokia, though he still didn't quite have the hang of how the smartphone worked. Laboriously, he sent a text.

Awake?

The answer came back immediately:

Why?

And before he could compose his reply, another message:

Still with Marloes.

Posthumus steeled himself. Anna wasn't going to like this, but it was worth a try.

Can you send me photo of Zig's painting?

Again, a reply within seconds:

?????

No go. Posthumus did not reply, but he'd scarcely reached the bridge across the river when his phone chimed the arrival of a text. The photo. And a message.

What for? I really hope u not up 2 anything.

He gave a slight grimace, and cycled on to the Rijks.

The struggling sunshine had already brought people out to the terrace tables around the café on Museumplein. Children clambered all over the giant letters of the **I am**sterdam logo beside the pond on the square. As Posthumus had thought, there was no ticket queue this late in the afternoon. It infuriated him that one of the leading art collections in the world remained largely under wraps, while the Rijksmuseum limped through an interminable renovation, way over budget, years behind schedule. But it did mean, at times like this, when the museum wasn't too busy, that the 'greatest hits' selection, spread through the handful of rooms that remained open, took on an intimacy that the old building never had.

Posthumus lingered momentarily over a few favourites. Frans Hals's wickedly happy wedding portrait of Isaac Massa and Beatrix van der Laen, Johannes Verspronck's wistful *Girl in Blue*, in her shiny dress and delicate lace. But he hurried on to *The Syndics of the Drapers*. He took out the printout he'd made at the office, compared it to the original, like one of those spot-the-difference puzzles he had done as a child. Then to the Vermeer, surreptitiously checking the image on his phone, one eye on the guard. So *that* was it. Odd. How very odd. But *why?*

Posthumus was still frowning when, well after five o'clock, he walked in to the Italian deli to buy what was left of their antipasti.

Merel was brimming with her news. Posthumus had barely popped the cork from the prosecco, when she took out a letter.

'Just take a look at this!'

The letter was typed, over a page long. Posthumus turned the first leaf to see who it was from.

'Who is Lisette Lammers?' he asked.

'Read it.'

Twenty minutes later, Merel had hardly touched the antipasti, and was still talking excitedly. Posthumus leaned back in his chair, and grinned at his niece.

'Didn't I tell you that you'd get your big story one day?' he said.

And this story would be big: an exposé of a rogue secret service official, planting an *agent provocateur* among suspected terrorists. The arrest of the 'Amsterdam Cell' two weeks earlier had been top news.

'But you're absolutely sure it's true?' he went on. 'That this Lisette Lammers is for real?'

Posthumus felt a protectiveness over his niece kicking in. Already, he thought, he had put Merel in danger, when he had unwittingly entangled them both with the cell by asking too many questions after the case of Amir Loukili – then just an anonymous corpse, drowned in a canal – landed on his desk at work.

'I've spoken to her,' said Merel. 'She's for real all right.'

'Couldn't she have done this through the internet? Social media or something?' said Posthumus. 'Or one of the big networks? Look, I don't want to rain on your parade, but, I mean, why *you*?'

'Those Amsterdam Cell pieces I wrote? Apparently, the security service had their eye on me, too, for a while. Believe me, she knows stuff about me that few other people could. And I got the feeling that she'd actually *targeted* me, you know, picked me on purpose to write the letter to because she thought that would be the most effective way to do it. And, maybe . . . maybe because she also thought I might be in touch with Aissa and could, you know, apologise?'

'Be careful, Meertje, it could be a hoax. I mean, you had some sort of insider tip-off for that first story, right? You're not going to be flavour of the month on either side, Cell or spooks. Someone could be setting you up. From either side.'

'Hey! Mr Negativity! I'm good at my job. I spent the whole of last week background-checking. I've spoken to Lisette twice on the phone, and we're meeting on Monday. It's all there. She was in on what was happening, but against the idea all the time, and she's resigned from the service. My very own whistleblower! I'll break the story next week.'

'It'll probably blow the Amsterdam Cell case out of court.'

'And Lisette will most probably be arrested. But she's OK about that. She's going public, I can quote my source. I wouldn't have shown you the letter otherwise.'

'And you're all right about that, about members of the cell maybe going free again? Your source risking arrest?'

'Such underhand – *criminal* – ways of operating *cannot* be allowed to go on.'

'Even for the greater good?'

'Absolutely not!'

'And if a week after they were released there was a bomb, and people were killed? Children? How would you feel then?' Posthumus asked.

'And if some other group were incited to violence, because they thought they had a mole in their midst, and were living in a society that did not do something about that, how would *you* feel?' asked Merel. 'It's the same with torture, Guantanamo Bay. Lisette is right, we have to uphold the standards we are supposed to be fighting for, otherwise we have lost.'

'No grey areas?'

'No compromise on that.'

There was a moment's silence. Then Posthumus laughed.

'God, you remind me of your father when you're like this,' he said.

'Like what?'

'Enthused, flinty, idealistic. Beneath that angelic blonde exterior, a streak of steel.'

Reminded him so strongly that it hurt. Merel got up to help clear the antipasti dishes, and gave Posthumus a hug around the neck.

'Well, this won't be the only good that has come of the past few weeks,' she said. 'Who'd have thought that I would not only get back together with my long-lost, much-maligned, evil uncle, but that I would *like* him so much.'

Posthumus was silent.

'*And*,' Merel went on, putting a pile of plates near the dishwasher, 'this story will probably save me my job. And . . . who knows, maybe Aissa will even answer my calls.'

Posthumus looked across the kitchen at Merel, as he carried the casserole dish to the dining table. Her voice had grown softer.

'You haven't heard from Aissa, then?' he said.

'Only a text right at the beginning to say that Najib was missing, and the police were looking for him. I mean, would *you* reply to somebody you thought was somehow to blame for your brother's disappearance?'

'She can't think that.'

'And Khaled?' Merel went on. 'I'm sure she blames me for that, too. And you think she can just carry on being friendly with me as if nothing had happened? *Not.*'

'You'll sort it out, she'll be back in touch.'

'You think? I hope so. I rated her.'

Merel came back to the table and sat down.

'PP, that smells *delicious*!' she said.

Posthumus had lifted the lid on the chicken casserole, releasing aromas of aniseed and thyme. He was glad he'd added that dash of pastis to the marinade. He let the subject of Aissa drop. Merel was quiet as he dished up.

'So, tell me, just how *is* this long-lost, much-maligned, evil uncle of mine,' said Merel, after a while. 'Beginning to sort himself out?'

Posthumus opened another bottle. He told Merel about Zig. About the flashbacks. How Willem was getting mixed up in them. About his dream the night before: Zig, the cherub crashed to the floor; Willem, the broken angel twitching on tarmac. And guilt. And yes, he was at last trying to stop beating himself up about it all, but, no, after twenty years, it wasn't suddenly going to go away. It was a sombre meal, after the first burst of excitement at Merel's news.

★   ★   ★

'Come on,' said Posthumus, after they had finished. 'Let's go and sit at the front. There's no pudding, but I've got chocolates from Puccini.'

'Perfect!'

Merel moved over to the sofa, Posthumus fetched the chocolates, and came back also carrying a couple of pieces of paper and his new phone.

'I've got something interesting to show you,' he said, sitting beside her. 'Look – Zig was painting this when he was killed.'

Posthumus handed Merel his phone, the image of Vermeer's *The Milkmaid* enlarged on the screen.

'And this is the original.'

He gave her a postcard he'd bought at the museum.

'And this is a painting that was hanging on the wall in the apartment of my first ever case . . . and the original.'

He handed Merel another postcard, and the printout he had made at the office.

'What do you make of them?' he asked.

Merel seemed puzzled.

'Look closely,' said Posthumus. 'See, in the Vermeer the woman is actually pouring the milk. In Zig's painting, the bowl on the table is full, and she's tilted the jug back up again. In the original Rembrandt, the book that they're all gathered around on the table is open, and there's one person half rising from his chair. In this painting, the book is closed, and two of them are getting up. And the guy at the back has his hat on. He's the only one who doesn't in the original.'

Merel laughed. 'Two minutes later!' she said.

'What do you mean?'

'It's the original scene, a few minutes later. Or here, even seconds. There was something like this at Schiphol once. In the Arrivals hall. But it was with *The Night Watch – The Night Watch, Two Minutes Later*, it was called. Everyone doing something else, the whole composition still there, but also disrupted. Such a clever idea! I loved it.'

'When was that?'

'Oh, quite a while ago. 2005, it would have been. I was still on the foreign desk in Rotterdam, travelling a lot.'

'That couldn't have been Zig's though.'

'Well, no, but maybe he liked it. It was there a long time. Months. All over the papers, too, you don't remember it? Maybe Zig was inspired by it. Did both of these.'

'That's what I had been thinking,' said Posthumus. 'And this other guy was also from eastern Europe. And died horribly. And was possibly involved in the underworld. I'm sure there was something at the time about him being a *loverboy*, you know, luring young girls into prostitution, but I'd have to check up.'

'PP, PP, PP,' said Merel. 'I can see where you're going. Not again. Not after last time. Take it to the police, if you have any suspicions.'

'That's pretty much what Anna said, though she put it more forcefully.'

'Well, do it.'

Posthumus took back his phone, the postcards.

'Promise?' said Merel.

Posthumus nodded.

Merel stayed on till after eleven. When she had gone, Posthumus tidied up, poured himself a glass of wine, then fetched a black, cloth-covered box from the work-corner behind the spiral staircase that led up to his bedroom. His ponder-box. He picked up the printout, and the postcards from the Rijksmuseum, walked to the front of the long apartment, and dropped a cushion on the floor in the opening of the tall window, once the door through which goods were hoisted from the canal three floors below. Centuries ago, this had been a warehouse. Sometimes, Posthumus fancied, he could still smell scents of spices impregnated in the doorposts and beams. He sat down on the cushion, lifted the lid off the box.

On top of the curious collection of mementos of cases from his old job, ones that had bothered him, were the objects that had first set him puzzling on the Funeral Team. Started him wondering about Amir drowned in a canal, about Bart Hooft dead in his attic room – the photo of a tattoo, of a Namiki pen, of Amir himself. Of Khaled. Posthumus picked up that one. So Khaled had been a mole, stirring things up. And maybe the scenario Posthumus had come up with was right. He cradled the photo in his palm for a long while, deep in thought, then slowly replaced it in the box.

And Zig? These two paintings? The body in the sauna? He reached for the printout and postcards, held them for a moment, his hand hovering over the open box. Then, moving swiftly, he took his hand away, closed the box, and stood up, still holding the images.

Anna and Merel were right. Enough was enough. He would go to the police in the morning.

4

Detective Inspector Flip de Boer walked out of Central Station, negotiated the chaos of criss-crossing trams and pedestrians, and worked his way through the remains of Stationsplein, still a war zone of a building site for the new metro line, after eight hopeless years. Under his denim jacket a green polo shirt fitted flatteringly over tight pecs and biceps. He was in good shape. Quite good shape. De Boer was aware that his belly was beginning to push a little at the waistband of his jeans. He'd had to let his belt out a notch a few weeks ago, for the first time since he was a teenager. But jogging and a few extra visits to the gym would soon see to that. He might be in a job usually filled by an older man, but he wasn't going to look like one. Wasn't going to fill it like one. De Boer gave half a laugh at his own joke, and waited for the light to change to walk over to the Damrak.

Fast-food wrappers lay strewn about the pavement, abandoned bottles crowded the bases of overflowing litterbins. The dumpings of another Saturday night, of the hordes that swooped down on the Damrak for eateries that held out long after everywhere else was closed. De Boer walked on towards the Beurs, past the hoardings of tour-boat companies, queues already forming for the first trips of the day. He'd been hoping to spend Sunday with the kids. Till the call from the Bureau. An unexpected development. He turned left at the end of the small harbour, on to a scrappy stretch of street that ran behind the Beurs and disappeared into De Wallen. De Boer was from out of town, but he'd learned to use the Amsterdammers' term for the red-light district. It looked to him somehow even sleazier when deserted, in the unforgiving light of a Sunday morning, than it did at night. So, the city council wanted to clean things up? Buy properties back from dodgy syndicates, put art and pretty dresses in the windows instead of prostitutes, convince restaurant owners to sell proper food instead of pizzas and chips-with-everything. Nice try, but fat chance.

De Boer stopped to light a cigarette. Steak and pizzas made money, paid the rent. He couldn't blame them for not wanting to change. Those who wanted their business to make money, that was, not launder it. Now *that* was the real problem. The big boys behind it all. De Boer inhaled deeply and turned into the narrow street that ran down the side of the old stock exchange, towards the Beursstraat Bureau. De Boer rather liked the fact that his first days heading his first investigation team were going to be at the bureau where he'd first been on the beat. The team was based here for a few days, while proper space was being sorted at the IJ Tunnel office. But he had to admit to a twinge of nerves. He really wanted to get this right.

De Boer walked on down the alley to the Bureau, his mind moving over the scene in the guest-house room like a video playback. Stop. Rewind. Change angle, zoom in. Bruising. So probably a fight. Severed temporal artery. De Boer didn't need forensics to tell him that – the gash on the side of the head, all that blood. On the sharp corner of the radiator, he'd bet his last cent – but for that they would have to wait for pathology and the full report. He took another drag on his cigarette. A fight in the room? Accidental, or a deliberate attack? Motive? De Boer knew the sort who ended up in that guest-house. The lad didn't have form, but he did have a past.

Some sort of retribution, maybe? An old score settled? De Boer paused outside the door, took a few final draws. And now this new information. A link to a past case, Bas had said on the phone, and a new witness. He stubbed out the remains of his cigarette, and went inside.

'Morning, Flip.'

'Bas. This had better be good, ten o'clock on a Sunday morning.'

'Wait till you hear. This'll make your day.'

De Boer was glad that he'd been able to get Bas on the team. They went back a long way, the two of them, had joined the force at the same time – Bas always just a step or two behind in the promotion stakes, but a good ally, even when rivalry stirred the waters a bit. The two men walked to the room that the Beursstraat Bureau had made available to them. Three more of de Boer's team were there, sitting at a conference table. He nodded greetings all round.

'What's up?' he asked.

'First this,' said Bas. He handed de Boer a signed formal statement. 'Scraggy bloke comes in late yesterday afternoon, after you'd left. Jelle Smits. Looked like a junkie to me. Says he was visiting Tina, the other resident at the guest-house, on Friday evening. The nature of the visit we can leave to your imagination. Says he saw who did it.'

De Boer skimmed the statement, and raised his eyebrows.

'"Heard shouting and thumping,"' he read aloud, '"few minutes later when I left Tina . . . saw running from Zig's room . . . down the stairs and out into the street."'

De Boer looked up from the statement and across at Bas.

'And we're to believe this?' he said. 'A credible witness?'

Bas shrugged.

'And he didn't hang around, this Smits?' asked de Boer.

'Didn't look the sort who'd like to meet with the police,' said Bas.

He indicated to de Boer to turn the page.

'Says he didn't think anything of it at the time, had things to do, so left. Then when he heard people talking about a murder, thought he'd better come in,' said Bas.

De Boer gave his colleague a sceptical glance. 'A sudden twinge of public spiritedness?' he said.

'Or he sees *more* up there,' said Bas, 'beats it at the time, because he doesn't want to be involved, then the next day worries that he might have been seen, and be implicated after all. So thinks it best to overcome his allergy, pay us a visit and have a little chat.'

De Boer slid the statement across the table. 'Check it out,' he said to one of the junior officers. 'See if there's anything in it. And I want to talk to that Tina girl again. Did she mention anything about a visitor?'

'Nope,' said the officer, 'but she was so out of it, she hardly seemed to know she was there herself.'

De Boer turned again to Bas. 'This worth a Sunday call-out?' he said.

'There's more,' said Bas. 'Eight o'clock this morning, Pieter Posthumus comes in.'

'The witness, Posthumus?'

'The same. He's with the city council, works at Emergencies and Internment. Some of the boys here have dealt with him before.'

'Bit of a meddler,' chipped in a young officer who was on secondment from Beursstraat. 'So at first no one takes him seriously – he's going on about paintings, flashing postcards around.'

'But in the end it turns out he's found some sort of link with an old case,' Bas resumed.

He tapped a key on the laptop in front of him, and two photos appeared on a screen at the end of the room. A mug-shot of a twenty-something man, and a blackened, bloated corpse.

'Antoni Wojciechowski,' Bas went on. He'd clearly been practising the name. 'Known as Tony. August 2010. Found dead in a sauna at the FitFast gym, in there all night. He'd died of respiratory failure and a heart attack. Was one of the last customers of the day, no one bothered to look.'

'And *that* happened in what, ten, twelve hours?' said de Boer.

He grimaced and indicated the blackened corpse with his chin. He noticed the young Beursstraat officer was grinning.

'Sauna was on all the time,' said Bas. 'At first, a gym employee was suspected of negligence, but there were suspicious circumstances. The timer had been tampered with. Wojciechowski had ingested large amounts of cocaine, traces were found in the bottle he used to mix a protein drink. He was a *loverboy* – well, brought in for questioning late 2005, procuring minors, but it never got to court. Mid-2006, he testified *against* one László Kiss. Good name for the job. Similar sort of thing – trafficking, procuring. That one did go to court. Kiss was convicted, got five years, was released a week before Wojciechowski's death. He was seen in a café with Wojciechowski two hours before Wojciechowski went to the gym, on the night he died. Kiss was arrested, but there was insufficient evidence. No prints on either the timer or the bottle, and he had an alibi for the rest of the evening. The gym attendant claimed he was there, but there were no other witnesses, no CCTV, and the attendant was possibly trying to cover his own back. So Kiss remains prime suspect. But take a look at this.'

Bas ran the cursor down the screen, clicked twice.

'Fellow witness against Kiss,' he said, with the flourish of a head waiter at a ritzy restaurant lifting a silver cloche off the food, 'one Stefan Zagorodnii.'

'And this Posthumus came up with all that?' said de Boer.

'No, no, he put us on to the case,' said Bas. 'Some sort of link between the painting that was in the victim's room, and one on Wojciechowski's wall. That's what the postcards were all about.'

'And Posthumus remembers that after nearly a year?'

'He's that sort of bloke,' said the Beursstraat officer. He pursed his lips, and with a thumb and two fingers imitated a chicken pecking little bits of grain off the ground. 'Does memory games, too.'

De Boer moved to the laptop, and began navigating through Wojciechowski's file.

'And where's Kiss now?' he asked.

'That's the bad news,' said Bas. 'Best alibi of all, apart from being dead himself. Currently in police custody. Has been since last Wednesday. Charges of procuring, again.'

'That's very convenient,' said de Boer. 'For him.' He frowned. 'Or maybe he's not alone in this,' he said, and began scrolling through notes on Wojciechowski's movements, and statements of witnesses who had fallen from the main focus as the investigation closed in on László Kiss.

De Boer's finger stopped dead on the touchpad. He scrolled back a little.

'Or perhaps,' he said, 'we've been barking up the wrong tree completely.'

He double-clicked. A typescript flashed up on the large screen across the room.

'Take a look at that,' he said. 'At where Wojciechowski was on the afternoon before he died. Twice. And who he was having a bit of aggro with.'

'Don't forget to pick up my ciggies!'

Pia Jacobs's voice echoed down the stairwell.

'You can smoke yourself to fucking death. Do me a favour,' muttered Marty, as he opened the street door. It was drizzling. He rubbed at his eyes, still grainy from a Sunday morning sleep-in, smelled his fingers, and let the door slam behind him, not bothering to answer. Marty glowered at the empty butcher's window as he passed. She just wouldn't let go, would she. Thought the whole lot would hit the rocks without her. Wouldn't let him near the orders, wouldn't let him do the books, wouldn't even let him cash up. He was thirty-two for Chrissakes! His father had been the same. Blanked him out, no talk of him ever taking over.

Marty glanced back up at the apartment. Streaks of rain scudded off his cheap leather jacket. He'd show her, oh yes, he'd show her, with her lizard-skin tan, and her girly pink, and her hair, and fake leopard skin, and her voice. Fetching cigarettes on a Sunday was all he was good for, was it? Cleaning the butcher's floor? She had a big surprise coming to her one day. They all did. Marty smiled as he padded round the corner on to Warmoesstraat. The backpacker café up the other end served full English breakfast till one o'clock. He might just make it in time. He liked a good English breakfast, as comfort food when things were going badly . . . or as a quiet private celebration when something had gone especially well.

By three o'clock, Marty was on his fourth coffee, and feeling drowsy. Too much caffeine had a reverse effect with him. That and a double breakfast. The rain had stopped. The Kester cow would have closed up the tobacconist's by now, he thought. But no matter, he knew where to find her. She'd have taken his mother's weekly carton along with her, and where else would she be on a Sunday afternoon?

* * *

Posthumus picked up the apple tart on his way over to De Dolle Hond. Anna usually did that herself in the morning, but she'd been with Marloes. Posthumus enjoyed Sunday afternoons at De Dolle Hond – the familiar faces, the apple tart, the good coffee Anna put in the machine especially for the regulars. The café became her parlour for a few hours. And today, of all days, he was looking forward to its comforting cosiness. It had been quite a weekend.

Carrying the large cake-box with both hands, Posthumus swung round and pushed the café door open with his back. He heard a musical chime and a clatter, as the fruit machine paid out a win, and he smiled. Mrs Ting was at her post as usual, incorrigible, playing the thing till her hands were black, never saying a word. Posthumus turned, and let the door swing shut behind him.

Simon, the casual who helped out on weekday mornings, was at the bar. Talking to Paul. The musician was becoming too much of a fixture, thought Posthumus, hanging around Anna all the time. The trio didn't even play on Sundays. He barely disguised his sour glance.

'Anna still next door?' he asked Simon, as he put the tart down on the counter.

'Should be back any minute,' said the young barman, looking up at the wall clock. 'Least, I hope so. I've got a match soon.'

'A coffee for me, please, when you've unpacked this,' said Posthumus. 'And do me a slice with cream, while you're about it.'

He noticed Marty come in, and go across to the Kesters.

'Young Simon here has been telling us that the efforts to clean up De Wallen are all a mistake,' said Paul.

Posthumus saw that the 'us' was the woman from the new boutique down the alley, Marie her name was, if he remembered rightly, sitting alongside Paul at the bar. He nodded to them both.

'I was just saying that it's been a red-light district for five hundred years,' said Simon, giving Posthumus his coffee. 'It's part of what Amsterdam is about, of the spirit of the place.'

'Ah, but it wasn't *solely* a red-light district,' said Posthumus. 'I mean, these days the coffee shops, the windows, fast-food restaurants, tacky bars, head shops, the whole caboodle that goes with it all – they've taken over everywhere. We need to get some variety back.'

He felt a little guilty about his curt behaviour earlier.

'That's why the council's encouraging people like Marie,' he added.

She smiled at him. Well, at least he'd got the name right.

'It's not just that,' said Marie. 'They think a lot of the businesses are simply fronts for organised crime.'

'And *we* get tarred with the same brush! "Potentially criminogenic business", just because we sell a few souvenirs. Souvenir shops a criminal danger! It's scandalous!'

It was Irene Kester, sailing by on her way to the Ladies.

Simon dumped the cake-box under the counter, and gave the cream-siphon a shake.

'I hardly think they mean you,' said Posthumus to Irene. 'It's more exchange bureaux, mini-supermarkets, restaurants that are always half-empty and mysteriously go on for years, that sort of thing.'

'They said souvenir shops,' said Irene.

'And fast-food places.'

It was John, the Englishman who ran a snack bar near the Dam.

'You too?' said Irene. 'We had them in the other day, asking all sorts of questions. Us! I gave them a piece of my mind, I can tell you.'

She turned to Simon, who was handing Posthumus his apple tart.

'Marty over there is having a beer.'

Posthumus looked over to the Kesters' table, where Marty was showing every sign of wanting to leave.

'No you don't, young man!' Irene called over to him. 'Sit down. You and I are going to have a talk.'

She turned back to the bar.

'"Criminogenic", indeed,' she said, and disappeared through the door to the Ladies.

Simon rolled his eyes. 'Donna Kester-Corleone,' he said, pouring Marty a beer.

'It's no joke,' said Paul. 'The council's right. There're a lot of evil bastards about, especially where the window-girls come into it, and the tourists just trail through, going, "Ooo, isn't it naughty, isn't it nice?"'

'But at least the girls are safe,' said Simon. 'It's better than being on the street.'

'Bullshit.'

'Don't you think that's a bit of a rosy view of things?' Posthumus asked Simon.

He moved closer to the wall, to make room for Marty, who had come up to collect his beer.

'From what I understand, they're all under the thumb of pimps, and landlords who demand exorbitant rents for the rooms,' Posthumus went on.

'And some crisps,' said Marty, when he saw the beer was going on to the Kesters' tab.

Simon obliged.

'My point was,' he said, 'that Amsterdam's always been a gritty sort of place, attracting gritty sorts of people. That's its *strength*. What they're trying to do in De Wallen is part of a wider move, trying to sterilise the city, make it all nice and neat and clean.'

'Dude, you're clueless,' said Paul.

He took advantage of the CD coming to an end to walk over to the podium, and start improvising half-heartedly on the piano, leaving Marie to Posthumus at the bar. Marty noticed Irene re-emerge from the Ladies, and turned to go back to the table.

There was a sudden crash, a commotion of voices. Posthumus spun round. It was Anna. She'd flung open the café door, and was striding towards him.

'*You!*' she said.

Posthumus had never seen her look at him in the way she did.

'*You!*' she said again. 'They've arrested Marloes. *Marloes!*'

Posthumus looked over Anna's shoulder, out through the café window. There were two police cars in the street. Anna walked right up to him. She was standing very close, her voice almost a whisper.

'And they took Zig's painting. This is something to do with you, Pieter Posthumus. I *know* that this is something to do with you.'

FEBRUARY 2012

5

On the first day of Marloes Vermolen's trial, ice gripped Amsterdam, thrusting stiff fingers through the canals. That night, Tom and Tinneke, who presented their *Crimebusters* TV programme with relentless relish, as if it were a game show, appeared wearing earmuffs, and couldn't resist mention of the topic that was on everybody's lips: whether waterways up north would freeze solid enough for skaters to reach all eleven cities of the *Elfstedentocht*.

Then, in perfect synch, Tom and Tinneke removed the fluffy headwear and threw it off camera, as the orange and pink studio backdrop transformed into an image of the guesthouse on Nieuwebrugsteeg, with superimposed flashes of lightning, and rivulets of blood dripping from the windows. The words 'The Witch of De Wallen' were emblazoned across the screen like a horror-movie title.

'Do we have to watch this crap?' said Posthumus, leaning hard back against the wall in his favourite spot at De Dolle Hond.

Simon was behind the bar. Anna had been at court all day, and still wasn't back. Simon gave a nod towards the other customers, all glued to the television set that he and Paul had dug up from somewhere.

'Cause a riot if I turned it off now,' he said. 'Irene's on in a minute, or so she says. She's been sounding off about her three minutes of fame for weeks.'

Irene Kester sat pink-faced, four-square in her usual chair, feet planted apart. Posthumus could swear that she had dressed for the occasion. *She* had changed her tune since trying to comfort Marloes with platitudes on the night of Zig's death, he thought.

'And if it's what the customers want . . .' said Paul, up the other end of the bar.

Posthumus looked around the café. Everybody sat, necks crooked, looking at the television, except for Mrs Ting, at her usual post at the fruit machine.

Posthumus turned away. But the duo on screen were strident. Insistent.

'Not just one murder, but *two*,' said Tom.

'Both attractive young men in their twenties,' said Tinneke. 'Did they fall foul of this lonely, middle-aged, *single* woman?'

'Who filled her house with misfits and lowlife,' said Tom.

'Most of them young,' said Tinneke.

'Nearly all of them male,' said Tom.

'Were these the only victims, or are there more?' said Tinneke.

'That's blatant nonsense,' said Posthumus to the café in general, but no one appeared to hear him.

A new face flashed on to the screen, billed as a 'neighbour'. A witness, apparently.

'Such comings and goings from that place!' said the face. 'All times of day and night. Weirdoes. And her, always some young man in tow. I don't want to think about what went on in there.'

'Who the hell is *she*?' said Posthumus. 'I've never seen her before.'

Again, nobody answered. John, the Englishman from the snack bar, had come up to order a drink.

'Cold enough for you out there?' he asked. 'You're not going to be gracing our screens with an appearance, then?'

Posthumus scowled.

'I'm surprised you're not in court,' said John. 'Aren't you going to have to give evidence or anything?'

'It works differently here,' said Posthumus.

'But there's got to be witnesses and defence and stuff?'

'That's already happened. These past few months, before a *rechter-commissaris*, an examining magistrate I think you'd call him.'

John was trying to catch Simon's attention, but Simon was riveted to the screen.

'These few days in court are to summarise everything – the evidence, forensic findings, that sort of thing – and to reach a decision,' Posthumus went on.

'And that's it?'

'They might call witnesses again, but it would be exceptional,' said Posthumus. 'And Marloes will be able to give a statement.'

'But no theatricals? No dramatic cross-examination, no moving speeches to the jury?'

Posthumus shook his head. 'No jury, even,' he said. 'Just the judges.'

'No wonder you lot need Tom and Tinneke to perk things up.'

They both glanced involuntarily at the screen.

'It's no joke,' said Posthumus. 'Not for Marloes. She's barely coping with things as it is, Anna says.'

The neighbour was on again. Talking about the evidence she had given to the *rechter-commissaris*.

'Sitting right next to me, she was, I could hear every word. Going on at the poor boy because he wanted to go and live in Berlin. She was having none of it! Quite a row it was.'

'They're allowed to say that sort of thing on TV, even if they're a witness?' asked John.

Posthumus nodded. 'Do *you* know who she is?' he asked John, with a toss of his head towards the screen.

'Not me,' said John. 'Someone said she's something to do with where Zig worked. The bar. She was on earlier, on the news.'

'And she's a *neighbour*?' said Posthumus. 'I've never seen her.'

'Down past the guest-house, on the corner, according to Irene. Top floor. Probably a curtain twitcher.'

'And it was the same with the other one,' the good neighbour was saying on screen. 'The sauna one. Threw him out of the house. Yelling at him in the street. I *told* the police at the time, when they showed me the photo, but they didn't do nothing.'

The sauna. Posthumus tapped a cardboard coaster so that the lettering on it ran parallel to the edge of the bar counter. From what had emerged over the past few months it was clear that the unsolved sauna murder was what had clinched the case against Marloes. Parallels. Links with Zig. That Marloes even knew Wojciechowski had taken Posthumus by surprise. But that she'd had a blazing argument with him only hours before he was killed, and thrown him bodily out on to the street – that he could believe. She was a big woman. Thickset, strong under those baggy dresses. But having a physical fight with Zig, as the police claimed? Hitting his head in a rage on the radiator, leaving him to bleed to death? Surely not. Not Marloes. Posthumus placed his wine glass carefully on the coaster, lining up its base with the circular logo. Anna had a point. If it hadn't been for his meddling . . .

'John, I'm sorry. What can I do you?'

Simon had come across at last. He was holding his phone.

'Text from Anna,' he said to Posthumus. 'She'll be here in about twenty minutes, she says. Just after nine. Seems it all started really late this morning 'cos of the weather, then went on into extra time, or whatever they call it. Something big happened at the end, delayed it more. She's been waiting to speak to Marloes's lawyer.'

Posthumus checked his own phone. Nothing.

'Ah, some drama after all,' said John. He ordered two beers, and turned back to Posthumus.

'So,' he said. 'What do you think? Did she do it?'

Posthumus was silent.

'I don't think Marloes is capable of something like that,' he said at last.

Simon sliced a foamy head to level it with the top of the glass.

'Anna sees it very clearly,' Posthumus went on. 'Marloes is innocent, therefore Marloes will be freed. Simple as that. Of course Marloes didn't kill those boys, so of course the authorities will see that. It couldn't be otherwise. Anna can't understand why the affair has gone on for so long, how come the case wasn't thrown out ages ago. She wants the trial over as quickly as possible to clear it all up. I don't feel as positive about it.'

'So you *do* think she did it.'

'No. No, I don't think so. I don't know. Something's not quite right.'

'I guess it's not for us to judge, despite programmes like that,' said John. He nodded up at the television, and turned to take the drinks back to his table. 'As you say, it'll all be over in a couple of days, and we'll know.'

Posthumus checked his phone again. Still no message. Things were better now with Anna than they'd been in the days after Marloes was arrested, but he felt something had slipped away from him, that she still blamed him for the push that had set all this in motion. For a while the dinners they had together on her Monday nights off had stopped. She had hardly spoken to him. But they went too deep, the two of them, for that to go on. Things were . . . well, not quite back to normal. Back to the shape of normal, perhaps. Strained, but not broken. And he'd promised, for once, to hold back, not to interfere – to make things even worse, Anna had said.

Posthumus looked up. A new face on the screen. Now *he* was familiar. Skinny. Scrawny, looked like a junkie. Standing shivering outside the courtroom, with the odd snowflake wafting on to his face. Posthumus was sure he'd seen him before. 'Jelle Smits' according to the screen caption. But that didn't mean anything. Also a witness, it seemed. He was going on about hearing sounds of an argument from Zig's room, on the night of the killing, and seeing Marloes run down the stairs. Posthumus frowned. He was sure the landing had been empty when he got up there, after Marloes came banging on the café window. And later? When the others were up there with him? Perhaps. Posthumus could not picture who had been on the landing. The image of Zig came back to him. Again. Vivid, like a sudden close-up. After all these months, he still could not shake that. But no, the scrawny guy was familiar from somewhere else, he was sure.

'Direct from the courtroom earlier this evening!'

The television grabbed Posthumus's attention. Tom and Tinneke at their upbeat double act again, but with something new.

'The judge extended the trial to nearly half past seven,' said Tinneke.

'And the reason was,' said Tom.

'He wanted to finish the summary of the psychiatric report!' said Tinneke.

'Which was completed only yesterday,' said Tom.

'Now why *did* it take so long?' said Tinneke.

'And the news from the experts is,' said Tom.

'That the Witch of De Wallen is unstable!' said Tinneke. She drew the word out twice its normal length.

'Severe personality disorder,' said Tom, brandishing a piece of paper. 'Borderline psychotic.'

'Tendency to denial,' said Tinneke. 'Disturbed relationships with men.'

'But we knew that all along,' said Tom. 'Earlier this week, we were speaking to people in the neighbourhood.'

Irene Kester, seeming even larger and pinker than in real life, flashed up on the screen, just as Anna came in the door.

Anna stood very still, as the on-screen Irene, against a lurid 'Witch of De Wallen' backdrop, began to say how everyone in the neighbourhood had always thought there was something not quite right about Marloes, and all those young men.

'What's that television doing here?' Anna asked Simon. Her voice was quiet.

'I thought . . .'

'Off. *Off.*'

Anna turned to Irene. 'I think you had better drink up and go.'

Irene began to protest, but her husband took her by the elbow, nudged her up and towards the door. He fumbled in his wallet and left a €20 note on the table. No one else said a thing.

Anna walked up to the bar. 'How could you?' she said to Simon. '*Crimebusters*, of all things.'

Simon looked across to Paul, then turned back to speak to Anna, but she cut him off.

'I'm going upstairs,' she said.

She glanced back at the others in the café.

'Actually,' she said to Simon, 'I think we're closing for the night. Get everyone to drink up. And get rid of that thing.' She gave a sharp nod at the television. 'Clean up, then just go. I'll cash up later,' she said.

Simon turned to the café at large. 'Home time, everyone. I guess,' he said, with an exaggerated shrug.

He avoided Anna's eye. Paul put a hand on her shoulder.

'You, too,' said Anna to Paul. 'Goodnight.'

She walked over to Posthumus. 'PP,' she said. 'PP, can we have a chat?'

'That *woman*, I could strangle her!' said Anna, throwing her woollen scarf aside and tugging off a thick overcoat.

Posthumus had followed Anna to her sitting room upstairs. The room seemed bare, almost minimalist after the clutter of the café. Furniture by IKEA, one wall given over to Anna's LP collection, a couple of covetable autographed music posters. Anna had given the apartment a complete clean-out after her parents died, but interior décor was not one of her strong points. Posthumus poured out two glasses from the bottle of wine he'd brought up from the bar, as Anna flopped on to the sofa.

'Strangle Marloes?' he asked. His brow furrowed.

'Of course not, don't be an idiot. Sorry, sorry, sorry, I didn't mean that. I'm just *totally* stressed out. That blonde bitch supposedly kick-ass lawyer.'

Posthumus said nothing. Anna had gone all out to get the services, *pro bono*, of the top-shot lawyer, just after Marloes was arrested. She'd seen it as quite a coup. Back when she thought that the whole affair would be over in days, that all it needed was a good professional to sort things out, clear up misconceptions, and Marloes would be free. He handed Anna her glass, and sat down in one of the armchairs.

'What's she done?' he asked.

'What *hasn't* she done, more like,' said Anna. 'She's done *nothing*. I don't know why. Lost interest maybe, too busy, didn't really care. Whatever. Or maybe she just likes getting her face on television. My fault, I suppose, for thinking that just because she was famous, she must be good. Anyway, that's why I'm so late. Sat there waiting in the wings while she did her star act.'

Anna took a sip of her wine.

'*Useless*,' she said. 'And OK, it's a bit my fault, too. I suppose I let things ride a little. But I thought, Marloes didn't do it, she's got a good lawyer, things will be fine, even when it dragged on for months. I should have been more on the ball.'

'You're the last one who can be blamed for not doing anything.'

'What? One visit a week? For an hour? Out of a sort of duty? In the end only half listening to what Marloes was saying, because it was the same week after week after week.'

Anna got up and strode over to the window that looked out over the Nieuwebrugsteeg, the heels of her boots clacking angrily on the floor.

'Reporters outside,' she said, and took a step back. 'But no, I'm not blaming myself,' she went on. 'I'm more furious than anything. With that bloody lawyer.'

'So what is it she hasn't done, exactly?' asked Posthumus.

Anna swung back round to face him. 'That Jelle Smits guy, the one who looks like a junkie, and Tina from next door, they both made witness statements, and she doesn't even question them. Not a thing. And he's saying he overheard Marloes and Zig having a fight that night.'

'I'm pretty sure he wasn't up on the landing when I got there,' said Posthumus. 'No one else was.'

'*Exactly*. Somebody should have asked these things.'

'But I saw him on television,' Posthumus went on. 'He did look familiar, I just don't think from there.'

'I'm sure it was him who ran off down the stairs just as I arrived with Marloes, looking like he was about to spew,' said Anna. 'But does anybody *ask* about this?'

Posthumus walked over to join Anna at the window.

'And Tina was so out of it, I doubt she remembers anything,' he said, 'or even had a clue what was going on.'

'That's what I'm *saying*,' said Anna.

It was snowing again.

'And it's not just that. There's us, too,' Anna went on. 'She should have had me go before the examining magistrate for one, as a character witness. She should have had me testify about Marloes's relationship with Zig. And OK, so Marloes was covered in blood when she came running down that night, but she'd been holding the poor little shit. She was busted up about it. You and me, both of us could have testified that she didn't behave like someone who'd just killed a man. The woman should have sorted that, had us both in as witnesses. There's a whole *list*. I was speaking to another lawyer while I was waiting outside the courtroom. A really nice guy. He was gobsmacked none of this had happened.'

'And now?' asked Posthumus.

'It's too late now,' said Anna. 'Marloes is fucked. I'm sorry, but she is. She didn't do it, and she's going to be sent down.'

In all the years they had been together, Posthumus had hardly ever seen Anna cry. No one ever did. But these were tears of rage, frustration.

'We can do something, surely,' he said.

'We'd need something really big to happen, before a judge would agree to call us. Or something that would blow the whole lot out of court.'

'What about an appeal?' said Posthumus. 'Even if she is found guilty now.'

'And who is to say that would make a difference? That it

won't be the same mistakes all over again, even with a better lawyer? The guy I was speaking to says an appeal is like going into the second half of a football match ten–nil down, before you even start. Meanwhile Marloes gets branded mad, and stays on in jail. That alone is cracking her up. It'll *destroy* her. Who says there isn't a death sentence any more?'

Posthumus looked down into the street. Simon had just locked up below, and was talking to a reporter. Anna made a move forward to open the window, but Posthumus put a restraining hand on her arm.

'Best not,' he said. 'They're probably snooping around because of the psychiatric report, trying to get more dirt. It was on the telly.'

Anna walked over to the LP wall, pulled a disc off the shelf, and put it on the turntable: the Velvet Underground. Music she had always played after she and Posthumus had had a row. It calmed her down, she said, though he could never understand how those grating voices could be soothing.

'And this "Witch of De Wallen" thing is being tweeted all over the world by now,' said Anna, as the first notes of 'Heroin' began to play. 'That is *never* going to go away. Can you imagine what that will do to Marloes if she finds out? We've got to stop it all *now*.'

She leaned back against the record shelves and closed her eyes.

'Nothing beats vinyl,' she said, 'and the Velvets.'

They had made an odd couple back then, the pair of them, when they visited markets, he heading for the vintage clothes, she flipping through piles of second-hand LPs, cleverly building up a collection that was now probably worth more than everything downstairs in the café put together. Posthumus felt the urge to go and put his arms around her, but he knew it would be the wrong thing to do.

'There was someone tweeting next to me on the tram,' Anna said, 'then going on about it to the friend next to her. *Horrible*. It's just salacious gossip.'

'Well, *Crimebusters* was hardly the model of insight and information. But they were saying something about a personality disorder, and disturbed relationships with men.'

Anna straightened herself up, opened her eyes. 'That's the problem, isn't it?' she said. 'It's sort of true, but not. We all know Marloes. She's just a bit odd, that's all, it's not a big psychological disorder or anything. And that's the other thing! Why did this come so late? Why didn't the lawyer do anything about it? Why did I get to hear about this just *now*, in court? I want to *see* that report. All of it. And before this so-called expert witness appears to give details on Thursday. Surely we can challenge him. I mean, if they lay an insanity thing on Marloes, it's a prison sentence, then a psychiatric institution. Throw away the key.'

'Not necessarily.'

'Pretty much. Psychiatric detention can go on for ever, if they don't think she's improved. And they won't. "In denial", they said. Of *course* she's in bloody denial! She keeps saying she didn't do it.'

'And she didn't.'

Posthumus tried to keep his voice absolutely neutral. Not a hint of a question, or a 'did she?'. This was difficult.

'Look, I'm standing by her,' said Anna. 'I am 100 per cent sure she is innocent. *I* know – and you know, *really* – that Marloes could never have done something like that. Either of those horrible, *horrible* killings.'

Anna picked up the wine and poured herself another glass.

'I'm going to ask if they'll let me see her tomorrow,' she said. 'Change my normal visit from a Thursday to a Wednesday. She's free tomorrow, court's not sitting, but she'll be back in there again on Thursday, so it's my only chance. They'll *have* to let me. And then I'm going to tackle that lawyer. Properly. Head to head.'

Anna sat back down on the sofa. She crossed, then uncrossed her legs. When she spoke again, her voice was quieter.

'But PP,' she said. 'I did some thinking on the tram. I want to ask you something.'

Posthumus turned his back to the window, and leaned against the sill.

'We're going to have to do something about this ourselves,' said Anna. 'The lawyer's useless, Marloes is bewildered by it all, she's in no state to do herself any good, and now, with this psychiatric report . . . they've got it all *wrong*.'

Some wine slopped from Anna's glass, as she jerked her hand in emphasis.

'Shit!'

'I'll get a cloth.'

Posthumus slipped out, and came back with a damp tea towel.

'Lucky it's white,' he said.

Anna reached for the cloth, but held instead on to Posthumus's wrist.

'PP,' she said. 'These past few months . . . I know I said back off. With Marloes, and all. And I meant it. But maybe I was wrong. Maybe what we need here is some good old Pieter Posthumus meddling after all, don't you think?'

Posthumus went back to the window. Anna mopped at the wine.

'You *do* think something's not quite right, don't you?' she said. 'I can see. I know you.'

Posthumus nodded.

'What is it? Can't we start looking? Into the paintings, into Zig's life, into the other guy in the sauna. Some other connection? Some other person? *Please.* The trial could be all over in a few days. There's got to be *something* they're just not noticing . . . Will you?'

Posthumus walked slowly across the room, and sat down beside Anna on the sofa.

'You're right,' he said. 'There's a . . . a *disproportion* somewhere. There're these links, these parallels, pieces that *seem* to fit together, but they don't, quite. Like a kid cheating at a jigsaw. As if the pieces have been forced together a bit, but there's something missing, a piece or two that should be in between, which would make a whole different picture. But what that can be I just don't know. I've been trying not to think of it, pushing it out of my mind.' He gave a little smile. 'Obediently,' he said.

Anna smiled back. 'And now?' she said. 'Would you? We could both. No one else is going to do anything for Marloes.'

Posthumus did not meet her eye. He was looking over at the window, which was beginning to steam up slightly, as another flurry of snowflakes did a slow pirouette outside, over the Nieuwebrugsteeg.

'Let's speak to the lawyer,' he said. 'And I'll have a think. Come up with some specific questions you can ask Marloes. I'll have a look at Wojciechowski's file at work.'

He stumbled over the name.

'Doesn't he have a first name?' said Anna. 'Something easier?'

Posthumus's mind clicked back to the moment when he was holding the file, after he pulled it out searching for the painting that reminded him of the one in Zig's room.

'Antoni, I think it was,' he said after a moment. 'Tony. I guess that's the place to start. And I'll see what more I can find out about those paintings.'

'Thank you, PP.'

Anna leaned over and gave him a hug.

74

'And . . . sorry,' she said.

Posthumus pulled back slightly. 'There's just one thing,' he said.

Anna cocked her head to one side.

'If I *do* look into it, and . . . and if I find that Marloes somehow *was* involved, then you are – we both are – really going to have to accept that.'

6

'It looks a little like the opening scene of a dismal drama,' said Cornelius. 'Upon a wooden coffin we attend . . .'

The poet was standing, shoulders slightly hunched, outside the chapel portico, his hands in the pockets of an old, but clearly very well-tailored dark cashmere overcoat. Posthumus was beside him. On the other side of the arch stood a pair to match: the cemetery superintendent and the funeral director, both formally dressed. There was nobody else.

A low-slung hearse had that moment pulled up between the pillars of the graveyard gate. Four pallbearers, in top hats, were falling in behind it, two by two, to follow it at walking pace to the chapel. A shroud of snow. A few flakes wandering this way and that, falling from a frigid sky. Grey stone, gaunt trees – even the evergreens seeming black. Cornelius had a point, thought Posthumus, as the four dark figures crunched in step over the gravel, circled the fountain – desultory, frozen – then turned to face each other in two lines, as the hearse reached the chapel and came to a halt. The pallbearers removed their hats.

'And who do we have here?' asked the cemetery superintendent, lifting his heels off the ground slightly, then dropping back.

'Mrs Bep van Tonder. Died at the admirable age of ninety-six, in full command of her senses, at the Zonhof old people's home,' said Posthumus. 'Outlived her only daughter, and all her family and friends.'

The men at the chapel portico stood, hands behind their backs. The pallbearers replaced their hats and, at a nod, stepped forward in unison to remove the coffin from the hearse.

'Every turn of ceremony, every dignity observed. Even if there's no one to see,' said Cornelius. He glanced up at the grey sky. 'What a god-fearing nation we are,' he said.

The pallbearers shouldered the coffin and swung to face the chapel door.

'And, thanks to you, my dear Charon, a small moment of significance for me, too,' said Cornelius to Posthumus. 'This will be my twenty-fifth poem for a Lonely Funeral.'

Posthumus smiled. Over the past few months, he had grown used to Cornelius's nickname for him – the ferryman who carried souls across the Styx. It certainly beat the usual tired old gag about his surname.

'Twenty-five already?' he said. 'I wouldn't have thought.'

The crunch of car tyres on gravel again. Crisp. Urgent. A white mini-bus drove in through the graveyard gate, turned into the car park, and stopped abruptly in the Disabled bay.

'Well, maybe not outlived *all* her friends,' said Posthumus. 'She made some new ones at the end. Looks like the old biddies from the Zonhof have come after all, despite the cold. They said they might.'

'Take her on through,' the cemetery superintendent told the pallbearers.

The mini-bus driver jumped out of the driver's seat, went around to the back door and began to operate a wheelchair lift. The frail group took a while to assemble beside the bus, and made slow progress across the gravel. Quietly, the cemetery superintendent began to tell a story, hitting the punch line seconds before the old women – and one old man – reached them. Cornelius and Posthumus struggled to keep straight faces. The funeral director had perhaps heard it before. He stepped forward to greet the new arrivals, to invite them to sign the condolences book, and usher them into the chapel. The cemetery superintendent surreptitiously checked his watch.

The music was Handel – the CD that had been in a battered player in Bep van Tonder's room. The volume on the player was not set that high, Posthumus remembered. Mrs van Tonder's hearing must still have been good. Only large-print books, though. Cornelius stood up to read his poem. He began:

> 'She did not bend a knee to death,
> Drop the meek curtsey, opening the door to
> Admit the silent, anticipated stranger
> Unbidden . . .'

The funeral director leaned forward and murmured in Posthumus's ear that one of the mourners, the old man, had prepared something to say. Posthumus noticed the cemetery superintendent tap his left wrist. As Cornelius concluded, Posthumus folded the paper on which he had written his own speech, and slipped it into an inside pocket.

After the ceremony, the woman in the wheelchair stayed behind in the coffee room with a friend. The others from Zonhof braved the cold to follow the coffin to the graveside, the funeral director up front, Cornelius and Posthumus a few paces behind the group.

'So what were you saying, about the lawyer?' said Cornelius.

They had been talking about Marloes's trial on the way to the funeral.

'Seems she's totally incompetent. Or plain uncaring,' said Posthumus. 'And now this psychiatric report. Apparently that could really tip the case against Marloes, according to some lawyer bloke Anna was talking to at the court.'

'Mad as the mist and snow, in the words of my favourite Irishman. Yes, even little Lukas was going on about the Mad Witch. One of the older boys got it off Twitter. I had to give him a severe talking-to.'

Posthumus grimaced. Cornelius's son could not be older than twelve. He reached into his pocket and pulled out his own phone.

The little cortège was far enough away, and focused on the coffin up ahead.

'Look, I know this is really bad, but I must,' said Posthumus.

He had switched the phone to silent before the funeral. It indicated a text message from Anna, and some missed calls. He checked the message.

Seeing Marloes 10.00. What u want know?

Ten minutes to go. She might still have the phone with her.

'Sorry. Got to do this,' he said to Cornelius. 'Anna. She'll have to lock away her phone in a minute.'

He rang. Anna answered immediately.

'PP. Be quick. I'm just about to go in.'

'Ask her what it was between Zig and Tony. Any links. Anything she can think of. And see if you can get to the bottom of why Tony was around the guest-house. If there's anything she hasn't told us, or the police. Even if it doesn't seem important.'

'Got to go.'

'Oh, and if there's anything she can tell us about Zig's paintings. Anything.'

The line had gone dead. Posthumus slid the phone back into his pocket.

'My apologies to Bep van Tonder,' he said.

'Somehow, I don't think she would have minded,' said Cornelius. 'I have the impression she was a game old bird. Quite the sort who started wearing purple at sixty.'

'And clearly still able to create a flutter in that old boy's heart, the one who gave the address,' said Posthumus. 'She had quite a spark in her, from all accounts. Your poem really caught that, I felt.'

'Thank you, mild Charon. It certainly helps now that I can come along exploring with you beforehand.'

'You don't mind poking about dead people's things? My colleague Maya thinks I'm a macabre snoop.'

'On the contrary. First-hand impressions, rather than someone else's hazy sketches over the phone. Infinitely preferable,' said Cornelius.

'Suits me, too, to have you rather than Maya along on the house-visit.'

'Fearsome harpy, I agree,' said Cornelius.

The cortège had come to a halt, and the coffin was being lowered into the grave.

'Locking her phone away?' said Cornelius, as the two of them joined the back of the group.

'Anna? Visiting Marloes. I'll tell you later,' said Posthumus.

One by one the mourners threw a trowel of earth on to the coffin. Posthumus and Cornelius did the same, and joined the little group on the walk back. A thin, tired-looking woman accepted Cornelius's offer of an arm.

'A quick coffee, then out,' said Posthumus to the poet, as they went into the reception room beside the chapel. 'I need to get back to the office.'

Ten minutes later, the two tall men were folding themselves somewhat awkwardly into the department Smart.

'From what I glean,' said Cornelius, 'from these crumbs you are so tantalisingly dropping beneath your table, you are about to play detective again.'

'Anna has asked me to help,' said Posthumus. 'She thinks it's the only way.'

He started the car, and steered out through the cemetery gate.

'And you're certainly not reluctant,' said Cornelius. He peered at Posthumus over the top of his half-moon spectacles. 'That much is plain. This is very much your sort of thing, as they say.'

Posthumus dipped his head in acknowledgement. 'You have me in one,' he said. 'But then, you see, I made a link between the two deaths in the first place. So I feel responsible, too, I guess.'

Posthumus explained to Cornelius about the two paintings, why he had first gone to the police, about *The Night Watch* at Schiphol and Merel's idea that the paintings represented the original scene two minutes later.

Cornelius pursed his lips. 'Any chance of another mind throwing light in dark corners?' he said.

Posthumus looked across at the poet. Cornelius's eyes had a glint in them.

'You'd like that, wouldn't you!'

'I dare say I could help,' said Cornelius. 'In my modest way.'

Posthumus grinned, and slowed for a traffic light.

'Those paintings, for instance,' Cornelius went on. 'I take it that's where you're going to start?'

'I thought I'd try to find out more about the other murder, first. Just who this Tony was, what he had to do with Zig. And Marloes. Something doesn't fit in all that, not the way it's put together at the moment, anyway.'

'It's the paintings that interest me,' said Cornelius.

'I'm not sure what they tell us,' said Posthumus. 'The police didn't seem to think anything of them at all. Not about the paintings themselves, not once they'd made the link between the two cases. They released the one that had been in Zig's room – it ended up with some of his other effects, back at the office.'

'And now?' asked Cornelius.

'Things like that we'd usually send to auction if they looked valuable, or simply ditch. Or we'd hand them over to relatives, if we could find any. But we couldn't trace any family for Zig. And no will, except for a scrap of paper leaving everything to Marloes.'

'I imagine *that* wouldn't look good, if our Zig had a secret stash of gold.'

'Not even enough to cover the funeral, poor lad,' said Posthumus. 'In the end I gave the painting to Anna to keep for Marloes. If she can ever bear to be reminded of all this.'

'And both paintings are by Zig?'

'Seems likely, don't you think? But somehow Tony had one. That's puzzled me all along. I want to get to the bottom of *that*, but I thought I'd start with Tony himself. The paintings bother me, but I'm not sure where they get us. The paintings themselves, I mean.'

'Quite the contrary,' said Cornelius. '*Quite* the contrary. I'm thinking that if the painting were mine, if it were a *poem*, there would have to be a reason for it. The act of creation – it's not a mere whim, random emotion. There must be a reason. He's applying structure. To what? Now *that's* our question.'

They both fell silent. The traffic moved slowly along the Haarlemmerweg.

'I do remember that painting at Schiphol, the mutated *Night Watch*,' said Cornelius, after a while.

He took out his phone, tapped in to Google.

'Albert,' he said, then held the phone a little further from him. 'No, Aldert. Aldert Mantje, and Jan Maris. *The Night Watch, Two Minutes Later.*'

They had reached the Haarlemmerpoort. Posthumus hesitated in the centre lane.

'Straight on, or right?' he asked. 'Can I take you home, or are you going into town?'

'Dare you play truant?' said Cornelius. 'Do you dare to eat a peach?'

'I really do need to get the car back for Maya.'

'In that case, right,' said Cornelius.

He had pursed his lips again, and was drumming his fingers lightly on the car's rounded dashboard.

'Yes, right. Please,' he said again. 'But not home. You had photographs of those paintings you say? Could you ping them across to me as soon as you have a moment? And would you mind dropping me off in the Jordaan? There's someone I want to see.'

Posthumus backed the Smart into a parking bay twice its size, across the way from the department. A woman in the houseboat moored alongside gave him a smile and a wave from her kitchen window. Posthumus always picked that spot if it was free. He positioned the car very precisely towards the rear of the bay, allowing room around the houseboat gangplank, but not enough to tempt another motorist to squeeze in. He switched off the engine, and glanced up at the department's spout-gabled canal-house, just in time to see Maya's face disappear from behind their office window.

Today, he was simply not in the mood for Maya, Posthumus thought, as he let himself into the building. Sometimes he wished the department would go ahead and make her leader of the officially leaderless Funeral Team. She so clearly already saw herself in the role. But the department head had let drop in Posthumus's ear that if there were to be a restructuring, it would be Posthumus not Maya who'd be up for the job. Now the consequences of *that* didn't bear thinking about. Unless, of course, it were to make Maya resign.

Alex was behind the reception desk, straight-backed, eyes shining, her black hair cascading on to a green mohair jacket – and on the phone. She gave him a flutter of the fingers, and mouthed, 'Speak later,' as he crossed to climb the stairs to the Funeral Team office. Posthumus went straight to the coffee machine in the small kitchen off the landing. Let Maya sweat a bit. He dropped a capsule into the machine and pressed the button for a double espresso. He was intrigued by what light Cornelius might throw on this whole Marloes affair. And glad in a way that Cornelius was on board. God knows they needed to move fast, so could use all the help they could get. He hadn't liked the man at first. Thought he drank too much, for one, was irritated by the constant secret joke Cornelius seemed to be sharing with himself. And, Posthumus had to admit, he had a prejudice against men who wore bow ties. But he'd begun to see another side, had warmed to him over these past months.

Posthumus carried his coffee into the office. As he came through the door, Maya gave a single rap to the return key on her computer, and sat back in her chair with an air of triumph that made him pity the recipient of the email she had just sent. He jangled the car keys and dropped them on to her desk as he passed.

'A good ten minutes to go,' he said, before she could turn the same time-frame into a complaint.

'All right, mate?' he said to Sulung, across the room.

Sulung nodded a greeting. His desk was a mess.

'You haven't seen the Muller file anywhere?' Sulung asked.

'Sorry,' said Posthumus.

He crossed to his own desk, near the window, and turned on his computer. Sulung really shouldn't be back. It had been hell, having Maya undiluted during all those weeks Sulung had taken off after his wife's death, but the poor man was simply not coping. He'd been disorganised before, now he was completely adrift.

'What's the problem?' asked Posthumus.

'Some relative complaining. Says his uncle always wanted to be cremated.'

'The uncle whose funeral he wouldn't pay for,' said Maya, from her corner. 'To which he didn't even come.'

'That's unfair,' said Posthumus. 'People have reasons.'

He turned to Sulung. 'The Muller from Boomstraat, that you and I did a couple of weeks ago?' he asked. 'He left instructions. Chose his own music, everything. There was a note.'

'That's what I'm looking for,' said Sulung. 'There's nothing in the computer file.'

Maya gave a sharp sigh. She picked the car keys off her desk, clicked shut her smart leather attaché case, and stood up.

'You off on the house-visit with Maya, right?' said Posthumus to Sulung. 'I'll see what I can do.'

Posthumus crossed to the shelves where the Closed Cases hard-copy files were kept, as Sulung followed Maya out of the door, and down the stairs. Nothing under M for Muller. He tried B, for Boomstraat. There it was.

'Sulung, Sulung, Sulung,' he said aloud, and pulled out the file.

Then he moved to the Ws, selected Wojciechowski, and took both files back to his desk.

The whingeing relative took only a few minutes. There had been a note, stipulating burial. Could be worse. Could have been the other way around. Posthumus telephoned, and with perfect politeness offered to have the body exhumed and cremated at the nephew's expense. That got rid of him. Posthumus put the Muller file aside, settled back in his chair, and opened the one labelled Antoni 'Tony' Wojciechowski.

Arriving at Nieuwersluis, Anna always had the feeling she was visiting a stately home, or minor royal palace: the grand brick façade of the main building, with its double lines of windows; the decorative gable and gilded coat of arms over the door. It had been something military, a century or so ago, she remembered reading. It was only when you looked left or right, to the cell-wings with huge cage-like extensions covering the outdoor areas, that it came home to you with a thump where you were. Or when you got inside.

Anna switched off her phone, and slid it hastily into a locker beside her bag and coat. She had to get a move on. The icy weather may have thinned out visitor numbers at the prison, but there was always a bottleneck going through the metal detector, and she knew that the stopwatch started ticking from the minute her hour with Marloes was scheduled to begin, whether she had reached her or not.

Anna wished now that she had paid closer attention to what Marloes was saying on earlier visits, but Marloes did tend to go on a bit, jump from topic to topic, then get bogged down in some total irrelevancy. Anna felt a guilty twinge, as she admitted that she had at times switched off while Marloes was speaking. But then – stupidly, that was now clear – she had trusted the lawyer, left it all to her. With Anna, Marloes had talked mostly about her feelings, how she was coping with Nieuwersluis. It had upset her to talk of Zig, or anything to do with the killings. Anna had never thought anything other than that Marloes was innocent and that the lawyer was sorting it all out. Now she had to crush weeks' worth of lost conversations into an hour. Less than an hour.

She joined the queue for the detector and body frisk. She'd missed the first surge, when the doors opened; every minute that passed now was a minute wasted. The warders were polite enough. Unsmiling. They always managed to make her feel guilty. Tacitly accused, as if the next time she came, she would be going through all this because she was about to be detained, not simply a visitor – that it was merely the luck of the draw that she could choose to leave, and when she was next outdoors look up and not see wire mesh between her and the sky. Anna handed over the little purse she'd bought especially for these visits – she knew the rules by now, coins only, no notes, no cards. She retrieved it on the other side of the detector arch, and walked on through the security doors, feeling a momentary surge of irritation at the few seconds' delay as the one door closed behind her before the other opened in front.

Marloes sat at the far end of the thin, long table that twisted through the room. Warders called it 'the snake' – Anna had overheard two of them talking on her first visit. In her baggy, orange and mauve home-made dress, Marloes stood out startlingly in the sea of jeans, tracksuits and sweatshirts around her, even more of an oddity here than in De Wallen. Anna looked up at the wall clock. Seven minutes gone already. She crossed quickly to the vending machine, picked up two coffees, and went over to Marloes. A brief hug. That was all that was allowed – over the table, across the ridiculous plastic barrier in the middle, barely taller than the coffee cups. Anna supposed it was there to prevent you sliding objects across to the prisoner, but it seemed to her a needless underlining of the division between them. Between a clear sky and one viewed through a cage.

'They don't have skimmed milk in the shop any more.'

Marloes launched straight in to her grievance. 'I must have skimmed for my health. They know that. They're doing it on purpose.'

'I'm sure they'll be getting it again soon,' said Anna. 'The weather's been really bad.'

At first Anna had thought these outbursts of Marloes's were one of her oddities, but after a few visits she'd begun to pick up on similar discontents being aired all along the table. The woes of worlds turned upside down, controlled entirely by others, shrunk to a size where a missing magazine, or the availability of skimmed milk, meant more than anything. Anna guessed it was all about the tiny things, over which you thought you might still try to exert control.

'It's been five days now. I want to file a complaint.'

'You must speak to the lawyer about that, Marloes, not to me.'

'She never listens to me. You don't either. Sometimes. You think I don't notice? I can see.'

'Oh Marloes, Marloes.'

Anna longed to reach across the table and hold her hand, but felt the gaze of the warders, perched in the corners of the room.

'Your hair looks nice,' she said instead. 'In court yesterday, too. Quite neat and chic. That's good.'

'Maria did it for me,' said Marloes. 'For yesterday, special. She's kind. Better than the others.'

Anna didn't think anyone at Nieuwersluis treated Marloes badly. At least, she never mentioned anything. But no one much seemed to care for her, apart from this Maria.

'Ordinary things, that's the worst,' said Marloes. 'I think of people doing ordinary things. Carrying home shopping, stopping at a café. I feel jealous.'

'That's hard, I know, you've said.'

'Not jealous, really. Nostalgic. And I want to walk, walk for no reason, nowhere special, no one watching. Then go home. *My* home. Everything here is strange.'

They had covered this ground before. On nearly every visit.

'I've brought you some more clothes, and warm things to sleep in,' Anna said. 'It's been freezing. I don't know how cold you get in here. I was a bit rushed this morning, but I'll leave them with the warders before I go. So you'll get them later, or tomorrow.'

'They'll all smell of home, again, like the last ones. I still think of Zig, you know. All the time. I hated yesterday. Those things they said. They think I've flipped. They do, don't they?'

'Marloes, you must try to concentrate, focus on just one thing at a time. Sometimes . . . sometimes, you jump all over the place. People find it hard to follow you. I can, I've known you a long time. But you must try, especially when you speak in court.'

'But they *do* think I'm mad. And Irene, and Pia, and all that lot. Just because I'm not like them, never have been. You've always been good to me, but I know. I know what they say behind my back. They think I don't, but I know.'

'Marloes, I need to ask you some questions, we don't have much time. PP's going to be helping me, we want to get you out of here, to get to the truth of all this, as soon as we can.'

'But I've *told* them the truth. Why don't they believe me? What am I supposed to say? How do they think I could kill little Zig? And I didn't even know that Tony boy. Hardly.'

'That's what I want to ask you about.'

'Tell them, tell them, please, tell them I'm not mad. Do you think I've flipped? Do *you* think so?'

'Marloes! One thing at a time. No, I don't believe you have. I want to get hold of that psychiatric report for a closer look.'

'So you do think so.' Marloes's voice was quiet.

'Marloes, we've got to get this sorted. What was it between Zig and this Tony guy, the other one?'

'Even you,' said Marloes.

Her hands were spread wide, fingers stiff but interlocked, moving rapidly in and out of each other.

Anna gave her voice a sterner edge than she really felt. 'Marloes, I'm on your side.'

'*I didn't do it!*'

Warders were starting to look their way.

'Can't they just see that? The judges will see. I just want this to finish. Tomorrow. They can finish tomorrow. They'll see it's all wrong. Why are they taking so long? Why will no one *believe* me? This way, *trapped*, that way, *trapped*.'

'Marloes!'

Anna leaned forward over her side of the table.

'I need to know about Zig and Tony.'

Marloes was silent for a while, sullen, like a little girl reprimanded. Anna felt the eyes of the warders move off them.

'He was from the past. Zig's past.'

'When Zig was . . .'

'Yes, before I found him.'

'So they worked together?'

'Yes. I don't know. Maybe. I didn't like that Tony,' said Marloes. 'So rude. I said I'd help him, like I helped Zig, and he laughed. Horrid laughter, like . . . like boys when we were younger.'

'Just think about Zig, Marloes. Did he like Tony?'

'Not like that! Tony liked girls, Zig said. Some do, you know, even if they work like Zig.'

'They were friends?'

'Tony was his first friend, Ziggie came here all alone. But Tony was older.'

'What do you mean, Marloes?'

Anna glanced up at the clock on the wall.

'Then they weren't friends. Something happened,' said Marloes.

'Marloes, I need you to fill in the gaps. What do you mean by saying Tony was older than Zig? Not much, surely?'

'Not much, but I think he brought Zig into it, into . . . you know.'

'But those men were all arrested, weren't they?'

'Tony wasn't one of *them . . . evil* men. They had Tony working for them too I think, like Zig, but before him. Tony testified against them, after the police got them. But that was a surprise. Zig had dropped him by then, he didn't know . . .'

Something brushed against Anna's thigh. She looked down. A little kid, maybe only two or three, had his hand on her leg and was staring transfixed at her dishevelled mass of auburn hair. His father, next along on the snake, was leaning at the boundary of what was permissible over the table, talking to a sulky-looking woman on the other side. He noticed the child at the same time as Anna did.

'Remi, here!' he said, and pulled the child back towards him. 'Sorry.'

He turned back to the woman. Minutes were not to be wasted on strangers.

'But he never told me.' Marloes had not stopped speaking.

'Sorry, Marloes.'

Anna pointed downwards, below the level of the tabletop, to where the child had been. Perhaps Marloes had not seen.

'A little kid,' said Anna. 'So Tony testified against Zig's pimps, and the two of them were friends?'

'In the beginning. Then suddenly they weren't. Something happened, I told you, but Ziggie would never talk about it.'

'When?'

'Soon. Very soon. Just after he came.'

'Came to you, to live in the guest-house?'

'Yes.'

'And you've no idea what happened?'

'Just that they fell out. Something really, really upset him, but he wouldn't tell me, even me. That was when he began his paintings, maybe that had something to do with it, I don't know. But Tony went. They all go, in the end, don't they?'

Anna tried changing tack. 'What did you argue about?' she said. 'That day they say you and Tony argued. The day Tony was killed.'

'Now you sound like them! I've *told* them!'

'Tell *me*.'

'He came back.'

'Tony?'

'Yes, I was glad he stopped coming, but he came back. After all those years. He hadn't been.'

'That day? He came back that day?'

'No, before. And Zig didn't like it, I could see. There was shouting. And Zig told me not to let him in again, and I wouldn't. But sometimes one of the others did. Sometimes even Ziggie did, like he couldn't resist, and then there'd be shouting again.'

Marloes was beginning to get agitated once more.

'What didn't Zig like about him?' said Anna.

'He wouldn't say, but that's why he wanted to go to Berlin, I'm sure. He said it was for his painting, but it wasn't. It was after Tony came back, that's when this Berlin thing began. Berlin, Berlin, Berlin. They *all* go, Zig said.'

'That day that Tony visited, you had an argument?'

'Oh yes. Yes, indeed. I threw him out.'

'About what, the argument?'

'That. Throwing him out. I answered the door, he tried to push his way in, and I wouldn't have it. I told him what I thought of him and that Ziggie didn't want him. I told him if he was going to see Zig it would have to be somewhere else. And I threw him out. I can do that, it's my house. Mother did. All the time. I *told* them this.'

'And that's all?'

'He got back in again.'

'That afternoon?'

'Ziggie had gone out, and they came back together.'

'And you threw him out again, was there another argument?'

'No, I felt bad about earlier I guess, getting cross like that. And with Ziggie right there, it was different. That's when I told Tony I could help him, like I helped Ziggie. That's when he laughed at me. But I *told* them all this, again and again. You, too. No one listens.'

Nearly time. Anna did not have to look at the clock. You could feel it. The pitch of the general hubbub seemed to rise a tone or two, as the urgency crept in. The little kid from alongside had come over again, was grabbing on to her knee.

'Hello, Remi,' she said, and put an arm around him.

What was the other thing PP said she should ask? She turned back to Marloes.

'Zig painting, that started after he fell out with Tony?' she asked.

'It was his love,' said Marloes. 'He took so long, so much care with each one.'

A few people were already getting up to go. Saying goodbyes in their own time, before the rush.

'Were they all the same, Zig's paintings, copies, I mean?' said Anna. 'I know . . . I know that Tony had one, that's how . . .' She couldn't finish.

'Zig wouldn't have given him it!' said Marloes. 'They were his children, like he was mine. Every year, one. He made them with love . . .'

'Ladies and gentlemen, it is eleven o'clock. That's your lot.'

The visitors knew the procedure. They seemed resigned to it. Chairs began to scrape back even before the guard had finished. No dramas today. Not even from the little guy clutching on to her knee, it seemed. Anna ushered him back to his father, and stood up. Marloes, too. Anna leaned over to give her a hug. She held on for a moment, squeezing Marloes as tight as she could.

'Tomorrow or the next day, my dearest, when you give your statement in court, just remember, *please*, one thing at a time.'

7

As he flipped open the Wojciechowski file, Posthumus gave a half-smile. Tony Wojciechowski may have been his first case in a new job, but right from the start he'd been interested in the story behind a name, in the person who'd once inhabited a corpse. A thin wad of newspaper clippings, and some hand-written notes jotted on a sheet of A4 already clearly indicated the path Posthumus would take. It hadn't been long before he started calling cases 'clients', putting together orations for their funerals – private sacraments that somehow acknowledged a life spent on earth, marked its passing.

Posthumus picked up the police photo of Tony's blackened, blistered corpse from the top of the pile of papers in the file. Did he believe in an afterlife? It was hard to shake off a Catholic upbringing. Perhaps he still did. Or perhaps what he did for these clients was a way of dealing with his own uncertainty, taking hold of what he *could* be sure of, and making something of it. Giving an identity to someone, when it has been lost or obscured. Fastening a memory. Of course someone like Maya saw it all as a waste of time. Cornelius got it, though. And Alex downstairs.

Posthumus examined the photo, more closely now than he had done a few months before, when he'd pulled out the file in the hope of finding out more about Zig's painting. The image was gruesome. The body barely recognisable. He looked again at the Case Report. Cause of death, 'drug-induced hypoventilation and heart failure'. An overdose, then, in layman's terms. Posthumus skimmed some of the newspaper clippings, most saying that Tony's death was triggered by his being in the sauna, that the heat heightened the effect of the drug. Cocaine, said some reports, heroin another.

Posthumus frowned, took a clean sheet of paper from a drawer in his desk, and made a couple of notes. That must have been the police line: if Tony had been in the guest-house just before going to the gym, then Marloes had somehow slipped him the drug. But how? Cocaine could be ingested, and be fatal, he knew – like with the drugs mules who died trying to smuggle the stuff by swallowing it packed into condoms that sometimes burst. But how could Marloes sort something like that, or get her hands on coke? He knew that the guest-house wasn't always squeaky clean, as far as drugs went. That Tina girl, for one, up on the landing on the night of Zig's death, was clearly out of her head on something. But such cold planning just didn't seem like Marloes. Or not the Marloes he thought he knew, anyway.

The early clippings focused on the horror, on the body left overnight in a 110°C sauna, on the faulty thermostat and time switch. And on the attendant who had shut up for the night without checking the sauna was empty. Posthumus flicked through a couple of the reports. *De Telegraaf*, of course, 'the newspaper for the wide awake', had weaselled out the attendant's name: 'Robbie K. (23)', reported with the coy abbreviation the Dutch press used for criminal suspects. Posthumus let out a dismissive sniff. *De Telegraaf* was also the only paper to have somehow got its hands on a photo of the corpse. He noted the name nevertheless, and the name of the gym, FitFast. He knew it. Not far away, on the other side of Waterlooplein, on the way up to the IJ Tunnel.

Posthumus returned to the clippings. A few weeks later, there had been another wave. The papers suddenly full of revelations about Tony's shady background, speculation that he had been a *loverboy*, recruiting adolescents into prostitution. Lads like Zig, maybe? And that he had gang-land connections, that his death was no accident. There was a photograph of Tony drinking with a notorious crime boss, across a number of the papers. Then one report from quite some time after his death. Posthumus checked the date he'd handwritten across the top of the clipping, and cross-refer-enced the Case Report. After the funeral. The arrest of one László K. on suspicion of Tony's murder, released without charge.

The phone in Posthumus's jacket pocket beeped. He took it out. A text from Anna.

Managed at last nail down lawyer. Seeing her 12.30. Will ask copy psych report and Tina/junkie witness statements. What else?

He texted back.

Give me five minutes.

He picked up the notes he'd been making, and swung his chair round to face the window. The line of gables across the Amstel stood out against the low, dull sky. Elements. Individual. Yet pulled together by circumstance, here and there by design, into a sequence. Posthumus held the sheet of paper in one hand, moving it in a slow, fanning movement, not reading the notes but continuing to stare out through the window. The timing? Surely the police would have taken that into account? If Marloes had given Tony the drug, it would have had to have been enough so that he didn't die on the spot. Could she have known that he was on the way to the gym, that he would take a sauna, and administer a dose accordingly? That seemed way out of Marloes's zone. And clearly the police had suspected this László K., and probably worked on the assumption it had all happened at the gym. What made them change their minds about that?

Posthumus swung his chair abruptly back to the desk and picked up his phone. He texted Anna:

Get Tony pathology report. And for Zig.

He paused for a moment. The arguments Marloes was supposed to have had, with Tony and with Zig? Maybe. He tapped on:

And statement that neighbour made to the r-c – Marloes argument Tony.
Marloes police statement, too, if poss.
Everything you can.

The reply came within seconds.

Will do what I can. Bitch owes us!!

Posthumus picked the handwritten A4 from the file. The notes were mostly from his attempts to trace friends and family, plus a couple of jottings after the house-visit. He skimmed them. He hadn't taken down very much back then.

B&O! Dolce & Gabbana! Diesel.

He remembered. It had been a fairly ordinary apartment, just beyond the zoo, yet brimming with expensive stuff. A huge flatscreen TV, a sound system he couldn't imagine how to operate, three wardrobes crammed with designer clothes, trainers enough for a family of centipedes. Well, that certainly supported the criminal-contacts idea. Even then, the bounty had struck him and Sulung as suspicious.

Bond apartment.

'Designed to seduce,' Sulung had said. Or to impress. Had they known about the *loverboy* speculation at the time? Posthumus thought not – but it all fitted.

Mxx.

What that was Posthumus could not recall. Mexx? Possibly. And that was it as far as the apartment went. The rest was mostly names and telephone numbers. He'd have to check the computer file. They had photographed extensively, which they always did, and especially in an apartment stocked like this, where families were apt to make claims about missing valuables. But there had been no family. Or, rather, Tony was one of the disowned ones, whose family would have nothing to do with him, whose friends were lying low, whose enemies, perhaps, were silently gloating.

'I have no son.'

The last words Posthumus had written on the page. They had found family, all right, but Tony's father would have none of it. It had been an awkward phone call, not made any easier because the father's bad English meant Posthumus had to be blunt. No softening of the edges. He remembered the boy's mother sobbing in the background, calling out something in Polish that he couldn't understand, but certainly got the gist of. But the father was adamant. 'I have no son.' How *could* someone do that? Cut off so completely, so vehemently. Posthumus sighed, shook the beginnings of a shudder from his spine, and placed the A4 face down in the file. It wasn't too long ago, till Merel tracked him down last summer, that *he* would have said, 'I don't have any family.'

Posthumus tapped his mouse to wake up the dormant computer. Mail from Alex.

Anything happening up there? Quiet week, no? Nothing much doing after your funeral this morning and M's house visit. Not enough people dying. Am stuck down here. Himself Upstairs has loaded me with a whole pile of paperwork. Chat?

He replied.

Down shortly. Much to tell. Early lunch? Then think might take afternoon and tomorrow off. Officially. Maybe Friday, too. I'm owed a few days. Can you sort it? Will fill you in.

Alex held the reins of the Funeral Team diary, and was deft at steering it this way and that as circumstance required. If she liked you.

Posthumus opened the Closed Cases folder on his computer, scrolled down to the Wojciechowski file, and clicked through to the apartment photos. There was the close-up of the odd painting of *The Syndics of the Drapers* he'd printed out a few months before, the six soberly dressed grandees, he now knew, painted as if captured a few minutes after Rembrandt's original. Cornelius had wanted to see it, Posthumus remembered. He 'pinged' one across, as Cornelius had put it, and from his phone sent the photo that Anna had taken of the painting in Zig's room. Returning to the computer, Posthumus clicked a few photos back in the sequence. He raised his eyebrows slightly, and jotted an addition to the notes he was making. Zig's painting was on the floor, propped up beneath a blank space on the wall. Posthumus zoomed in, moved the cursor around: a stick-on picture-hook on the wall, one of those you had to leave for twenty-four hours before using. The torn-open pack lying beside the painting on the floor. By whatever means Tony had come by Zig's picture, he had not had it for long before he was killed.

Posthumus clicked the first photo in the file and started Slideshow, pausing it occasionally, zooming in, making a note. The apartment was much how he remembered it. Immaculate. No books, the music clearly all stored digitally. A line of only four or five CDs. There was a close-up. Posthumus could read the titles, but there was nothing he had heard of, apart from a curiously incongruous Spice Girls album. The other names all sounded like rap or heavy dance music. Even the bedroom – or possibly especially the bedroom – was like a film set, or a catalogue photo. Unreal, perfectly laid out, pristine except for a half-open sports bag, dropped untidily on its side at the foot of the bed. Photos of the wardrobes, doors opened wide to display their contents. A photo of a drawer empty but for a thick wad of cash. They'd needed a key from the ring Tony had had with him for that one. Sulung had joked that for once the department might cover the funeral costs, would even make a profit. In another drawer, there'd been a batch of photos, each showing Tony with his arm around a different girl. The slide show flicked through them one by one. Nine. And beside the bed, another – the same size – in a heart-shaped frame. A cheap seduction device, he and Sulung had thought – the replaceable love photo. Even at the time he'd thought they were sweet-looking girls for such a tinpot Lothario. It sickened him now, to realise what Tony had been up to.

Posthumus closed the file and shut down the computer. He tutted to himself, handwrote a note to Sulung saying that he had dealt with the complaining Muller relative, and put the Muller and Wojciechowski files back on the shelf across the room – in the correct places. He had tidied his desk and was on the way downstairs to Alex, when his phone beeped in a message from Anna.

I'll kill her. I'll KILL her!

'Aldert Mantje? The *Night Watch* piece at Schiphol? Yes, that was Mantje. Him and a couple of others, if I remember correctly. Nice work, clever. Well painted, too. That still matters to some of us.'

Floris de Wit shrugged off his overcoat and hung it on a rack made from the back of a wooden chair, fixed midway up the wall. Cornelius had spent well over an hour in the badly heated café across the road from Floris's gallery, waiting for him to open up. His cheeks glowed pink. Floris switched on a small electric heater in the screened-off corner of the room that served as an office.

'Your coat?' He held out a hand.

'I'll keep it on for a bit,' said Cornelius.

Floris, without asking, poured them both a genever, and slid Cornelius a glass across the table.

'*Proost*! And you say these paintings are similar?'

'But certainly not by Mantje,' said Cornelius.

He took out his phone.

'Here. The *Syndics* . . . and a Vermeer. That's the one that was in the apartment, unfinished.'

Floris took the phone, put on a pair of round, horn-rimmed spectacles, looked at the pictures, and smiled.

'Subtle,' he said. 'You know the originals, of course, in the Rijks?'

'Not well enough to play spot-the-difference, I must admit. Pieter told me,' said Cornelius.

'Well, I'd say these are certainly inspired by Mantje. *Homage* to. Direct crib of.'

'But why? If we can work out what this boy was up to – why

he was *painting*, why *these* paintings, why doing *this* with them – then we're moving somewhere.'

'Maybe he simply liked Mantje.'

'That much?'

'So then it's the question you lot always loathe to hear,' said Floris, topping up their genevers. 'What is the artist trying to say?'

Cornelius was silent.

'Well, in Mantje's case, I imagine it was a cheeky take on a national symbol,' said Floris, 'with a wink at photography. The moment. Or if I were to put it in catalogue-speak, "a statement of transience and the illusion of time".'

Floris gave the last phrase a hollow, breathy tone. Cornelius grimaced.

'These are actually not that bad,' Floris continued, zooming in and out of the paintings, flipping between them. 'I'm presuming from what you say that the lad had no formal training. But look here, even on the resolution this phone gives.'

He zoomed in on a detail of *The Syndics*, and turned the phone towards Cornelius.

'The brushwork's quite crude. I mean, he's got an eye and this looks OK in a photograph, but I don't think it would if you actually saw it. But this . . .'

He brought up the Vermeer.

'Now this is very fine. I'd say someone has been helping him, his technique's improved markedly. Odd though . . .'

Floris was back on the detail of *The Syndics*. He switched to the Vermeer for a moment, then back to *The Syndics*. Cornelius waited.

'At first I thought he'd dated them,' said Floris. 'No signature, just the year, and on the front of the canvas, which is unusual. That would work for the Rembrandt.'

He slid the phone back across the table. Cornelius checked.

In the bottom right-hand corner of *The Syndics* was the date 2012.

'But then have a look at the Vermeer,' said Floris.

Cornelius did. There the date read 2015.

'Dating it in the future?' said Cornelius.

'And before he'd even finished the painting.'

'Come to think of it,' said Cornelius, 'even *The Syndics* has a future date. Our artist died in 2011.'

Floris shrugged, and knocked back his genever.

'Lord knows what that is about,' he said. 'But tell you what. We could take a little walk.'

Cornelius glanced around the corner of the screen, and out through the gallery window. The narrow Jordaan street, which usually carried a steady stream of cyclists, shoppers, people wandering in and out of other galleries and cafés, was deserted. Flakes of snow flew almost horizontally past.

'Or maybe I'll phone,' said Floris. 'Carla Spiers. Gallery O, around the corner?'

Cornelius shook his head.

'I don't think it's Mantje's gallery as such, but there were a few of them involved with that project. Some of the old Seymour Likely group.'

Again Cornelius shook his head. 'Not entirely *au fait*, I'm afraid,' he said.

'One of the Seymour Likely lot is hers, I'm pretty sure,' said Floris. 'I know she had something to do with that *Night Watch*, anyway.'

Cornelius wandered out into the gallery while Floris telephoned, and stood looking at a portrait of a boy with full lips and almond eyes, done with a sombre palette of maroons, deep greys and a soft olive green. It was as if an abstract painting – a Rothko, someone like that – had resolved itself into a face. Something Gabrielle would like. Perhaps they should commission a portrait of little Lukas. Cornelius bent his head to peer at the price tag. Not on a poet's poor scrapings, nor even on Gabrielle's rather healthier whack, they wouldn't. He carried on walking around the gallery. He could hear Floris going through the usual socials, then telling Carla about Zig's paintings. Followed by a short silence. Floris chuckled, and dropped into what was clearly gallery gossip. A moment later, he appeared around the corner of the screen, brandishing a piece of paper.

'Quite possibly, you're in luck,' he said.

After lunch, Posthumus tried Anna's phone again. It continued ringing then flipped over to voicemail. He left another 'You OK? What's up?' message, and crossed the street to FitFast. The gym had occupied the same spot on Valkenburgstraat for years. Well, almost the same spot – and it hadn't always been called FitFast. Posthumus remembered it first as Henk's, a rundown neighbourhood weight-lifting centre. He'd looked in once, as it was close to home, but free weights, peeling paint and grunting musclemen had made him ill at ease, and in the end he'd opted for swimming to keep himself in shape.

In the past few years, he had seen the place transform itself, expanding first into the building on one side, then on the other, as the gym fad caught hold of Amsterdam – and as the patch between Waterlooplein and the IJ Tunnel was redeveloped and gentrified. Free weights and body builders had given way to fitness machines and clients in chic sportswear. The blanked-out window that Henk's presented to the street had become a moving frieze of figures on treadmills behind lightly frosted glass. Somewhere along the way, Henk's had changed its name to suit its new image. But Posthumus still preferred the cosy, early twentieth-century ambience of the

Zuiderbad pool. He stood to one side, as the gym door swung open and a couple of young women walked out into the street. It was going on for two o'clock; the last of the lunchtime crowd would be leaving.

Inside, four men with identical sports bags were bantering with the attendant as they handed in their locker keys. As they passed, Posthumus thought he recognised a face. The man caught his glance, nodded, and left with the others. Posthumus looked back over his shoulder at the logo on their sports bags, and it clicked. It was one of the police officers who had been around on the night of Zig's death, the one who had taken charge when Posthumus let them in to the guest-house. Of course. The big IJ Tunnel police bureau was just up the road. Still, the coincidence unsettled him. Posthumus walked up to the counter. A lean young man stood at the till. Shaven head, tiny ears. Not an ounce of surplus anything.

'Welcome to FitFast!'

The words almost bounced out of him.

'I'm thinking of joining,' said Posthumus. 'You have some sort of day ticket, so's I can try it out?'

'Not been before, then?'

Posthumus smiled encouragingly. Perhaps that *wasn't* entirely obvious from his initial request.

'I used to know the place a while ago, but looks like things have changed a lot,' he said.

'If you fill in the form you can have a free trial visit.'

The young man flourished a sheet of paper.

'Thank you . . .' said Posthumus, keeping eye contact, and cocking his head to one side.

'Oh, Pogo. Everyone calls me Pogo.'

Posthumus could see why. The lad looked as if he was worked by a spring.

'Thank you, Pogo.'

The counter also served as a juice bar. Posthumus pulled a stool nearer to the till, sat down and began filling in the form.

'You worked here long?' he asked, as he wrote.

'Couple of years,' said Pogo.

Dive in at the deep end, thought Posthumus. Worth a try.

'Robbie still work here?' he said.

Pogo turned to look directly at Posthumus. 'Robbie? Robbie Kramer, you mean?' he said. 'No.' His bathtub-smooth brow crinkled slightly. 'What you asking about Robbie for? You a journalist or something?'

Posthumus laughed. 'No, no no. I live nearby,' he said.

He remembered 'Robbie K.'s' age from the *Telegraaf* article, did a quick calculation.

'My son used to hang out with Robbie,' he said. 'Nice guy.'

God, that made him feel old. Pogo grinned. He looked as if he never lost his bounce for very long.

'Robbie left a while back,' said Pogo, 'After, you know, after all that in the newspapers, and all . . .'

'That thing with the sauna?' said Posthumus. 'Yes, I can imagine that must have been hard on him.'

Two box-built men in tracksuit bottoms and puffa jackets dropped off their locker keys. Clearly some of the old Henk's crowd were still around. Posthumus paused over the form.

'Robbie wasn't sacked or anything, was he?' he said, with a look of concern. 'I mean, it wasn't really his fault, after all.'

'Too true it wasn't! He was well cut up about it. And we all told the boss it wasn't, an' all. Poor Robbie.'

Pogo warmed to what clearly had been, maybe still was, a cause.

'I take it that he did have to go, then. That hardly seems fair,' said Posthumus.

'*Yeah*, tell me,' said Pogo.

Posthumus signed the bottom of the form, and handed it back to Pogo. Another gentle prod.

'You know what people were saying, though.'

'Yeah, but what could Robbie have done, I ask you? Like, *all* the keys were back in, Robbie said he checked the change area, and there weren't any clothes or bags or *nothing*. I mean, OK, so he didn't go *inside* the friggin' sauna. You don't, do you?'

Posthumus shook his head.

'But that didn't cut shit with the boss though, did it?' said Pogo. '*Out*. On his friggin' ear.'

A clutch of young women, gossiping about an office colleague, handed in their keys. Pogo turned with Posthumus's form to a computer beside the till, his face taut. Posthumus sensed Pogo did not like his boss.

'Tell you what,' said Posthumus. 'Give me a strawberry and banana smoothie. I could do with a bit of energy before I start.'

Pogo left the form on the counter, and turned back to Posthumus. 'We've got energy drinks, too, if you like,' he said, 'or I can mix you a protein shake. Build you up.' He nodded to a shelf of dumpy plastic bottles, with names like Whey-In, PerfectPec, and Hi-Hunk.

'A smoothie will be fine,' said Posthumus, suppressing a grimace.

Pogo walked to the other end of the bar to fetch the fruit.

'So the whole blame gets dumped on poor Robbie,' Posthumus continued. 'Shouldn't someone else be responsible for locking up and all that? Wasn't the boss around?'

'On a Saturday night? You gotta be joking. Dunno why we even friggin' open. There's never anybody here, hardly. Not later on, anyway.'

Pogo dropped the fruit into the liquidiser, and gave Posthumus a grin. 'Anyone who's keeping themselves nice and trim is out having fun Saturday night, aren't they?'

For a moment the machine drowned out conversation. Posthumus checked his phone. Still no reply from Anna to the 'What's up?' messages he'd left earlier. Pogo brought him his drink.

'That was very hard on Robbie. Especially when it turned out that it wasn't, you know, an accident . . .' said Posthumus.

'That someone did that guy in, you mean?' said Pogo.

He leaned over the counter towards Posthumus, and lowered his voice. 'The geezer that did it was a regular. László, his name was. *And* he was in that Saturday night, Robbie said. Told the cops an' all.'

'So they got him?' said Posthumus. 'Surely that made Robbie a bit of a hero.'

'Couldn't make it stick, could they? *He* said he was with his girlfriend all night. No one else would say they saw him, so it was Robbie's word 'gainst theirs. Still, he's doing time anyway, isn't he? László. Locked away all safe and sound, as we live and breathe. Not that that stops him. Does it all by phone now, doesn't he. With a phone that was magicked into his cell. Fucking pimp. Sorry. Language.'

Two young men came in. Late teens, early twenties. Cocky. Good-looking. Pogo slid them a couple of locker keys without a word. The younger one held Posthumus's gaze cheekily as he passed. Posthumus took another sip of his smoothie.

'Couldn't anyone back Robbie up? What about CCTV?' he asked.

Pogo laughed. 'Here? You gotta be joking,' he said. 'Boss is a mean asshole. All fake. In there at least.' He pointed a thumb over his shoulder towards the door marked Fitness Rooms.

'Just to make the customers happy, think we're watching them all attentive like, in case they snuff it on a treadmill. Only one that works is this one here, close focus to make sure we're not nicking from the till. Besides, László had powerful friends, know what I mean? Still has. And now I saw on telly they're saying this crazy lady did it. Huh!'

Pogo whisked Posthumus's form from the counter, and began entering the data into the computer, then the printer whirred into action. Pogo flipped back into professional mode.

'I've done you a free-trial day ticket, then if you find you like FitFast and join, you'll get 10 per cent off the registration fee, but you must do it within a week. Here you go.' He handed Posthumus a bright yellow sheet of A4. 'All the info is on there,' said Pogo.

Posthumus glanced at it. 'Personalised Welcome and Price List,' it read. Posthumus grimaced slightly. 'Welcome to FitFast PIETER POSTHUMUS,' it went on. There followed an enthusiastic lauding of the gym's features and amenities, and a price list.

'If you decide to join, you'll need a photo for the membership card, but we do that here,' said Pogo.

'Then all I need do is show my card when I come in, and the rest is free?'

'Bingo! Except the sunbeds.'

Posthumus drained his drink. 'Couldn't that have helped Robbie?' he asked. 'Membership cards, I mean. You keep a record or something?'

Pogo nodded and tapped a small device beside the computer. 'Magnetic strip,' he said. 'Checks you're still valid. But some don't have cards. Friends of the boss, a few of the old crowd been here years, the likes of those two just came in.'

Posthumus looked at him enquiringly.

'Boss runs an agency. They get in free,' said Pogo, his voice hard. 'Enjoy your workout.'

Posthumus swung from the stool, and picked up his sports bag. 'Thanks,' he said, 'and say hi to Robbie, if you're still in touch.'

'Don't hardly hear from him no more,' said Pogo. 'He buggered off, and he's got a new phone.'

'Any idea where?' asked Posthumus.

'Dunno. New job. Germany, I think.'

Posthumus turned back to the bar. 'Germany? Not Berlin?'

'Search me. But hey, what about your son, doesn't he know? Does ever hear from Bobbo?'

'Don't think so.'

'What's his name? Do I know him?'

Posthumus felt his gut tighten. He should have seen that coming. 'Willem,' he said, without a beat.

Pogo glanced at the computer screen. 'Willem Posthumus?'

Posthumus's gut knotted further.

Pogo shook his head. 'Nope,' he said.

'I'll ask,' said Posthumus, and walked quickly to the door through to the fitness rooms.

'Men's locker room down the passage to the left,' Pogo called after him.

What the *hell* had made him use Willem's name like that? Posthumus walked down the corridor and pushed open a swing-door stamped with the silhouette of a male weightlifter. Just when he thought he might finally be laying his brother and all of that to rest. He'd had that dream again last night. Zig the fallen angel somehow melding with Willem, twitching, dying on wet tarmac.

The locker room was clearly part of the original Henk's. Long and narrow, with scuffed walls, the floor water-stained. Lockers down one side of the first section; benches and clothes hooks along the other. A couple of sports bags, too large for the lockers, under the benches. Then a row of showers facing a line of wash basins. Someone in the showers – Posthumus could hear splashing water. The sauna was at the far end of the room, its door facing the entrance. There was a glass panel in the door, but the light inside was dim. Posthumus could barely make out the interior, couldn't say whether there was anybody in there or not. The glass, anyway, gave a view of only a small part of the sauna. He walked on past the showers. Steam rose from behind one of the pairs of saloon-style doors, and Posthumus caught sight of a man's thickset neck and hairy shoulders under a cascade of water.

To the left of the sauna door was a small cooling-off alcove, which gave the locker room a stubby L-shape. Benches around the edges, more coat hooks. An elderly man held on to a hook with one hand, as he leaned and pulled up his underwear with the other. His towel lay crumpled on the floor, the legs of a pair of trousers dangled from a supermarket bag beside him. A towel and another set of clothes were hanging from hooks across the alcove, a sports bag under the bench. If Robbie had simply looked in at the door, and Tony Wojciechowski had left his stuff here in the alcove, then of course Robbie would have thought the locker room empty. And might not have seen anyone in the sauna.

The old man turned, still hanging on to the coat hook, and gave Posthumus an unfriendly look. Posthumus returned to the other end of the room, found his locker, and sat down to slip off his shoes. He'd have to make some show of a workout, at least. The pattering water stopped. A man with a large beer gut banged out of the shower, strode across to the sauna, and slammed the door behind him. A few seconds later he was out again.

'Bloody motherfuckers, they never put the fucking thing on! We pay all this money and they never put the fucking thing on!'

Still wet from his shower, a towel barely reaching round his midriff, he stormed past Posthumus and yelled out into the corridor.

'Pogo! Pogo!'

'Shall I go?' said Posthumus. 'I'm still dressed.'

Pogo shrugged apologetically and came out from behind the counter.

'Boss does it,' he said. 'Resets the time switch to turn off during the quiet patch between lunch and five, and *we* gotta take the flak. I'll come with you.'

'Can't you sort it from here?' said Posthumus.

'Switch and stuff is in there,' said Pogo. 'Electrics in this place is like spaghetti, with the expansions and all.'

They returned to the locker room. Posthumus went back to getting changed for his workout. The man with hairy shoulders let forth a torrent of abuse at Pogo, who countered it cheerily, walked up to the sauna, and unlocked the flap of a wooden box attached to the wall beside the door. Posthumus could see a switch and a couple of bulky dials. Thermostat and time switch, most likely. He noticed that while the switchbox was as battered as the rest of the locker room, the lock, hasp and staple on it still looked shiny new.

Posthumus was hanging his jacket in the locker when his phone beeped. A message from Cornelius. Posthumus read it, and turned to Pogo as he passed on his way back to Reception.

'Pogo, I'm sorry,' he said, 'but do you think it might be possible for me to take a rain check on this free trial? I need to go, something's cropped up.'

8

Marty slid a calf's liver off the shelf, backed out of the refrigerator and kicked the door shut. He looked over his shoulder, into the shop. His mother had come down. Ten past three, about fucking time. Checking on the day's totals, of course. He could see her knobble-fingers and bright red nails tapping away at the till keys. Well, it was her turn to listen to the Kester cow now. He'd had enough of the woman, spluttering on about being barred from De Dolle Hond. Bad move on their part. It would probably drop the place's takings by half. Marty gave a wheezy giggle, and padded back up to the counter.

'I mean, who does she think she is?' Irene was saying, now for Pia's benefit. 'Just because I chose to speak my mind to the television people. Not that I'm bothered, I'm sure. She can keep her blasted café, there're plenty of others in town.'

'She's got a temper on her that one,' said Pia. 'Always has had. Learned it from her mother. It'll blow over, don't worry.'

'Oh, I'm not going back. You wouldn't catch me dead in there now. It's the principle of the matter! And she doesn't even tell me herself. Has that nice Simon do it, when I went in for my little lunchtime pick-me-up. Poor boy was so embarrassed.'

'Bet he enjoyed it,' said Marty, slapping the liver down on the cutting table.

Irene shushed him.

Pia wagged the till slip with the day's total at him, puckering her lips as if she had swallowed a lemon. 'Not very exciting,' she said. She turned to Irene. 'Don't know what he gets up to when I'm not down here. Certainly not selling any meat.'

Marty jabbed at the liver with a giant pair of scissors, releasing it from its vacuum seal. What the fuck was he supposed to do? Stand outside in his striped apron like the Jolly Butcher, calling in the customers?

'Not even a single slice of pastrami over lunchtime,' said Pia. 'Too lazy, even, to make any *broodjes*.'

Irene lowered her voice, conspiratorially. 'If you ask me,' she said to Pia, 'it's because he always seems in a bit of a grump. Lacks the friendly touch.'

Hello, thought Marty. I'm *here*, close enough to slit your ugly old throat. He sliced off two pieces of liver.

Irene leaned over and looked at them sceptically. 'Not like his father,' she said, now clearly directing the remark at him. 'Now *there* was a man for you.'

'God rest his soul,' said Pia, catching her reflection in the decorative mirror behind the counter, and wiping off a smudge of lipstick with her middle finger. 'I saw your big moment on the box last night, giving them the heigh-ho about Marloes. Good programme. "The Witch of De Wallen", I liked that.' She gave an odd, suppressed hoot of a laugh.

'Saw it, did you? Then that's more than I did,' said Irene. 'That Anna had it switched off, just as I was coming on. Up on her high horse.'

'She's on some sort of crusade to rescue the woman,' said Pia. 'Rita was telling me about it. St Marloes the Innocent, the Saver of Souls.'

Irene let out a snort. 'We all know she did it,' she said. 'Mad as a hatter. And that place of hers. It's a disgrace! All those weird types in and out all the time. At least *that's* stopped.

They should lock her up and throw away the key, that's what I say.'

'Interfering old bat,' said Marty, 'meddling in people's lives.'

'My God, it talks!' said Pia. She faked a look of astonishment in his direction.

'Well, at least there's *some* sense in you,' said Irene.

Marty thwacked the slices of liver on to the till scales. His mother could sort it from there.

'I'm going out,' he said.

He shrugged off his apron and dropped it on the floor.

'Out? In *this* weather? Where?' asked Pia.

'*Out,*' said Marty. 'My afternoon off, isn't it?' He glowered at the clock. He was thirty-two for Chrissakes, couldn't she get off his back?

Pia rolled her eyes at Irene, picked up the apron and began to fold it. 'You'd think he was sixteen, wouldn't you?' she said. 'The way he goes on.'

Marty turned to go upstairs and fetch his coat. The Kester cow had plonked her fat ass on the bench against the wall. The two of them would probably be at it all afternoon, customers or no.

'I wouldn't be surprised if that Anna herself had something to do with it all,' she was saying. 'And I could tell you a thing or two about *her*. She's got something going with that skinny musician in the bar, I'm sure. Rita says he's married and all, to a singer. *And* she's never really stopped with that Pieter Posthumus . . .'

Marty shuddered as he stepped outside. It had been below zero for weeks on end now. Still, not far to go. He looked straight ahead as he passed the butcher's window. She would be trying to catch his eye, to give him another of her 'so where do you think you're off to' looks. He stopped to buy a custard pastry, and ate it as he pushed his way past dawdling knots of stoned young tourists on Warmoesstraat. Even in this weather. In the middle of winter.

The sky was low and dark. Most places had their neon lights blazing, even though it was mid-afternoon. Marty breathed in deeply as he passed through the weed cloud outside a coffee shop, and turned to walk around the side of the Oude Kerk. Then he ducked down a dark street off the church square, one that frayed into a network of red-lit alleys, a world of its own, detached, even from the rest of De Wallen. No traffic, no shops, no bars, not even any bicycles. Just files of men, trudging back and forth past girls in windows.

Marty's eyes ran along the windows at pussy level as he walked. Here and there, he heard a murmured exchange about price. A door was unlatched, a customer slipped back out into the street, curtains were pulled open again. Left, and left again. A girl turned and wiggled her pert butt to lure a trick who was walking away. Last desperate try, thought Marty, but the trick was unimpressed and kept walking. An argument broke out down one of the dark passageways that led to a warren of indoor hutches. 'Twenty euros! I said *twenty* euros!' a woman was yelling. Marty walked on. He knew where he was going. He turned into an alley barely wider than a doorway. One of the girls rapped on the window as he passed. She must be new, he thought. The others recognised him, didn't even bother with the split-second smile. The black girl with the big boobs sat sending a text.

At the dead-end of the alley, a painted wall read 'MILORD – Bar – Girls – Live Porn Show – Exotic & Lap Dancing', with a picture of a woman in fishnet stockings and a silver top hat. The place looked closed, but Marty knew better. He pushed at the red door beside a column of framed photos, taken from porn mags, faded and bubbling slightly with damp. Inside, the old man in what counted as a ticket office nodded him through to the bar. Marty grunted an acknowledgement. Why did the place always stink of stale piss? He patted the thin wad of notes in his side pocket. Today, he had cash, was feeling flush, might even buy one of the girls a drink.

There were not many people in. Solos, mostly. Some with girls. One group of youngish men, workers, it looked like, builders probably. Polish. Something like that. Marty took a table near the dance floor. Tourists, and anything that counted as class, didn't come in here. They went to the big, glitzier places on the canals. He looked around. Two Middle Eastern-looking guys, drinking Cokes, between them a skinny little thing, with dead eyes. Someone passed out, or asleep, with his head on a table. The middle-aged couple who did the live sex show, standing at the bar in their street clothes. Coming or going. Just arrived, probably. They really were married to each other, someone had told him.

'Marteee, can I get you a drink?'

Marty looked up. It was blonde Barbara. Long legs, big tits, zesty. Not his type at all.

'A beer,' he said.

'Boss says it's on the house. Anything you like.'

'Whisky, then. A large one.'

Barbara was back in an instant, with a bottle, ice and two glasses.

'Boss will be joining you,' she said. 'Meantime, we've got something for you. Novelty act.'

She winked as she poured his drink, set down the bottle, and moved off towards the two Middle Eastern men.

Marty sat back in his chair and smiled. At least someone knew his worth. He took a slug of whisky. Call herself a mother? *Fuck* the way she treated him. The way she always had. Never right, never good enough. Never his fucking father, *that* was the problem. But he would show her. The background music stopped abruptly, coloured spotlights lit the dance floor, and loud, Arabic-sounding music blasted from a speaker somewhere behind him. Marty took another slug of whisky. Soon she really *would* have something to gossip about with the Kester cow. She'd see. He counted for something, could have some clout in the world. That interfering old bitch Marloes Vermolen was already beginning to find that out. Two birds with one stone that had been.

A little slip of a figure, dressed like something from the *Thousand and One Nights* stepped on to the dance floor, a scarf glinting with small metal discs veiling the lower half of her face, bare feet, a thin band of something satiny clasped with a big gold brooch over her almost flat breasts. She lifted her arms, and began the imitation of some sort of belly-dance. Marty's chair creaked, as he leaned back to watch. De Kok liked to put on different sorts of acts here. Try-outs, sometimes, for one of his bigger places. Or acts that catered for special tastes.

The dancer came towards him, her slim hips swaying like scales trying to find a balance, smooth skin dipping below her navel to pink bikini pants that barely covered her hairless little twat. Above the scarf, her eyes looked as if they were brimming with tears, and Marty noticed she was trembling.

'You like that, don't you?'

Marty put down his glass sharply.

For a big man, Henk de Kok moved very quietly.

'Maybe we can make her part of the deal. Your very own,' he said.

A dry chuckle was the only indication he might have meant that as a joke. Marty pushed down on the table to ease himself out of his chair. The table rocked, clinking the ice in the bucket.

'Couple of hours in the gym each week wouldn't do you any harm. Tell them I sent you,' said de Kok.

The dry chuckle again.

'Come!'

He indicated a table in the corner of the room. Marty struggled to his feet and picked up his glass. De Kok nodded at Barbara, then at the bottle on the table. She took a tray from the bar and walked across. Marty hesitated a moment, then put his glass back down. He was learning. He followed de Kok . . . Henk. They were partners, after all. Or would be.

De Kok strode ahead. Flat-top haircut, black leather jacket, jeans. Ordinary, really. Not at all flash. Marty wondered what he spent his money on. *All* that money. Two other places beside this one, then the gym, and nearly a third of the windows in De Wallen, people said. And Marty had been shown how much the windows could bring in. De Kok sat down. He had a sidekick. The sidekick did not speak. Remained standing. Marty tried not to look at him, to pretend he wasn't there. Natural as anything. Of course. He sat down too. Barbara poured the whisky, and walked away.

'Business,' said de Kok. 'Your junkie. He was on *Crimebusters* last night. I don't like that. Blabbing to the press. Tell him not to.'

'I'll . . . I'll try to find him,' said Marty.

This was not beginning the way he thought.

'You do that. I might have another job for him.'

Marty had no idea where Jelle Smits was. Shit.

'But . . . to more pleasant matters,' said de Kok.

Marty felt his shoulders relax. He leaned forward. De Kok rested a large hand on his back.

'The Vermolen woman. It's not going to be more than two or three days . . . she'll be sent down. As soon as she's properly out of the way, I want you to move. I don't want to risk the bitch getting off on appeal.'

He didn't touch his whisky. He pushed a business card at Marty across the table.

'Name of her lawyer,' he said. 'Don't deal with anyone else. Do the groundwork, make an appointment with her, she'll make sure the woman signs. That place is ideal. Lots of small rooms indoors, nothing on the street. And that's the direction things will be going now, if the council has its way – and those bastards are managing to give even Henk de Kok a headache.'

Buying up places, turning them into smart restaurants and fancy clothes shops, Marty knew all about that.

'Got to work round it,' he said. That was the tone to take. Knowledgeable.

'And we've got to move quick on the Vermolen place. We don't want anyone else getting power of attorney or anything. Then the other premises.'

'More?' Marty took a sip of whisky. He mustn't look too excited.

'Two at least. My other partners are fucked. The moment you've got some Egyptian or Hungarian trying to buy somewhere, the council's on to you. And they're on to most of my holding companies, already. But you, you're my man. Everything going for you. Good Dutch boy, family from the area, wants to open a cosy little hotel, then expand. Perfect. Just what they're hoping for.'

'What about permissions and things?' said Marty.

'You just get your hands on these places. Make sure the council thinks it's all kosher and cosy, so they don't try to buy. Or anyone else. Leave the rest to me.'

De Kok held out his hand to the sidekick.

'You don't have to worry about anything,' he continued. 'We've sorted out a little company for you. One that gets lost in the forest if you try to follow it. Sure, they'll get there in the end, but it will take them a while and by then I want it to be too late.'

The sidekick produced a wad of paper from a thin leather case.

'Contracts, company papers, that sort of thing,' said de Kok. 'All official and above board, my lawyer will sort it all for you from here on.'

He tapped the papers into a neat pile.

'I've put my scribble on them already, where it's needed,' said de Kok. 'But then I disappear. As far as Martin Jacobs Management goes . . .'

A little warm rush of pride.

'I thought you'd like that. As far as Martin Jacobs Management goes, you're managing director, landlord, the lot.'

De Kok pushed the papers across the table. 'I want to have this sorted tonight.' He patted Marty's shoulder.

It was dark in the corner. Marty angled the top sheaf out towards the dance floor. Still not enough light, and it looked like a lot of reading. Maybe he should take these home. He shifted his buttocks on the hard wooden chair.

'Take them home, take them home. Just make sure I've got them before morning,' said de Kok. 'You shouldn't trust me, you know. I've got a *very* bad reputation!'

Again the dry laugh. Marty joined in. He leaned back in his chair, so that his face was in the shadows. He didn't want de Kok to see the sweat he could feel beginning to prick on his forehead. The sidekick moved his weight from foot to foot. What the hell. Who understood any of this shit, anyway? And it wasn't as if he were going to say 'no'. Not now.

'I'm sure it's all fine,' he said.

Cool as anything.

'As you said, all sorted. And if you need it all back before morning . . .'

He took the pen De Kok was offering him.

'Show me where.'

Minutes later they were shaking hands. De Kok strode off, with a brief nod to Barbara, and to the Middle Eastern guys. Marty poured himself more whisky. Maybe he'd even force his mother to sell the butcher's. Become his tenant. That would be a good one. He smiled. The music had stopped. The little belly-dancer was walking towards him.

9

Posthumus put his sports bag on the floor, and with one foot edged it under the table, wincing as pain jabbed at his knee. It had been a classic Amsterdam winter mishap. Cycling too fast over a hump-back bridge, slipping on ice as he was taking the corner afterwards. The sort of mistake you made only once. Supposedly. Like getting your front wheel caught in the tramlines, or dropping your keys into a canal while you were unlocking your bike from a bridge railing. Posthumus had ticked off all three years ago, but he'd been distracted today, thinking about what Pogo had said at the gym. And wondering what it was that was making Cornelius so excited.

'Just a coffee please,' he told the waitress.

She gave him a look of polite surprise and put away her notepad.

'For the moment, anyway,' he said. 'I'm waiting for a friend.'

People crossed town for the cakes here. Was that what had made Cornelius pick the place? Surely not. It seemed an odd choice. Around him, women, mostly, sat chatting over dark wedges of chocolate, thin pastries topped with elaborate mounds of glacéed fruit. Relaxing after a quiet afternoon at the Rijksmuseum, most likely, or from browsing the galleries and antiques shops round the corner. Smart. Lots of tailored tweed, mohair, the odd modest string of pearls. Posthumus pushed the sports bag further out of sight. He checked his phone. Not damaged in the fall, thank God. And at last a message from Anna.

All OK, don't fret. More than OK. Been v busy. Didn't have to kill her. Ax

With an x, no less. She must be in a good mood. Anna didn't scatter her kisses lightly. Posthumus sighed, and closed the message. Nearly three thirty. Where *was* the man?

Cornelius came blustering in from outside, the long coat he'd had on at the funeral now damp, and flecked with snow. He hung it on one of the overladen coat hooks at the door, looked around vaguely, straight past Posthumus, then smiled and came over.

'Pardon, dear Charon, pardon,' he said as he sat down, 'I humbly do desire your grace of pardon. Delayed at the Rijks. Might have met you there, if it still had a café.'

'Don't get me started on never-ending museum renovations,' said Posthumus, raising an arm as if to fend off a blow. 'The Rijks?'

'Tell you in a minute. All in good time.'

Posthumus's coffee had arrived.

'Same for me, please,' said Cornelius. 'No cake.'

Posthumus eyed a glistening *Sachertorte* as it passed.

'So, what's all the excitement?' he asked.

'The short version is, I've found more of Zig's paintings,' said Cornelius.

'Already? Good man! Where?'

Cornelius held up a hand. He had that look on him that he wore when he'd made a joke that no one else understood.

'The longer version,' he went on, 'begins in Floris de Wit's gallery in the Jordaan.'

Cornelius told Posthumus of Floris's agreeing that Zig's paintings were done in imitation of the one at Schiphol.

'His take on that one is that it toys with photography,' said Cornelius, 'plays with the idea of the moment. So, for our young man, maybe those "two minutes" are important, a moment that swung things one way or another.'

'What do you mean, exactly?'

'You know, like those movies where if a character catches the train one series of events occurs, but if she misses it, that leads to another set of consequences entirely. Life is completely different.'

Posthumus was not convinced.

'More broadly,' Cornelius went on, 'you could say the painting is playing with the idea of time. Of transition. Significant, perhaps, in that our young artist appears to have dated his work rather eccentrically. Did you spot that?'

Posthumus shook his head.

'Well, possibly they're not dates,' said Cornelius. 'Or, rather, they're *future* dates. But they're there on the two paintings you pinged me, on the front where the signature might be, and on the others, too.'

'These others . . .' said Posthumus.

'Good Charon, have patience!' said Cornelius. 'Floris phoned a fellow gallerist, one Carla Spiers, who had something to do with the artists involved with the Schiphol project. *She* remembers a young lad, foreigner, couple of years back, who on the strength of this involvement had tracked her down, wanting a gallery. Small portfolio, only two or three paintings, Carla not interested. Said the paintings were derivative, but she liked the boy, an "angel" apparently, thought he had skill, and put him on to an art-teacher friend. Floris *did* point out that Zig's technique had improved, between the *Syndics* and the Vermeer.'

'*Cornelius*, the other paintings!'

'Take care, dear Charon. Walk with me. Who knows

which step along the path is the one that brings you to enlightenment?'

'You're incorrigible.'

Posthumus grinned at him, shrugged, took a sip of coffee, and leaned back in his chair.

'OK, I'm with you,' he said, 'but can we keep it to journey highlights?'

'Very well,' said Cornelius. 'Art teacher remembers. Young man is indeed our Zig. Takes lessons. Improves. Considerably. But output is low. And he will not change his *idée fixe*. Won't paint anything but variations on the Schiphol theme.'

'Such as?'

Cornelius stared at Posthumus over the tops of his spectacles, and continued. 'Is obsessed by as many people seeing his paintings as possible. Doesn't want to sell them, but won't keep them, either. Wants them out in the world. Art teacher puts him on to the SBK.'

'I thought that had been wound up when subsidies to artists stopped,' said Posthumus.

'Not at all. It no longer disperses the works the poor souls handed over in return for their daily bread, but it's still an art library. And, *voilà*!'

Cornelius produced an iPad from the slim leather case he had carried his poem in, to the funeral that morning.

'Amazing, isn't it?' he said, holding the tablet between thumb and forefinger. 'State-of-the-art, as thin as air. One benefit of fatherhood. Young Lukas is all of eleven, yet he firmly instructed me what to buy, and of course works the thing better than I can. But for now, only the bare minimum of competence is required. I've downloaded these from their website. Look.'

Posthumus leaned forward.

'Two more,' said Cornelius. 'Another Rembrandt. *The Jewish Bride*, but Zig has her respond just a little more to her husband's touch. See? She's turned towards him, is looking up at his face. Not so the original. Two minutes later. The second one took a little more tracking down. Reason I was late. *The Cnoll Family*, it's called. Main point of note is that in the original those two little dogs aren't fighting, but one is cradled in the young girl's arms, looking down and about to jump. Again, two minutes later.'

He handed Posthumus the tablet.

'Extraordinary,' said Posthumus.

'*The Syndics* wasn't on the website,' said Cornelius. 'Registered as borrowed, but not returned. As we know. And there's one more, lent out. It seems the SBK fulfilled young Zig's desire to spread these paintings widely. It lends not only to private individuals, but to businesses, to the city council, public offices . . .'

The smile that had been twitching at the corners of Cornelius's lips spread into a grin.

'*And*,' he continued, looking over Posthumus's shoulder, 'to a certain patisserie.'

'You mean?'

Posthumus followed Cornelius's glance. On the back wall of the café hung a still life. Not a particularly good one. He'd barely given it a second glance when he came in.

'I imagine someone thought it whimsically appropriate décor, here in the shadow of the Rijks, and with all that fruit,' said Cornelius. 'I don't think the Old Masters did cakes. I thought a closer look might add a little piquancy to our meeting.'

'I *wondered* why you wanted to meet here,' said Posthumus. 'How did you find out where it was?'

'They weren't *too* reluctant to tell me, as it's in a public place. But I did have to do some fast talking, and take Floris's name in vain. Invent a little exhibition. Come! I've bought a postcard of the original from the Rijks. Let's have a look.'

He rose, and strode across to the painting. Posthumus winced as he got up, his knee still giving him hell.

Posthumus felt like a misbehaving schoolboy, as the two of them, mumbling an apology, crowded over an elderly woman at the table beneath the painting. She said nothing, drew her lips tight and did not give way an inch, exuding moral superiority. Cornelius dipped his head at her slightly, then ignored her completely.

'Passable, though not nearly as competent as the others,' said Cornelius.

'Well, it was a bit ambitious on Zig's part to try a still life,' said Posthumus. 'Naïve, almost, especially if he was untrained. Artists used still lifes to really show off their skills – painting different textures, surfaces, that sort of thing. He hasn't got that at all.'

'I'd say it's one of his first,' said Cornelius. 'And *that's* intriguing . . .' He indicated the lower right-hand corner of the painting. 'See, 2011,' he said. 'The lowest number so far, and if it is a date, the only one not in the future.'

The elderly woman gave an audible sniff and, still not compromising in any way by leaning back, raised a fork of cream cake to her mouth, narrowly missing the cuff of Cornelius's jacket.

'But how on earth do you apply the two-minute rule to a still life?' said Cornelius.

He held up the postcard for comparison.

'There's a plate missing,' he said.

'Of course!' said Posthumus.

He pointed to a half-moon shape at the bottom of the canvas. Those rainy afternoons with his father's coffee-table books, his first art lessons. He could almost hear his father's voice, gently explaining.

'Often there'd be a plate at the front of the painting, teetering on the edge of the table,' said Posthumus. 'It helped give a sense of depth, of reality, almost as if you needed to grab it. Look, here the plate's fallen off.'

'And there are a couple of apples missing from the bowl,' said Cornelius, 'and more debris on the table.'

He showed Posthumus the postcard. A few more nutshells had been added to those scattered on the tablecloth in the original painting. The woman they were looming over put down her coffee cup with a clatter.

'So sorry,' Posthumus said to her, 'we're being very rude.'

The look she gave him in return simply acknowledged that as fact.

Posthumus put a hand on Cornelius's arm, and nodded back towards their table.

'That does look like a date at the bottom, doesn't it?' said Posthumus, as they sat down again. 'And you say the others have something similar? I didn't pick up on that, looking at photos.'

'Not like Charon to miss a detail.'

'I guess I was looking at the big picture,' said Posthumus.

Cornelius scowled at him over the top of his horn-rims. '*The Syndics*, 2012, *The Jewish Bride*, 2013, the *Cnolls*, 2014, and the Vermeer from Zig's room, 2015,' he said.

'So, a sequence of some sort. Serial numbers, perhaps? Or, say they are dates, then a different calendar?'

'None that I know of,' said Cornelius. 'Not Jewish, not Muslim, and the difference between Julian and Gregorian is only a matter of weeks.'

'Merel said that *Night Watch* was at Schiphol in 2005. She remembers it, she was travelling a lot,' said Posthumus. 'So there wouldn't be one before then. And that was about the time Zig came to Amsterdam. So, say he started then. Five paintings . . . not quite one a year, if those are sequential dates of some sort. Maybe we're still missing some.'

'Somehow, I suspect this is our lot,' said Cornelius. 'From what both Carla Spiers and the art teacher said about Zig's slow output. And there's certainly nothing more at the SBK.'

Posthumus sighed. 'And where does all this get us, anyway?' he asked. 'As far as Marloes goes, I mean.'

'I reiterate my argument of this morning, m'lud,' said Cornelius. 'There is a *reason* for these paintings. It's not the *when*, but the *why*, not a question of when Zig began painting, but for what reason. And why this *particular* painting? There lies the way forward.'

'I need to think,' said Posthumus.

'And I,' said Cornelius, checking his watch, and leaping abruptly from his chair, 'need to go! Have to pick up Lukas!'

He hastily scrabbled together his belongings.

'You and your paintings,' he said. 'I completely lost track of time.'

Posthumus checked his own watch. 'I'm meeting up with Anna later, at De Dolle Hond, to talk everything through,' he said. 'You able to join us, you think?'

'I'll try,' said Cornelius. 'Depends what time Gabrielle gets home from work. And in what mood.'

He was already halfway towards the door.

Posthumus pushed the two empty coffee cups on the table to one side, against the wall, then brushed the detritus of sugar and coffee-creamer sachets into a pile. He stared at the coffee cups a while, a slight furrow between his eyebrows, then, with his forefinger, tapped at the handles, till the cups were aligned in the same direction. He placed the teaspoons in parallel.

'Anything more I can do for you, sir?'

Posthumus looked up at the waitress, blinking. 'Um, yes,' he said. 'I'd like another coffee . . . and a slice of *Sachertorte*.'

Reaching into his jacket pocket, he took out a pen and small black notebook, and made a list. He left the notebook open in front of him as he devoured the *Sachertorte*, looking long at what he had written.

1) 2011 *Still Life*
2) 2012 *The Syndics*
3) 2013 *Jewish Bride*
4) 2014 *Cnolls*
5) 2015 *Vermeer*

It was a series, clearly. And Posthumus could not shake himself free of the idea he had raised with Cornelius that the figures were dates, rather than simply numbers in the sequence. Why was that? Because they were positioned where a signature would be? Because they included current dates, 2011, 2012? He shrugged, and tapped the tip of his cake-fork on the edge of the plate. One, two, three, four, five. From what Cornelius had said, one painting a year was quite feasibly the rate of Zig's output. So, what if the numbers were dates, or referred to dates? How did they then relate to reality? The date he knew for certain was for the Vermeer which had been in Zig's room when he was killed. He took a last mouthful of cake, pulled the notebook towards him, and adjusted his list, working in reverse.

1) 2011 $_{2007}$ *Still Life*
2) 2012 $_{2008}$ *The Syndics*
3) 2013 $_{2009}$ *Jewish Bride*
4) 2014 $_{2010}$ *Cnolls*
5) 2015 $_{2011}$ *Vermeer*

Then he asked for the bill.

The Zuiderbad, that's what he'd do. It was just five minutes away, and he had his trunks in the sports bag. A long swim, before heading over to De Dolle Hond. That would help clear his head. And it might be good for his knee.

It was counting the lengths as he swam up and down that gave him the idea.

10

Posthumus slung his sports bag over one shoulder, and opened his front door. A good swim always gave him a lift. A bonus. Like starting the day again, fitting two days into one. Especially with a hot shower afterwards. It seemed to have sorted his knee, anyway. And had set him thinking. He picked up his post and newspaper from the mat, and quickly climbed the steep stairs to his apartment. As he passed Gusta's door on the first floor, he heard it open behind him.

'Parcel for you!'

Posthumus turned round. He smiled weakly; he really wasn't in the mood for Gusta.

'I had to sign for it,' said Gusta, beckoning him in. 'I was just pouring a glass of wine.'

'Sorry, Gusta, I've a lot on my plate at the moment . . .'

But he didn't finish. Gusta had already gone in, in a waft of coloured silk. He followed, inhaling the familiar odour of face powder and tobacco that filtered from her apartment. A padded envelope lay on the table, and beside it two wine glasses. Gusta was already filling the second.

'No, no, Gusta, I can't, sorry. I'm pretty much doing a U-turn, I have to go out again in a minute,' he said.

Posthumus managed to stop her halfway, clinked glasses in a toast, but remained standing, as if he were at a cocktail party. Gusta glanced at the envelope.

'It says "Contents, book and a pen",' she said. 'Gift. From America.'

She didn't actually *say* 'Aren't you going to open it', but he knew he would have to. It was the quickest way out. And if he didn't, she'd probably find some excuse for coming upstairs later.

'Is it what I think it is?' she asked.

Posthumus smiled, and tore open the envelope. He had no idea what Gusta might think it was. He didn't have a clue himself. He pulled a slim volume from the envelope. The pen, further wrapped in tissue paper, fell on to the table. Unabashed, Gusta picked it up, and pulled off the paper. Posthumus looked at the book, and felt a lump come to his throat. *Selected Poems of Bart Hooft.* Gusta was cradling a beautifully lacquered fountain pen, its black body flecked with gold, a Bird of Paradise design down one side.

'It is, isn't it?' she said. 'It's the Namiki you showed me a photo of last summer!'

Posthumus glanced up, but did not answer. He looked back at the book. There was a handwritten letter slipped inside the cover.

'Have you *any* idea what this is worth?' said Gusta, cradling the pen in one hand.

Posthumus nodded. 'Vaguely,' he said.

'Vaguely! *Vaguely*, ten grand at least, and he says *vaguely*.'

Gusta spoke to the heavens, as if imploring help from her insane neighbour.

Posthumus read the letter.

Dear Pieter Posthumus,

As you see, I have followed up on your suggestion and published a selection of Bart's poems. It's a small edition, done privately through a contact at the university, but I'm

sure you'll agree they have made a beautiful book. Bart's
mother and I would like to thank you – most *heartfelt*
thanks – for the quite extraordinary lengths you went to in
finding us, and in ensuring that Bart did not merely fade
from this earth in anonymity.

Even though the news you brought us was the saddest a
parent can hear, we both feel, in some way, reunited with
our son through your efforts. That means more to us than
words can express. We hope you will accept, as a rather
inadequate expression of our gratitude, not only a copy of
Bart's book, but the pen that was instrumental in your
tracking us down.

Yours, most warmly,

Jan and Nathalie Hooft

Posthumus downed his wine, thanked Gusta, retrieved the
pen, and with a hurried apology for his rudeness went on
upstairs to his own apartment. As he unlocked the door, he
glanced at the newspaper headlines. 'The Witch of De Wallen.'
Even they were at it. He tutted irritably, threw post and newspaper together on to the dining table, placed Bart's poems
and the pen carefully beside them, and went up to the bathroom to hang up his wet towel and trunks. That done, he came
back down and switched on the television.

Marloes again. A dreadful picture of her, looking haggard
and aggressive, and in front of it someone going on about
yesterday's trial, speculating about her court statement tomorrow. Posthumus switched off the sound. What was it that so
grabbed public imagination about the case? The lonely middle-
aged woman and two pretty young men part, he guessed.
There was certainly something salacious about all the media
frenzy. Or was it that a woman was accused of such violent
killings? Well, OK, Tony's death wasn't violent, but it was pretty

gruesome. It was the whole messy mix. Throw in Amsterdam, and the way the rest of the country liked to see the capital, add De Wallen and a guest-house for rejects and miscreants, and you got a toxic brew. And in the middle of it, Marloes.

Posthumus flipped through the newspaper on the dining table. The sensationalist bilge on programmes like *Crimebusters* was one thing, but he couldn't believe that even a respectable paper already seemed to condemn her. Inside, one of the columnists took a more reasoned approach, but even he thought the case done and dusted. He focused on Marloes's psychological report as the tipping point towards a guilty verdict, and argued for a short sentence then TBS, indeterminate psychiatric detention. Pretty much what Anna predicted. And, as she'd said last night, in Marloes's case that meant throwing away the key – accused of being in denial, because she denied doing it, of disturbed relationships with men. Well, what could you say? Marloes and men. Marloes and the world in general. But being an oddball didn't necessarily make you a murderer. Necessarily.

Posthumus put down the paper and walked across to the window. The canal below had frozen over. A father was standing, bent to support his little girl as she set off shakily on skates. First steps all over again. Posthumus put both hands on the wall across the top of the window and leaned forward slightly, as if hanging there, face almost on the glass. And for himself? What did he really believe? Instinctively, and with most of his reason, he simply could not see Marloes killing those boys. But part of him, a small part of him, had – on the night she was arrested – asked: *Did she?* There was that grain of suspicion, try as he might to banish it, that there had to be something in it, or she wouldn't have been taken into custody. That thin edge of condemnation simply because she had been accused. But didn't everyone have that, to some degree?

Posthumus pushed himself away from the window and turned back into the room. Not Anna, it seemed. He glanced at the television. More snow forecast. He'd walk to De Dolle Hond. Anna's faith in Marloes was unconditional. But then that was what it amounted to, a sort of religious faith in her innocence. Anna had set him the task of proving her blind belief true. And he had two days to do it. He picked up his overcoat, turned off the light and, locking the door behind him, set off back downstairs.

As he turned the corner of Nieuwebrugsteeg, he thought he saw Merel walking ahead of him towards De Dolle Hond.

'Merel?'

She turned, her smile buried in the folds of a bright woollen scarf.

'PP!'

'A surprise to see you here,' he said.

'It's work, actually. I wanted a chat with Anna. I'm having dinner nearby, so thought I'd drop in rather than doing it by phone.'

He caught up with her.

'Fat chance at the moment, I'd say, if it's going to take up any of her time. She's deep in the whole Marloes thing. What about?'

Merel put an arm through his. 'Sort of a spin-off from that, really. The paper asked me to do an insider story on Marloes. They know I have some sort of connection and I think wanted me to dish the dirt, but I wasn't into doing that. Luckily I've still got some leverage after the InSec story.'

Posthumus smiled at his niece. Her story in the summer, blowing the whistle on a rogue secret service officer planting an *agent provocateur* in a terrorist cell, had been huge, with major repercussions – official enquiries, the officer sacked, the Amsterdam Cell released.

'So I suggested something else, a long shot,' Merel went on. 'It took quite some talking, and I've used up most of my Brownie points, but in the end I managed to persuade them instead to let me do a piece on families that have been in De Wallen for generations. Legit businesses. Marloes would have to be a part of it, and Anna, of course, if she agrees, and I thought maybe the Kesters. I wanted to pick Anna's brains for other suggestions.'

'The Jacobs, at the butcher's, maybe? There aren't many.'

'That's the point. A dying breed, count them on your fingers, that sort of angle.'

'Now that everything's owned by syndicates and front-men, you mean.'

'Yeah, I'll have to make it newsy, link it to the council's attempts to buy up properties from the syndicates and change the face of De Wallen, but I want mainly to take a human-interest angle.'

'And your editor went for that?'

'Sort of. I've still got to focus quite a bit on Marloes, but maybe I can work in something about what she was trying to do at the guest-house, rather than all this crap that's flying around about her at the moment.'

'You know that Anna's roped me in to help?' said Posthumus. 'To try to piece together what really happened.'

'Bit late for that, isn't it?'

'Not if we move fast. We've got to come up with something new, something convincing, before they slap TBS detention on her. Then it becomes really difficult.'

'And?'

'There's lots that doesn't fit. I've been doing some thinking, spent the day asking around a bit. I was holding back earlier, because of . . . well, you know. I thought I had messed things up enough. But now that Anna's *asked* . . .'

Merel stopped mid-stride. 'Don't try to kid me you're unwilling! It's what you've been wanting to do all along,' she said.

Posthumus laughed. 'Well, at least this time I'll be getting someone *out* of hot water, rather than dunking them in it, like I managed to do with us,' he said.

'Do you hear me complaining?' said Merel. 'It got me my big story in the end, even if you did make life a little, shall we say, eventful.'

'And something else good came out of it,' said Posthumus. He told Merel about Bart's poems, and the gift of the pen.

'So, you see,' she said, 'not all bad.'

They had reached the door. A more serious note came into Merel's voice.

'I heard from Aissa,' she said.

'And? Any news on Najib? How are they all, how's Mohammed?'

Posthumus felt guilty that he had not kept in touch with Mohammed, after his attempts to clear up mysteries around the death of Mohammed's young relative Amir had apparently provoked such mayhem. He'd phoned, but Mohammed hadn't answered or returned his calls. Not that Posthumus blamed him – with his son Najib gone missing, the family blown apart. None of that was his fault, but he was sure Mohammed held him somehow responsible.

'I'll tell you inside,' said Merel, pushing open the door.

Simon, not Anna, behind the bar. The place was almost empty.

'Anna's upstairs with some guy,' said Simon, as they hung up their coats. 'Been there all afternoon.'

Posthumus frowned. 'Who's that?'

'Dunno. Smart-looking geezer in a suit.'

Simon ducked down to stash away some bottles.

'I'll just run up and tell her we're here,' said Posthumus.

'She said she'd be down again at six,' said Simon, popping his head back over the counter.

Posthumus turned to the door that led up to the apartment. Merel put a hand on his arm.

'Perhaps let's wait,' she said.

'I should find out if she managed to get some documents about Marloes today. She could be going through them now. I ought to be there to help.'

He knew that was not the real reason.

'There's lots of time for going through papers later,' said Merel. 'Let's have a drink.'

Posthumus hesitated. Who was this guy in a suit?

'It's not long to wait,' said Merel. 'Come on, give me twenty minutes of quality uncle time.'

'The usual?' said Simon, from the bar.

Merel led the way to a table near the fire.

'No, I think I'd prefer a red,' said Posthumus.

'For me, too,' said Merel, sitting down, with a nod to Mrs Ting, at her post as always on the fruit machine.

'Italian OK?' asked Simon.

'As long as it's not Merlot,' said Posthumus, joining his niece.

'She means a lot to you still, doesn't she?' said Merel.

Posthumus looked at her a moment.

'We've known each other for years. Decades.'

He didn't go on.

'I'd say, from our girlie-talks, that smart men in suits are not her type,' said Merel. 'She has quite a wild streak, our Anna.'

'Tell me about it,' said Posthumus. 'I found out about *that* some years ago.' He cast a sour glance at the podium in the corner. 'Musicians, especially,' he said. 'Even ones who read X-Men comics.'

'So there *is* something going on with Paul?' said Merel.

Posthumus didn't answer, but leaned back as Simon approached with the drinks.

'Is . . .' Merel hesitated a moment, then went on with her question. 'Is Paul married?' she asked Posthumus.

'Paul? Naw,' said Simon, as he leaned over and positioned two beer-mats on the table. 'Used to be, though.'

Merel looked relieved. She didn't seem to mind Simon's invasion of their conversation.

'To that singer. Sarah Lindberg?' Simon went on. He put down the two glasses of wine.

'She's good,' said Merel, with a laugh. 'Now *that* would be nice, Sarah Lindberg unplugged at De Dolle Hond.'

'Not much chance of that,' said Simon. 'One of the other guys in the band, he tried to, you know, suggest it. Complete veto from Paul.' Simon's voice dropped, confidentially. 'He's a bit hung up that she made it and he didn't, you know?' he said. 'Whatever. I don't think they're even talking.'

'It's just that when I phoned Irene Kester,' said Merel, 'she was saying that—'

'Her!' said Simon with a laugh. 'I'm sure she was. Full of shit, that one. Anyway, she's barred. As of today.'

'From De Dolle Hond?' said Posthumus, chuckling. 'Well done, Anna!'

Right on cue, Mrs Ting had a win.

Posthumus raised his glass, and nodded a toast across to Merel, as Simon returned to the bar.

'But, you were saying as we came in,' he said. 'Aissa?'

'She's phoned,' said Merel. 'I had left a few messages, but didn't want to push her. I'd given up hope, almost. Then there she was. On the phone.'

'And?'

'Well, it wasn't easy. I mean, first I blow apart her relationship with her boyfriend, then I write a piece showing him to the world as a complete bastard and *agent provocateur*, hardly a recipe for friendship.'

'It could be *part* of the recipe for a very strong friendship, if you talk to each other.'

'Well, we're meeting up over the weekend, so we'll see.'

'And the rest of the family, how are they?' said Posthumus. 'Mohammed? Her mother? Have they heard from Najib?'

'They got a letter, a few weeks after he disappeared, posted in Pakistan, no address. He's at a madrasah. Ahmed Bassir – that's the other one of the group who disappeared – he's there too. That's all they know.'

They were both silent.

'So, it's possible, then,' said Posthumus after a while. 'There is some sort of terrorist connection. All the way to Pakistan, no contact address? Sounds as if it could be some sort of training camp.'

Merel shrugged. 'Mohammed is gutted,' she said. 'Her mother, too. Aissa . . . she just sounded angry, but maybe she didn't want to speak on the phone. Anyway, we'll talk on Sunday.'

Merel took a sip of wine.

'Anna's back down,' she said.

Posthumus turned around in his chair. Anna was coming through the door from the upstairs apartment, a young man in a dark suit in front of her. They shook hands at the café door. Posthumus felt his back muscles relax a little.

'But, please, remember, that was all completely off the record,' the man was saying.

'Thank you, all the same,' said Anna.

'Glad to be of help.'

Anna came over to them.

'Merel! Nice surprise. And PP,' she said.

She bent over and hugged him around the neck. He leaned back against her.

'Have I got things to tell you!' she said. 'That was the lawyer I told you about, the one I met at the trial yesterday, Marc van Tilburg. A really nice guy, and you wouldn't think so to look at him, but a fellow New Wave fan. I lured him here with my vinyl collection.'

'Come up and see my etchings,' said Posthumus.

Anna gave him a little slap on the ear.

'The real reason he came was that he can't *believe* how completely crap Marloes's lawyer has been, and he wanted to help,' she said. 'I can't quote him on anything, he was quite firm about that. He didn't want to be seen badmouthing a fellow lawyer, or interfering in someone else's case, so kept saying this was friendly advice, not a professional opinion. But he's been a great help with the papers.'

'We were going to come up,' said Posthumus.

'Just as well you didn't, he'd probably have shut up like a clam. But maybe we should all go up now.' She turned to the bar. 'Simon, Simon, *dear* Simon, any chance of another hour or two?'

'No way, I'm sorry,' said Simon. 'I've already pushed it by being this late. Now I've really gotta go, I was supposed to be there an hour ago.'

Anna wrinkled her nose. 'Don't worry. Thanks, anyway, for coming in last-minute,' she said.

She looked back to Merel and Posthumus. 'You wouldn't mind sitting at the bar?' she said. 'I'll go upstairs and fetch the stuff.'

Posthumus reached for his glass and stood up, turning towards the bar. Outside in the street, in a flurry of snow, a familiar figure passed the window, and stopped at the door.

Posthumus nodded to Merel. 'Here's a good one for you,' he said, as Marty Jacobs came in to the café.

★   ★   ★

De Dolle Hond was quiet. The weather had kept most people home. Posthumus sat at his favourite spot at the bar, on the stool he always occupied when he dropped in alone to chat with Anna, where the counter met the wall, beneath the collection of old medals, pins and badges. In front of him, part of the pile of documents that Anna had brought back from Marloes's lawyer; on a stool next to him, those he had already skimmed through. Quite a haul. Anna had created a stink when the lawyer wasn't there for the appointment, got her to give the OK to her assistant over the phone, then bullied the girl into photocopying far more than the lawyer probably intended. Anna could hit land like a hurricane when she needed to.

'Can I freeze the rest of that pasta, PP?'

Anna was wiping down the counter beside him. He'd knocked up a quick meal for the two of them, as he sometimes did, in the little kitchen at the back of the café. They'd eaten as Anna told him about her visit to Marloes, and he'd filled her in on what he'd learned at the gym.

'It should freeze OK,' he said. 'Merel sure she doesn't want any?'

He looked across the room. Merel was still talking to Marty Jacobs over in the corner.

'She says she's going out,' said Anna.

'Of course, a dinner date, she said earlier.'

'I'll help her with the story, naturally. Especially to make sure she gets it right about Marloes. Just not tonight. The pasta was lovely, by the way,' said Anna.

A Sicilian-style sauce. Just what he could find in the cupboard. Tomatoes, capers, sultanas, almonds, anchovies, whirred in the blender. Fusilli. All done in twenty minutes. Why some people said they hadn't the time to cook, he had no idea.

'You could try the rest cold as a salad, it'll keep a while in the fridge,' said Posthumus.

He picked up a new sheet: Pathology Report.

'But I can see to that, I'll do it after this,' he went on. 'You need any help with that kitchen?'

It had been a mess, boxes all over the place, piled high against one wall.

'That shouldn't all be in there, I know,' said Anna, 'but there was a snacks delivery this afternoon, and Simon did a big wholesale shop. He'll sort it all out for me tomorrow, don't worry. There are more important things to be getting on with.'

She glanced at the pile of documents. 'How far have you got?' she asked.

'I'm on Zig's pathology report,' said Posthumus.

'Case in point,' said Anna. 'Marloes's lawyer should have called her own expert witness to question that, to see whether Zig's wounds could have been inflicted some other way. Marc says she should have asked for a whole reconstruction of the crime scene, to try to show things couldn't have happened the way the prosecutor says.'

'And she didn't?'

'She did zilch,' said Anna.

She spread the pile of documents in front of Posthumus across the countertop. 'See?' she said. 'Clean. That's what Marc called them, "clean". Not a pencil mark, not a Post-it, no highlighting. She's hardly looked at them. Marc said anything a lawyer had been through properly would have marks, notes, *something*.'

Posthumus patted the documents back into a neat pile.

'And it looks like she didn't bother to question anything that witness said, the friend of Tina's, what's his name?' said Anna.

Posthumus picked up one of the sheets he'd placed on the stool beside him.

'Jelle Smits,' he said.

For a moment the image flashed before him. The scrawny man, up on the television screen last night, during *Crimebusters*. A familiar face. But not from among those on the landing the night Zig died.

'She didn't bother to go to the interrogation when Smits was called before the examining magistrate,' Anna went on. 'And Tina wasn't even called. She could have demanded that.'

Posthumus toyed with the box of paperclips he'd brought down from upstairs, rotating it between thumb and forefinger, like a square wheel, one edge at a time.

'Perhaps we ought to try to speak to them,' he said.

'How? I've no idea where Tina could be.'

'Didn't she say anything, when you had to close the guest-house?'

'She'd already gone. Flitted a day or two after Marloes's arrest, without paying rent, let alone leaving any forwarding address.'

Anna looked down, and wiped a smudge of water off the bar counter with the flat of her hand.

'Without Marloes looking after her, she probably went back to work,' she said.

'In the windows?' said Posthumus.

'I don't know, could even be on the street, a girl like her,' said Anna. 'That's where Marloes rescued her from. Before that, she'd been a window-girl. On one of those really horrible alleys near the Oude Kerk, Marloes said, but there was a fight. Drugs or something, I don't know. She was kicked out, or ran away, I can't remember.'

'And this Jelle Smits,' said Posthumus.

He looked again at the witness statement.

'He says he was in Tina's room, heard shouting and thumping, then when he came out a few minutes later to go, saw

Marloes running down the stairs. He didn't think anything of it at the time, so left, but came in to the police next day, when he heard there had been a murder.' Posthumus looked up at Anna. 'But you said someone ran off once we were up there. Him, do you think?'

'Could be. They keep showing that interview on telly, I'm pretty sure it was him. But there was so much going on, I only got a brief glimpse. I was trying to help Marloes, we were the last up there. I couldn't really see. It's hard to say for certain.'

Posthumus stopped rotating the paperclip box. The footsteps drumming on the wooden stairs. He'd heard that. Strange. An adrenalin rush, maybe, making everything so clear, so sharp. Sensations, mainly, but individual, distinct, etched into his brain. Mentally, he reconstructed the scene, placed himself at Zig's door, went back to when he came up the stairs from the street, and on to the moment he touched Zig's body. The light, the smells, the sounds. The group clattering up the stairs after him. The landing. Someone breathing close behind him, the hand nudging his back, 'You're used to it'. Zig. The blood. All that blood. Somebody gagging. And somebody running back down the stairs. But that was it, he'd *heard* it. He looked hard at Anna.

'Where were you standing?' he asked.

He knew the answer. He could see her, with her arm around Marloes.

'Near the back of the group on the landing, directly behind you.'

'And you couldn't properly see who it was because?'

'He passed round behind me, then he ran down the stairs.'

'Exactly.'

'Exactly?'

'You can't see the stairs from that part of the landing. Apart from maybe the first one or two, and then the stairway does a turn, anyway, completely out of sight. If this Smits had just come out of Tina's room, like he says, he couldn't have seen Marloes running down the stairs, *and . . .*'

Posthumus put the paperclip box down with a bang.

'If he saw Marloes *on* the landing,' he continued, 'I doubt he would have given her a second glance, because his attention would have been taken up by the sight that presented itself to him directly opposite, as he came out of Tina's door. Of Zig's body on the bed, and his room covered in blood. Zig's door was *open* when I got to the landing.'

Posthumus placed both hands flat on the bar counter, and leaned back on the stool.

'So either Smits left when he said he did, in which case he must have seen Zig's body, and we have to ask *why* he then left, or he was in Tina's room all the time, and was the person you saw leave,' he said. 'Either way, something is wrong with his story.'

'You think he did it, and he's trying to frame her?' said Anna.

She leaned forward over the bar, her eyes shining. For a moment.

'Hang on, sorry,' said Posthumus. 'It could be that . . .'

He hesitated, chose his words carefully.

'That whoever did it closed the door afterwards.'

'Then how come it was open when you got there?' said Anna.

'Marloes would have opened it when she went up to fetch Zig for a drink,' said Posthumus.

Anna straightened up again, picked up a cloth and began polishing glasses.

Posthumus frowned. Why had he assumed that the door had been open all the time? He turned to the stool beside him, and picked out the two statements Marloes had made to the police.

'But whatever the case,' he went on to Anna, 'it is question-able that Smits could have identified anyone on the stairs, not from outside Tina's bedroom. We've got to find him.'

He flipped through Marloes's statements, the one from the Friday night, the second, only slightly more coherent, from the Saturday morning.

'God, this is all over the place,' he said. 'She was a mess.'

He read aloud. 'We must clean. I have to clean. It's impor-tant that the room is cleaned . . . so much blood. I don't like that, so much blood.' He turned a page. 'Zig is asleep now. Just asleep. An angel. I used to sing.'

Anna turned away.

'You have to admit, Tijgertje, it does make her sound a bit cracked,' said Posthumus.

His voice was soft. He had not used his pet-name for Anna in years.

She swung round to face him. Burning. 'Cracked, nuts, loony! Don't *use* words like that!' she said. 'She's had that all her life. That's the problem. Don't you see? OK, so she is all over the place when she speaks. It was worse that night because she was frightened and upset, but she's *always* done that. Maybe it's some attention-deficit thing, but she's not *mad*. But they jump on that, and say she's erratic. They *twist* everything. They say she has problems with men. Of *course* she does. Guys used to laugh at her, her father was a bastard. That makes her a killer? Like this morning, she's going on about people talking behind her back. So suddenly she's para-noid? But it's *true*. Pia, Irene, that lot, they *do*. But the DA's bunch look at her and they look at the bodies, and they think, Well there's not a lot of evidence, and we can't really see any motivation, so maybe she's mad. So they pack her off for psychiatric evaluation. And the shrinks look at her odd behav-iour, then they consider the crimes and say, Well, she's borderline, but somebody who did that *must* be insane. So she's insane. And then the court gets her back and says, Ah, she's insane, so she must have done it! It's Catch 22, twice over! And what happens? She denies it. Again and again, *because she didn't do it.* And what happens when she denies it, and keeps saying she's innocent? They say the first step to getting better mentally is to admit what you've done, and that she's still in denial. *Trapped.* That's the whole big, monster, *fucking* problem. You know you are innocent, so you think the system will protect you but it *doesn't,* it *fucks* you!'

Anna banged down the glass she was holding, and stormed from the bar into the little kitchen. Posthumus heard the courtyard door slam while the swing-door into the kitchen was still flapping. There was a murmur through the café.

Merel came over. 'Everything OK?'

'It'll be fine,' said Posthumus. 'Don't worry, go back to Marty.'

'We were finishing up, anyway. I'll just go and say goodbye properly.'

Merel returned to the table. Two new customers came in and stood waiting at the bar. Posthumus went round to the other side of the counter to serve them. Marty left. Posthumus nodded a greeting, and received a glower in return. Merel came back, and sat on the stool Posthumus had vacated.

'Odd one that,' she said.

'Who, Marty?'

'Very smug and pleased with himself,' said Merel. 'Going on about some great plan, a new business venture of his, but wouldn't say what it was. Then went all moody on me. He seems to have it in for his mother, though; it was like talking to a teenager. Still, I got some nice background on growing up here.'

Merel stopped. Anna had come back in to the bar. She walked up behind Posthumus and touched him on the elbow.

'It was a bit cold out there,' she said.

Posthumus gave her arm a squeeze.

'I think I've just charged two of your customers 1990s prices for their beers,' he said. 'They looked very pleased, anyway.'

He went back round to his stool. Merel got up to go.

'I must be off,' she said, 'I don't want to keep my dinner-date waiting. At The Grand, no less!'

'You choose them well,' said Anna.

Merel wrapped her arms across her chest and gave a little swagger, as if she were showing off a fur coat. Then she laughed. 'Work-related, alas,' she said.

'We'll talk some time, about your article,' said Anna.

'If you could find a moment tomorrow, that would be lovely,' said Merel. 'I'll be around in the morning, interviewing some of the others. But if not, Friday or the weekend is fine.'

'Let's ring,' said Anna.

'Nearly forgot!' said Merel. 'Can I settle up? Whiskies. Expensive man, that Marty.'

Anna stood quietly as Posthumus and Merel pecked each other on the cheeks. For a moment after Merel left, she said nothing. Then: 'Sorry about all that just now. It's just that . . .'

'I know.'

'And it's another of the things Marloes's lawyer should have done,' said Anna, 'called her own expert witness to the hearing, to help counter the psychiatric report.'

'And she hasn't?'

'Seems not, and now it's too late.'

There was another pause.

'Zig's door,' said Posthumus, after a while. 'It *was* open. Or at least it was when Marloes got there. It's in both her statements. Implicit on the Friday, she talks of coming up the stairs, round the corner, and seeing him, all in one sentence.

Then on the Saturday she actually says lying there, in all that blood, with the door open.'

Posthumus's phone beeped. He reached for his pocket. Anna turned to serve some customers. Posthumus checked the screen. Cornelius. He opened the message.

Stuck at home. Had some ideas. Tomorrow? After morning school run?

The paintings. Posthumus hesitated a second, then replied:

My place OK? May have pile material. 9-ish? Will make hot breakfast.

He put the documents he'd been looking at into one pile, tapping the edges lightly to neaten it. De Dolle Hond was beginning to fill up, and was growing noisier. He'd ask Anna if he could take the papers home, read them properly there. His mind had begun moving around Zig and Tony. There was something there he couldn't quite fathom. About their having a past together. About what brought Tony back on to the scene, and why he had one of Zig's paintings newly in his apartment. And then the news that he had testified against Zig's pimps. Marloes hadn't told Anna much about Zig and Tony during Anna's visit, but that bit had come as a surprise. He needed to know more.

'Refill?'

Anna had come back, with a bottle of the Italian red Posthumus was drinking.

'Thanks,' he said. 'Then I think I might go. Maybe take all this with me and look through it more closely at home. That OK?'

'Sure,' said Anna. 'I wasn't planning to do anything more with it tonight, anyway.'

She topped up his glass.

'Before I do, there's something I wanted to ask,' he said. 'In the notes you made this afternoon, when you were talking to this Marc guy, one thing I didn't understand.'

He picked up a couple of sheets of A4, which he had fastened with a paperclip.

'Here,' he said, 'tunnel vision, what's that about?'

'It has to do with the police,' said Anna, 'whether they had any other suspects for either of the deaths, or whether they just had tunnel vision in pursuing Marloes.'

'Maybe they did, how would we know?'

'Her lawyer should also have asked for the officers concerned to be called before the examining magistrate, or at least requested the original file for Tony's case, investigated his background, seen if the police had other suspects there.'

'So she could come up with alternative scenarios,' said Posthumus.

'Yeah, your sort of game. Even if it was only for Tony, to get rid of one of the charges.'

'To separate the two cases,' said Posthumus. 'That's interesting.'

'Marc did say that the main motivation to prosecute Marloes would have been that they thought they could link her to *both* crimes.'

There was a pause. Posthumus looked away. The connection. The role he had played in that was still a raw spot between them.

'Zig and Tony, Zig and Tony,' he said. 'It keeps coming back to that. We need to know more.'

Anna put the wine bottle down on the bar counter. 'Something's bothering you,' she said. 'I know that look.'

Posthumus turned to her. 'Trying to remember something,' he said. 'When we were clearing Zig's room, there was a box of newspaper clippings about his pimps' trial, a box-file; didn't we put it to one side with some of his other things, in case Marloes wanted it?'

Anna nodded.

'And we still have it?' asked Posthumus.

'Everything we saved from Zig's room is on the dining table in Marloes's apartment. I put it all there when I was tidying up. I thought it best if it was all in one place.'

'I think I might take that with me, too.'

Anna dipped into a large beer glass beside the till, and brought out a bunch of keys.

'I haven't been over for a while,' she said. 'Could you bring back any post? There's probably only junk mail and more of those letters from estate agents, trying to get her to sell.'

She gave Posthumus the keys. 'The one with the orange plastic is the street door, green is for her apartment,' she said.

Posthumus placed the keys beside the documents.

'Hello, *moppie*, howdy pardner.'

The voice came from behind him. Posthumus tensed slightly, as Paul gave him a pat on the back, and leaned over the counter to kiss Anna on the lips.

'Got a little something to cheer you up, *mops*,' said Paul to Anna, pushing a black and white striped plastic bag across the counter. 'Something you said you wanted.'

Anna opened it, and pulled out a DVD. 'Brilliant!' she said, laughing. 'Where did you get it?'

'Took a bit of finding,' said Paul, 'but I thought we could watch it later. Well, some of it.'

He winked. Anna avoided Posthumus's eye.

'That's *so* sweet of you,' she said to Paul. 'And remembering I'd never seen it.'

She turned the DVD towards Posthumus. 'Look,' she said, 'isn't that brilliant!'

Posthumus did not answer.

'Soft Cell, live in Milan,' said Paul, as if explaining to a child. 'Tainted Live.'

Anna laughed again.

'Tainted Live, Tainted Love,' said Paul. 'Get it?'

Posthumus didn't, and he didn't particularly like the sound of it.

'I would have thought what you played here was more your sort of thing,' he said. He glanced at Paul's boots. 'Or maybe country and western.'

'I *play* all sorts, for the bucks,' said Paul, 'but I got wider tastes, man. And New Wave's got good memories. What did *you* listen to, back in the day?'

'Not that,' said Posthumus.

He knocked back a large mouthful of his wine.

'I was just saying to Anna that I ought to be going,' he said.

Anna was busy with customers again, up the other end of the bar. Paul stared after her, head slightly to one side.

'She's the best thing that has happened to me in a long time, man,' he said.

He leaned closer, and put an arm across Posthumus's shoulders.

'Dude,' he said, speaking softly, 'can't you get her to back off from this Marloes shit? It's doing her head in, man. And it's only going to be worse when they send the woman down. For Anna that is. Marloes, she'll be in a better place. Get some care and that. She needs it, you can see that.'

'I'm not so sure about that,' said Posthumus.

'But Anna,' Paul went on. 'She's like obsessed, man. She'll crack up. Not cool. Dude, we've got to help her, bring her down gently, get her off this crazy idea she's got. I've tried speaking with her, but no go. She'll listen to you, mate.'

Posthumus stood up, and gulped down the rest of his wine.

'Actually, I'm helping Anna try to get to the bottom of all this,' he said, putting down the glass. 'And I think we're getting somewhere. I'm behind her completely. Sorry.'

Paul had begun flipping through the documents on the counter, but Posthumus took the pile from him, and picked up Marloes's keys.

'Sorry,' he said again. 'But as you see, I've quite a bit of reading to do.'

He went up to the other end of the bar.

'I'm off,' he said to Anna. 'Can I sort out my tab? I'll just get a bag from the kitchen for this lot.'

'Don't worry about the tab. It's on the house tonight, of course,' said Anna.

'Thanks. Then I'll . . . I'll leave you to it,' he said.

Anna looked at Posthumus a moment, then as he passed the end of the counter on his way to the kitchen stepped out and gave him a hug.

'Oh PP,' she said, 'stop being such a *silly*.'

She's right, thought Posthumus, out in the street. Besides, what right did he have to be sour about it? Paul wasn't a bad sort of a guy. Of a 'dude'. Once you got past the cowboy boots and the louche rock-star image. But then Anna had a way of falling for guys like that, always had. Funny, Merel spotting that so quickly. Anna the wild one. *Tijgertje.* Little tiger. Her friends had called him 'Prissy Pieter', and wondered how they ever stayed together.

Posthumus reached the guest-house door. The orange key. It turned only a fraction, met little resistance, and the door clicked open. Posthumus frowned. The door was unlocked. He closed the door and tried again, this time locking it himself. The key clunked through two full rotations in the slot, then back again to unlock. Careless. That wasn't like Anna. Maybe Paul was right, maybe she was too stressed out. He let himself in, and felt for the hall light switch. A click. Nothing. A draught from some-where. The door swung shut behind him, taking with it the light from the street and submerging him in blackness.

The building was freezing. Colder, it seemed, even than outside. Posthumus felt for his phone, and took a step towards Marloes's apartment door, his leather soles slipping on enve-lopes lying on the floor. The green key. He found it using the light from his phone, and slid it into the lock. He paused. A noise from upstairs? Posthumus stood still and listened. There was a creak, and a scuttling sound. He shuddered slightly and opened the door. These old buildings moved and groaned to themselves like galleons, on Amsterdam's soft soil. And they had mice. Rats, even. He'd seen enough of that in the places he had to go to for work. Still, rats gave him the creeps.

The lights in Marloes's apartment also didn't work. Of course. Anna had probably switched off the mains, and only came here during the day so hadn't thought. A dim orange light managed to make some sort of way in through the paint-ed-out street windows. Posthumus could make out the shape of the box-file on the table. It fitted into the carrier bag he'd taken from Anna's kitchen to protect the documents.

Zig's painting stood propped against one of the table legs. Posthumus put the bag to one side, and picked up the paint-ing. It was too large to carry home, not with all this other stuff. He laid it flat on the table, looked at it as best he could in the light from his phone. He brought the phone up close to the bottom right-hand corner. There it was, 2015. But close up, with the real thing . . . was that just a mistake with the brush? It didn't seem to be. Not 2015, but 201.5. Interesting. Posthumus took up the carrier bag, and began to walk back towards the door. That fitted. He'd have to try to check the other paintings, but that fitted all right. He gave a half-smile, and headed back out into the darkened hallway.

It was going on for nine o'clock by the time Posthumus arrived home. He shed his outdoor coat and shoes, put the carrier bag of documents on the floor beside the dining table, and slid his feet into a pair of velvet slippers. In the kitchen, he took a jar of dried chickpeas from the cupboard. He unscrewed the lid, but then stood with his hand poised over a bowl. Would he have the time tomorrow? He emptied the peas into the bowl. He'd make time. Somehow. He really wanted to try cooking that lamb couscous. Posthumus half-filled the bowl with water, and put it to one side for the chickpeas to soak. Jacobs for the meat? He'd give them a try in the morning, but Pia wasn't that good on lamb. It might mean crossing town to one of the Moroccan butchers near the Albert Cuyp market. Posthumus gave a light shrug, and went back to the front of the apartment. He walked up to the window.

Snow lay thick, undisturbed on the streets beside the canal, and in long, thin crusts on the tops of branches, making a similar outline over the arc of the bridge railings. The canal was frozen solid, frosted white, criss-crossed by skate marks. An enterprising neighbour had set up a stand on the ice, selling *glühwein*. Posthumus angled one of his armchairs so that it faced out through the window, went to the dining table, and removed the contents of the carrier bag. He placed the box-file and pile of documents beside the armchair, and from the workspace under the spiral stairs that led up to his bedroom, he fetched his ponder-box. That went on the other side of the chair.

Before he sat down, he took his phone and notebook out of his jacket pocket. He tapped a few times on the phone, looked at the screen intently, ran his fingers over it to enlarge an image, and smiled. Then he opened his notebook and turned to the page on which he had listed Zig's paintings, adding a single dot to each of the entries.

1) *201.1* $_{2007}$ *Still Life*
2) *201.2* $_{2008}$ *The Syndics*
3) *201.3* $_{2009}$ *Jewish Bride*
4) *201.4* $_{2010}$ *Cnolls*
5) *201.5* $_{2011}$ *Vermeer*

But that, thought Posthumus, could wait until tomorrow, till Cornelius came. He left the phone and notebook on the dining table, and went over to sit in the armchair.

Focus. He needed to concentrate his mind. Posthumus began one of the mental exercises he had used with his father, after the virus had ravaged his father's brain, wrecked his memory. Posthumus still used the routines himself, but now almost as a form of meditation. And this time, the exercise would have a further purpose. Posthumus brought to mind an image of Jelle Smits's face. Where *did* he know him from? He held the image there for a moment. He must try to empty his mind of everything else. Posthumus closed his eyes, trying to shut down his senses one by one, so that he no longer heard shouts from skaters outside, the hum of the lamp behind him. No longer, even, felt the warmth of the room, or the softness of the chair. He pared all away, until his entire mind became a lens, honing in on the face of Jelle Smits. Nothing else. He let some time pass, just to be sure. Nothing. Then, gradually, he allowed his focus to expand once more, admitting Smits's scrawny body to the picture. A pause. Where *was* it? What had he been doing? Movement. Not Smits's but his own. He had been moving past Smits when he saw him. Posthumus allowed the sensation to take hold, he widened the focus. Cycling, he'd been cycling. But not easily. There was annoyance, noise. Trying to cycle through a crowd?

Posthumus paused again, he felt reason slipping in, and excluded it. He must allow the memory to rebuild itself. Smits. Cycling. Annoyance. He tried to widen the focus, include another layer. Shapes. He could see two shapes. Smits hadn't been alone. A contrast. The corners of Posthumus's eyes screwed tight, as he willed the shapes to take some form in the haze. Abstract at first. A circle. No, a disc. A disc and a vertical line. Then it came. Fat and thin. In a rush, as if he were being blown backward out of the scene into panorama, the details filled in. Marty, walking with scrawny Smits, on the Zeedijk, as Posthumus cycled past, making his way through jaywalking pedestrians.

Posthumus had to wait a moment for the memory to re-fix itself, and when it had, he could access it more consciously. It was in the afternoon, after he'd helped Anna clean out Zig's room. And the reason the image had fixed itself in his mind in the first place, apart from the absurd picture of Marty with such a skinny sidekick, was Marty's look of unbearable smugness, of seeming extraordinarily pleased with himself. Just the look he'd had on him when he came into De Dolle Hond this evening. Posthumus opened his eyes with a start, but remained perfectly still in the armchair. But *not* the look Marty had given him when he left the café, a sullen glower. And hadn't Merel said that Marty suddenly came over all moody on her? Had Marty overheard what Posthumus and Anna had been saying, about Jelle Smits?

Posthumus rose from the armchair in a single easy movement and strode swiftly to his kitchen. He'd certainly be
visiting Jacobs Butcher's in the morning. From the wine-cup-
board he selected a bottle of burgundy, opened it, and with a
bottle and glass in hand returned to his place at the window.
He picked up the pile of documents. Zig's pathology report
was still on top, he'd start with that. Posthumus poured himself
a glass of wine, and settled in for a careful read.

Anna woke first. Half awoke. She lay in the dark, curled on
one side, not quite surfacing, nor yet opening her eyes. She
could feel Paul breathing, his body close, one arm draped over
her, their legs intertwined. He'd been so concerned about her,
so attentive, letting her get everything off her chest. They
hadn't watched much of the DVD.

She tensed, abruptly aware of what had broken into her
sleep. Heat. And the sound of a smoke alarm from downstairs.
She could smell the smoke, already feel it catching at her
nostrils, at the back of her throat. Anna sat up and swung
round, her legs still entangled with Paul's and with the duvet.
An orange light flickered from behind the thick bedroom
curtains.

'Paul!'

But he was already awake.

'Fuck!' he said. 'Fuck!'

He leapt out of bed.

'Jesus!' he said. 'What's directly below?'

'The kitchen.'

'The floor's hot!'

Paul shot out through the bedroom door.

'For Christ's sake put some clothes on!' called Anna after
him, but he didn't stop.

'Call 112,' he yelled.

The smoke alarm on the stairway began to screech.

Anna threw off the duvet, and grabbed at the phone beside her bed. Dead. She tried the bedside light. Nothing. The electrics must have blown. She stumbled across the floor, groping for the jeans she knew she'd dropped there earlier in the night, found them, fished in a pocket for her mobile and hit the emergency speed-dial. 'Fire, fire!' she yelled, as soon as someone answered, pulling on her jeans with her free hand, then a T-shirt, as she ran out towards the stairs, trying to keep her voice calmer, giving the address.

A volley of explosions, like cannon fire, rocked the building. A sound of shattering glass. Anna had just reached the top stair.

'Paul! *Paul!*'

Glass! She turned around, ran into the sitting room, pushed her feet into the shoes she'd kicked off after coming upstairs with Paul. On her way back out, she grabbed the empty DVD cover and an armful of LPs from her collection. And the purse she'd left on the table beside the door. She ran blindly back down the stairs, almost dropping her phone, trying, with one hand, to stuff it and the purse into a pocket. Smoke, stinking acrid smoke, was filling the stairwell. Anna coughed and gagged as she pulled open the café door. A cacophony of alarms. Billows of black smoke, surging across the room from the kitchen. The fire-door open, fierce orange flames already reaching round and scorching the wood panelling. That beautiful old wood panelling! She ran forward, and hit a bank of heat.

'*Paul!* Oh my God, oh my God.'

Anna looked around rapidly. The dull white glow from the café's emergency lighting made it a little easier down here. She rushed back to the street entrance, wedged open the outside door, dumped the LPs and DVD box on the pavement, and turned to pick up a fire extinguisher from beside the coat-stand inside. A crash from the kitchen. Anna ran, cocking the fire-extinguisher nozzle, already beginning to spray. Another crash. Something was blocking the kitchen door. Flames leapt at her, the heat like a solid wall, like the flat of an iron branding her face.

'No, *no*! Paul!'

Anna hacked and gasped, felt the room turn. The extinguisher faltered. She dropped it, reached again for her phone.

Posthumus tried to ignore the ringing, thought better of it, and groped groggily for the handset beside his bed. He focused sleep-blurred eyes on the little screen. Anna! 2.38 a.m. He sat up quickly, pushed connect.

'What's up?' he said.

She was sobbing, almost choking. The line was bad, crackling with what sounded like static.

'Anna, is that you? Where are you? I can hardly hear you. Bad line.'

'PP come, *please* come. Fire.'

Then it sounded as if she had dropped the phone. Posthumus was out of bed in an instant. He slapped on a light. Taxi? Would probably take too long. The bike? Cycling fast in this weather would be treacherous. He'd run. Hastily, he pulled on a tracksuit and trainers, sped down the spiral staircase, and took a ski jacket off the rack beside the door. Keys, wallet, phone. He snatched them up, sprinted downstairs and out into the street.

The clouds had cleared, there was a half moon, but the air was icy, brittle. Posthumus began to run. Fast. He could hear sirens. Must be for Anna, engines from the IJ Tunnel station. He made the Nieuwmarkt in just over a minute. He was fit, breathing deeply, leaving a vapour trail as he exhaled. Zeedijk,

Wing Kee restaurant, the bridge. Three minutes. Already he could see flashing blue lights, reflecting off the snow and wet walls. He turned the corner. Emergency vehicles filled the alley outside De Dolle Hond. Posthumus shook off someone trying to restrain him, barged past a thickset fire officer, ignoring his 'I'm, sorry, sir, you can't . . .'

'She called, she called. She wants me here,' he said, as he felt himself forcibly pulled back.

Firefighters were knocking out the front window of De Dolle Hond. Posthumus stood, legs apart, hands on his waist, panting to recover his breath. The fire officer still gripped him firmly.

'Anna!'

She was being led out into the street, bent over forward, a masked fireman with an arm around her shoulders, holding breathing apparatus to her face. Her hair, her skin, her clothes, grimy but not burned.

'Thank God, thank God.'

Posthumus realised he'd spoken out aloud. He felt himself relax, and the hold on his arms loosen. Anna was being handed over to paramedics.

'May I go to her please?' Posthumus asked the man who had been restraining him, adding quietly, 'I'm family.'

He walked quickly towards them. A paramedic was helping Anna into the ambulance, wrapping her in a blanket. He began fitting an oxygen mask, the door to the vehicle still open. Anna snatched off the mask as she saw Posthumus approach, pushed herself up off the stretcher.

'PP! Paul, he's still in there.'

Her voice was hoarse, rasping. The medic firmly replaced the mask.

'Come on now, lie back,' he said, gently lowering Anna down. 'Those boys are good at their job.'

Posthumus reached in from outside the ambulance, held on to Anna's ankle through the blanket.

'Anna, Anna, what happened?'

Anna made to move again, but the paramedic beside her put a hand on her shoulder, shook his head.

Posthumus looked back at De Dolle Hond. Firefighters were going in and out, through both the knocked-out window and the door. Already, he could see the black smoke that had been pouring out into the street beginning to abate. Another ambulance had arrived. And more police. Posthumus climbed in to be beside Anna, at a nod from the paramedic shutting the door behind him.

'They're sorting it, don't worry. It looks like it's under control.'

The paramedic was talking with the driver.

'We're off,' he said.

'Shall I come?' said Posthumus, half to Anna, half to the driver.

Anna began to struggle again, reaching for the mask, trying to speak. Her voice was muffled. It sounded like 'stay, Paul, bar'.

'Where are you taking her?' Posthumus asked the paramedic.

'AMC. She'll be OK. They'll just need to check there's no internal-tissue heat damage. Monitor her for a while.'

Posthumus leaned over towards Anna, laying an arm gently across her.

'Don't worry,' he said. 'Don't worry about anything. I'll stay here, see everything is OK ... and I'll find out about Paul. Have you got your phone?'

Anna's hands patted the sides of the blanket. She shook her head.

'I'll get hold of you somehow,' said Posthumus.

He gave her hand a squeeze, and climbed back out of the ambulance, mouthing a kiss to her as he closed the door.

Immediately, the blue light started flashing, and the ambulance pulled off. Posthumus turned back towards De Dolle Hond. Paramedics were running out of the door alongside a body completely swathed in blankets on a stretcher. They loaded it into the ambulance, one of them shouting something about a defibrillator. 'Crazy fucker, tries to fight a fire starkers, then goes and rolls in the snow,' he heard another say.

Posthumus remained standing as the ambulance drove away. Smoke had stopped coming from De Dolle Hond. The pulse of the whole scene had slowed. More firefighters were coming out of the café than going in. Some were rolling up a hose. Posthumus took a step forward. What had been De Dolle Hond's front window gaped, cavern-like, the brickwork around the edges blackened by smoke. Black around the doorway, too. Drenched, scattered and trampled among the debris on the pavement outside were some of Anna's LPs and a splayed, empty DVD box.

Posthumus exhaled a deep breath, and walked up to the senior-looking fire officer, standing alone beside the door.

12

Four hours' sleep. He'd survived on less. Far less, back in the party days. Posthumus unlocked his bicycle from the bridge outside his apartment. The fire officer had persuaded him to go home, once the security people had boarded up the window. No electricity or heating, possible toxic substances, Anna's bedroom floor part collapsed – De Dolle Hond was no place to spend the night.

It pained Posthumus to think of the beautiful old café, its wood panelling blackened (completely destroyed around the kitchen door), one of the big Delft vases shattered, broken bottles, water damage, a stink of alcohol. And of gunpowder. The smell, and the scattering of bright scarlet paper on the floor – those were familiar enough from countless Amsterdam New Year's Eves. It didn't need a team of experts to tell him what that meant. Someone had set off one of those gigantic, multi-part Thunderclap fireworks. In the kitchen doorway, by the looks of things. But *why*? And surely that, even indoors, wouldn't have started such a fire. Did Anna know about that? She hadn't said anything on the phone earlier, and he hadn't mentioned it, hadn't told her the police were treating the fire as arson, only that there would be a forensics team there today, trying to ascertain the nature of the blaze. Posthumus mounted his bike, and cycled carefully over icy streets towards De Dolle Hond.

At least Anna was OK. She had inhaled smoke, but apparently there was no internal damage – though she'd still sounded croaky on the hospital phone, rebelling against the idea that they wanted to keep her in for observation. Back to normal, in that sense. Paul was a different matter. He was also at the AMC, Anna said – she'd got the nurses to find out. Severe smoke inhalation and second-degree burns. The doctors were debating whether he ought to be transferred to the severe burns unit in Rotterdam. Posthumus gripped the handlebars as the front wheel slid on ice, rounding a corner at the Nieuwmarkt. He had spoken to Anna only briefly, told her to get some rest, that he would see to everything, and come to the hospital as soon as visiting hours began, in the afternoon.

Posthumus turned his bike into the Zeedijk, fairly deserted at this time of the morning. At this time of the morning! Cornelius! He had forgotten. He stopped cycling, and took out his phone, checking the time: nine fifteen, he might just catch him. Posthumus texted:

> Sorry. Can't do breakfast. Fire at Dolle Hond last night. On way there now.
> Anna in AMC but OK. Will ring.

He replaced his phone, and rode on towards the café.

The door to De Dolle Hond stood ajar. Someone had already graffiti-tagged the hoardings boarding up the window. Inside, free-standing lamps drenched the room in a hard, white light. A crime-scene tape stretched across from the fireplace to the near corner of the bar. On the other side, a forensics team was poking about in the debris. Posthumus picked up Anna's LPs, which he had rescued from the pavement after the fire and left behind the door. And the DVD box. The DVD Paul had brought to watch with Anna. Funny the things people rescued from a blaze, Posthumus thought. He'd read about that somewhere. Crazy things, illogical. Often sentimental, rather than of any practical value.

'You are?'

One of the forensics men came up to the tape.

'Pieter Posthumus. I said I'd be back,' said Posthumus. 'I OK'd it with one of the officers last night. I'm a friend of the owner's, just want to check on things for her, upstairs too if that's all right.'

'Posthumus?'

Posthumus nodded, waiting for some forensics-humour wisecrack on his name. He got enough of that at work.

'Guv'nor wants you to give him a call. After ten.'

The man pointed with a gloved hand to a visiting card, left on the bar. Posthumus picked it up. His eyebrows raised slightly. The name on the card was familiar. Well, that was logical, he supposed, given that the incidents occurred next door to each other. It was the officer who had been in charge of investigating Zig's death, DI Flip de Boer. Posthumus walked towards the door up to Anna's apartment. Another voice called to him from the back of the café.

'Electrics up there should be all right, mate. Some rooms, anyway. I've isolated the damage.'

Posthumus waved a hand in acknowledgement, and went upstairs.

Flip de Boer turned his back and sighed, as the small team he'd put together for the Dolle Hond case filed out of his office at the IJ Tunnel police bureau. Not the brightest puppies in the basket, were they? Still, they were what he had to work with. He sat on the edge of his desk, pushed his hands into his pockets, thumbs hooked over his belt, and stared out of the window. There was something odd going on with that fire. De Boer was learning to trust gut feelings, and his gut feeling told him two things. First, that there was something wrong about this whole scenario, and second that Pieter Posthumus was a man worth talking to.

The fire was arson, clearly – there was certainly *something* deliberate behind it all, with that Thunderclap – but it seemed hopelessly amateur. He'd have to wait for forensics to get back to him officially, but at first glance, they said, it seemed as if someone had run a cord soaked in flammable substance across the kitchen floor. A piece of thick string and lamp oil, possibly, from the courtyard door to the Thunderclap, just inside the bar. It had been the makeshift fuse that had started the fire, first setting light to material in the kitchen, piles of cardboard boxes against one wall, and only catching the fire-work once the room was ablaze. Bungled, or what? Deliberate? Those boxes should not have been there. Idiocy? Someone sending a warning to the café owner? About what?

De Boer could not shake off the hunch that there was some connection between this and the Vermolen case, though what it could be he could not put a finger on. It just seemed too strange a coincidence that what had happened last night at the café, next door to Vermolen's guest-house, came in the middle of her trial, on the eve of her defendant's statement. Something was going on. And Posthumus was a common factor.

Pieter Posthumus, the man who first made the link between the two Vermolen killings. De Boer had been impressed by that. Surprised, and impressed. And now, his was the contact name left last night at the café. Not that Posthumus had anything to do with the fire. Not necessarily . . . though nothing should be ruled out. Clearly, Posthumus was a friend of the owner, but there was more to it than that. De Boer thought that here was someone, like a spider at the centre of a web, who watched, waited, was sensitive to distant twitching, drew things together.

De Boer's thumbs moved up and down over his belly, which was growing flat and muscled again, after a few months' extra gym work. He liked the man, had learned – through a couple of his own cases since the Vermolen arrest – what Posthumus was doing at the City Burials Department, and admired it. There was a humanity there. And integrity. De Boer felt that he should trust Pieter Posthumus. And he wanted to hear his take on things. He could do with a mind like that on his team, he thought, turning back towards his desk, as the phone rang.

De Boer picked up the handset. He glanced at his wrist. Ten o'clock, on the dot.

It didn't surprise him to hear the caller announce himself as 'Pieter Posthumus'.

Posthumus was a little thrown when the phone was picked up after barely one ring.

'De Boer.'

The voice on the other end of the line sounded gruff. Posthumus introduced himself.

'Thank you for calling,' said de Boer. 'You know of course that this is about last night's fire at De Dolle Hond, and you perhaps remember me from some months ago. The incident next door.'

'Naturally,' said Posthumus.

'The incident last night is being treated as a crime,' said de Boer.

'Clearly,' said Posthumus.

What with downstairs teeming with forensics officers. But he hadn't meant to sound quite so acid. De Boer appeared not to notice.

'I will be heading this investigation, too,' he said. 'I gather you were not at De Dolle Hond at the time of the fire, but arrived soon afterwards.'

'That is correct. Anna de Vries, the owner of the café, telephoned me soon after the fire woke her up.'

'One of my team will be contacting you for a formal statement,' said de Boer. 'As well as Ms de Vries, and the other man there at the time.'

Posthumus heard a rustle of paper. The detective consulting his notes, probably.

'Mr Paul de Vos,' de Boer continued, 'as soon as he is well enough.'

For a moment the conversation seemed to have run aground. Posthumus leaned over Anna's desk, and pushed up the window. The stench from downstairs clawed at the back of this throat.

'You asked me to phone you?' said Posthumus, aware that he was sounding more confrontational than he intended.

'Mr Posthumus . . .'

De Boer's voice had less of an official edge. More man to man.

'I wanted to speak to you . . .'

Again a silence, as de Boer hesitated.

'I wanted to speak to you . . . more informally,' he said, 'about whether anything struck you as odd about the fire.'

'Apart from the fact that someone set off a bloody great firecracker in the kitchen doorway?' said Posthumus. 'I'm sure you don't need your crack forensics team to tell you that.'

De Boer was silent.

'Sorry,' said Posthumus, trying to sound a little more relaxed. 'This has all been a bit of a shock, I'm still taking it all in.'

'*Was* it a shock?' asked de Boer.

It was Posthumus's turn to be silent. He shivered a little, in the chill air from outside.

'What do you mean?' he said after a while, his voice stiffening again.

'Could it have been a warning of some sort?' said de Boer. 'Not intended as a fire, but done to scare Ms de Vries?'

'Or me,' muttered Posthumus.

'Sorry?'

'Nothing. Thinking aloud.'

'Is there anybody you can think of who might want to do that?' de Boer continued.

'Scare Anna?'

Posthumus was silent. For quite some time. This was the conversation he had been wanting to have. Not under these circumstances, of course, but with de Boer. A conversation he'd been turning over and over in his head. He took the plunge.

'Anna de Vries and I are convinced that Marloes Vermolen is not guilty of the murders of either Zig Zagorodnii or Tony Wojciechowski,' he said. 'Last night, we came to the realisation that there is a major discrepancy surrounding the statement of one of the witnesses in the case, one Jelle Smits. In short, Smits's statement that he saw Marloes Vermolen leaving the scene of the crime is open to question. At the very least. Someone who . . . who I am *sure* I have seen talking to Smits, I think overheard that conversation, and left De Dolle Hond looking displeased.'

Posthumus paused. That had sounded rehearsed. De Boer, also, remained silent.

'The timing of this incident, in the midst of the Vermolen trial, had not escaped me,' de Boer said at last. 'Do you have a name for me?'

Posthumus pushed the window shut, and strode the few paces to the other end of Anna's office. Well, he'd come so far. Might as well.

'Marty Jacobs. Jacobs Butcher's on Lange Niezel. But this is only a theory.'

He heard de Boer make a note of the name.

'We will need to look into this a little more, and possibly speak to him,' de Boer said. 'Is there anything further you can tell me?'

Posthumus turned, and began to pace the room. There was no going back now. When he replied, he was aware that he was speaking rather too quickly.

'There are some things perhaps you can tell me,' he said. 'I should very much like to talk to you about the content of some of the witness statements involved in Marloes Vermolen's case.'

'As I am sure you know, that would be impossible,' said de Boer. 'Any queries should have been raised by Vermolen's lawyer, before the examining magistrate.'

'Precisely.'

De Boer took so long to respond that Posthumus thought the line had gone dead. When he spoke, his voice was hard.

'Thank you, Mr Posthumus, this conversation has indeed been helpful,' he said. 'I think that's all for the moment. One of the investigation team may be contacting you for a formal statement. About the fire itself.'

Posthumus rounded off the call and put down his phone. Well, he hadn't handled *that* particularly well, he thought. What was it after all this time, decades after the clashes of his squatter years, that still turned him prickly and uneasy when he spoke to a cop?

De Boer heard Posthumus give a terse goodbye, and hang up. He put down his own phone. Well, *that* wasn't very well handled on my part, he thought. He turned back to stare out of the window. What had he been hoping to hear? Some sort of affirmation that all was as it should be? The Vermolen trial had brought things to the surface again. Thoughts he had been trying to push away. He had so wanted to get it right with that case, his first as head of an investigation team, young for the job. Had he been too eager? The Zagorodnii boy had a murky background, and Wojciechowski was connected with it, but he hadn't pushed at that. There was a case against Vermolen, of course, but had he been too keen to nail her, get a quick result? It had always bothered him that though they had questioned Vermolen, every day for two weeks or more, she had never confessed. Had he been too hasty? It occurred to de Boer that, perhaps subconsciously, he had been waiting for a challenge from the examining magistrate that never came. For the questions that would somehow lift responsibility from his shoulders. Was he now expecting the same of Pieter Posthumus?

Posthumus sat down at Anna's desk and moved the little electric heater he had found in her attic storeroom closer to the chair. He picked up the phone again and rang the young barman Simon, to give him the news. Then he called Cornelius, giving him a quick outline of what had happened, and suggesting they meet up later. He'd ring once he had a clearer idea of how the day was panning out. He found Anna's insurance file, and slipped the documents she'd asked for into a cardboard folder to take to her at the hospital. At least her office was undamaged, she'd be relieved about that. He dug out the telephone number of the crime-scene cleaners who had done Zig's room, was passed on to someone who could cope with fire damage, and arranged for them to come in as soon as the forensics team was finished. That would probably be by the end of the day, the woman on the phone said. Posthumus glanced at his watch. Going on for ten thirty. He wished now that he had not mentioned Marty's name to Flip de Boer. If he were to get anything out of Marty, he ought to speak to him before he got a call from the police, go there now, perhaps, before the butcher's got too busy. His mobile rang. Posthumus looked at the screen as he picked it up.

'Merel,' he said.

'PP! There's been a fire at De Dolle Hond! It's terrible! Do you know? Is Anna OK? Can I do anything?'

'Hang on, hang on! I'm here at the moment. In Anna's apartment. Everything is OK. Well, not exactly, but at least Anna's fine. Where are you?'

'Downstairs! They won't let me in.'

'I'm coming.'

'I went to do the interview with Irene,' said Merel as she ran up the stairs behind Posthumus. 'You can see the kitchen from her back window. It looks a mess! I came straight over.'

The two stood together over the electric heater in Anna's cramped office. Merel did not take off her coat. Posthumus filled her in on what had happened, and on his conversation with Flip de Boer.

'So you think Marty has something to do with the fire?' said Merel. 'OK, so he did suddenly turn moody last night. And I remember he seemed distracted during the last part of the interview, you know, like at a party, when someone is talking to you, but really listening in to another conversation. But then what? That he didn't like what he heard you saying about Jelle Smits, and that the fire is some sort of warning? That seems a bit dramatic.'

'I'm wondering whether the fire wasn't a mistake.'

'What do you mean?'

'The Thunderclap. You know how loud those things are, and inside, too. I'm told they have the force of a couple of hand-grenades, some of them. What if it was meant only to scare Anna, do some damage? Not start a fire?'

Merel considered this a moment.

'OK, so a warning then,' she said. 'But a warning not to do *what*, exactly?'

'Jelle Smits. It all comes back to Jelle Smits. I have to talk to Jelle Smits,' said Posthumus.

He began pacing the small room. Three steps this way, three steps that.

'Can you find him?' asked Merel.

'Only two options,' said Posthumus. 'Through Marty, or through Tina. I haven't the faintest idea where she is, so it has to be Marty.'

'And he's hardly going to squeak. Not if he is tangled up in all this.'

'I was just about to go round, to the butcher's, when you rang,' said Posthumus. 'I need to speak to him before the police do, if there's going to be any chance at all. If Marty gets a whiff of cop, he'll shut up like a clam. I'd intended to drop in anyway this morning, to see if they had good lamb. Fat chance of any couscous cookery tonight, the way things have turned out, but I thought I could use that as a front.'

'And casually slip Jelle Smits into the conversation? I don't think so,' said Merel.

'Confront him, then?' said Posthumus.

'In the shop? With other people around? No way. And if he has the slightest inkling you think he had anything to do with the fire . . .'

Merel turned around and grabbed Posthumus's arm.

'Do *stop* that pacing!' she said. 'The room's too small. Look, I have an idea. *I'll* go.'

'And that won't look odd?'

'Not in the slightest. He's expecting me. I said I would drop round to interview his mother.'

Posthumus stood still.

'I can pretend I'm trying to get hold of Jelle Smits for the paper,' said Merel. 'To interview him for a story I'm doing about Marloes's trial. Ask Marty if he knows who Jelle is, where I can find him, obscure it a little by asking about the other witnesses, too, the woman who is a neighbour, anyone he can suggest for background on Marloes. It's a bit feeble, but it stands more chance than you would. *And* I could say I've just come past De Dolle Hond, and that there's been a fire. I could probably judge something from his reaction. It's unlikely that he's been near here himself this morning, so it should come as a complete surprise. Unless, of course, he did it.'

'Sharp thinking from the star reporter!' said Posthumus. 'You've your father's crafty mind, getting your story out of them somehow.'

He still hovered there, Willem, between the two of them, even though Merel seldom mentioned her father unprompted, and Posthumus felt, hoped, that he was at last banishing his sense of guilt.

'But can you do it right away?' Posthumus went on. 'I still think we should get to Marty before the police do. What about Irene? Don't you have to go back to her, finish the interview?'

'I don't think mornings are our Irene's best time of day,' said Merel. 'Not until she's got a few of what she calls her pick-me-ups inside her. I suggested we meet up later today instead. Oh, I nearly forgot!'

Merel took out her phone.

'I must tell her Anna's OK,' she said, texting as she spoke. 'She seemed really upset, contrite. Sorry that she had aggravated Anna, going on about how she'd known her since she was a girl, hadn't meant to put her back up. I had to promise I'd tell her how she was.'

Posthumus took his coat from the back of the office chair.

'You know where the butcher's is?' he said, as Merel slipped her phone back into her bag.

'On Lange Niezel, isn't it?'

'Yup,' said Posthumus, putting on the coat. 'I'll come with you as far as the corner. I need to get out of here. I could do with a walk, and a bit of a think.'

'As long as Marty doesn't see you,' said Merel.

Posthumus followed her back down the stairs.

'Your phone?' said Posthumus, as they walked up towards Warmoesstraat.

An unfamiliar ring-tone.

'Not me,' said Merel.

The tone followed them around the corner.

'It's coming from *you*,' she said.

Posthumus frowned and patted his pockets. Of course, Anna's phone. He'd forgotten he had it. He glanced at the screen. Unlisted number. He pressed connect.

'Pieter Posthumus,' he said.

'Good! I'm glad it's you.'

'Anna!'

'I was hoping you'd found the phone,' said Anna. 'I didn't get an answer at De Dolle Hond, and I don't know your mobile number off the top of my head, so took a chance.'

'Sorry. I picked it up last night, on the floor near the door. I forgot to say.'

'Miracle it's still working,' said Anna.

'You must have just missed us at the café, we've only this moment come out,' said Posthumus.

He attempted to give his voice a note of reprimand. 'I thought you were going to try to get some rest,' he said.

Merel squeezed his elbow, and mouthed something at him.

'Merel's here, she sends her love. How are you feeling?'

'I'm perfectly fine,' said Anna.

She didn't sound it.

'Any news?' she went on. 'Have you spoken to them? What caused it? What was that explosion?'

'They're still working on it,' he said. 'I'll tell you all when I see you this afternoon. Meantime, get some rest. Downstairs is not as bad as you might think, and upstairs is fine, apart from the bedroom. I've found your insurance papers. I'll bring them round when I come.'

'No need, I'm coming home.'

'They're letting you go?'

'I'm checking myself out.'

'An*na*! I'm dealing with everything, you really don't have to.'

'It's not that. There is just no way that I'm not going to be there for Marloes today, when she makes her defendant's statement, *no way*. I'm coming home to change, then straight to court.'

Posthumus knew not to argue. He tried pragmatism.

'The bedroom's in a bad way. I don't know about clothes,' he said.

'There'll be some in the drier or with the ironing. I'm going to try to see Paul, then I'll take a taxi. I'll be home in about an hour.'

Posthumus hoped his sigh was not audible.

'Anna, are you sure? It's not as if you can speak to Marloes, even if you do go. And I can cope with things here.'

'PP, you're a darling, and thank you. For everything you've done so far. It's horrible, but what's happened with the fire has happened. I have to face it, and I can deal with all that next week. Most of it. It's far more important, now, to keep going with Marloes.'

Anna broke into a fit of coughing.

'Will you? Promise?' she said as she recovered. 'Forget the fire, keep on with Marloes? How's it going? Are you getting anywhere?'

'Trying to track down Jelle Smits,' said Posthumus.

'PP, you're a saint.'

Posthumus could hear her trying to suppress another cough.

'Don't worry,' she said, 'the doctor's told me the danger signs, what to look out for, and I'll come back for a check-up after court. Kiss, kiss.'

The line went dead. Posthumus put the phone back in his pocket. They were getting close to the corner with Lange Niezel.

'You'd better go on alone from here,' he said to Merel. 'I'll carry straight on. I *really* need that walk now.'

Posthumus continued along Warmoesstraat, turned left towards the Oude Kerk. There would be no dissuading Anna, he knew that. The destruction at De Dolle Hond would hit her hard when she saw it, but when she found out about the Thunderclap, and what he suspected of Marty, that would, if anything, only make her sink her teeth in harder in her fight for Marloes. He began a circuit of the old church, an island between straits of alleys and the small lagoon of Oudekerksplein.

It was just like Anna to check herself out of hospital, he thought, as he passed the south door, glancing up at the haphazard outgrowth of side chapels, annexes and clerestories that clung to the church like barnacles. He'd google 'smoke inhalation', check on the danger signs so he could keep an eye on her himself. Phone the hospital, or maybe his own GP. But perhaps Anna was right. He had done what he could for her regarding the fire, practically speaking. And as for Marty and the fire ... well, he'd see what Merel came up with. But perhaps the fire wasn't a warning, after all, perhaps it was simply intended as a distraction, something to deflect him and Anna from their path. Even more reason, then, to turn his mind back to the odd pieces of the puzzle he had piled up reading the documents last night. Pieces that didn't fit, or seemed to belong somewhere else. Posthumus curled his nose as he passed a reeking metal pissoir, and bore left past the canal, circling the church anti-clockwise.

The other buildings of De Wallen crowded close to the rear of the basilica. Some toddlers were playing happily in a day-care nursery, which was flanked on either side by window-girls, already working though it had just gone eleven o'clock. No wonder some people were scandalised by Amsterdam, thought Posthumus, as he navigated the narrow alley. But they still came for a look. Fresh-faced young male tourists, with uneasy, bored-looking girlfriends in tow. Groups of middle-aged day-trippers in anoraks. Titillated, entertained, moral indignation reduced to tut-tutting. It could really bring out the misanthrope in him, he realised. They didn't have a clue, or didn't want to know, what life really was like for girls like Tina, for the women – most of them it seemed – who were here illegally, their passports held by minders who creamed off their earnings as rent for the window rooms. Or for those who didn't even make the windows, young girls lured by the likes of Tony Wojciechowski, the *loverboys* who posed as boyfriends, who flattered, seduced, spoiled with gifts, and then by violence, drugs, psychological blackmail, forced their girls on to the game.

Posthumus reached the point where he had begun his circuit, pausing on the edge of Oudekerksplein. Revulsion welled in him. For a moment, a feeling glimmered deep down that even if Marloes had killed Wojciechowski, he was totally with her on that. He stood stock-still, people milling around him. He turned his thoughts back to Marloes. Something Anna had said last night kept working its way to the surface. Something she'd said about tunnel vision, alternative scenarios, about the young lawyer saying that the main motivation for prosecuting Marloes was that the police thought they could link her to *both* crimes. Posthumus was painfully aware that it was he who had first made the link between Tony and Zig. So . . . what if he now undid it? Maybe he'd been wrong, his instincts off-target. Perhaps his skill at piecing parts together, making stories whole, wasn't all it was cut out to be. Maybe there were two, distinct, scenarios. Was attempting to link them confusing his thinking? What if he separated them, approached them as two individual cases, perhaps with different perpetrators?

Tony first. His link with Marloes was tenuous; how could she have got into the gym to slip him the overdose? A figure like Marloes would have caused comment. And he was part of the underworld, for certain. Posthumus wrapped his scarf more tightly around his neck, thrust his hands deep into his coat pockets against the cold. There could be any number of scenarios, all manner of people who wanted Tony dead. That shady László character that Pogo at the gym mentioned, the boss of the gym himself – he sounded pretty unsavoury, ran a rent-boy operation, if Pogo was to be believed, and who knew what else besides. Posthumus set off again across Oudekerksplein. Too complicated, he thought, too much he did not know, had difficulty getting access to. It would take too long, and he didn't have time on his side.

Zig, then. He'd forget about Tony for the time being, and focus closer to home. Literally. With Zig there was a direct connection to Marloes. Blow that one out of court, and he might be getting somewhere. And here there were two important strands of evidence, two large pieces of the puzzle that increasingly seemed not to fit: Jelle Smits, and Zig's pathology report. That, when he read it in detail, had come as a bit of a surprise.

At the far side of the square, Posthumus stopped outside a café. Walking cleared his head, set the train of his thoughts in motion, but warmth and a coffee were very tempting. His phone beeped. Merel.

No luck Marty/Jelle. Seemed surprised at fire. With Pia, can't talk. C u back DH,

mxx

So that meant Tina. Posthumus replaced his phone in a coat pocket. If there were to be any hope of tracing Jelle Smits at all, he would have to track down Tina. A narrow street ran off the square, down the side of the café. It led, Posthumus knew, to a network of alleys devoid of the tinsel of the rest of De Wallen, row upon row of women in windows, files of men trudging back and forth. It was where Anna had said Tina worked, before coming to Marloes, where she might have returned. What were the chances he'd find her here? Slim, thought Posthumus, with another momentary pang for a coffee, very slim. But not zero. He exhaled deeply, pulled his coat more tightly around him, and walked on down the alley.

13

Even by De Wallen standards, the alleys south of the Oude Kerk were seedy. Posthumus had glanced down them before, as he walked along the Oudezijds Voorburgwal canalside, but he had never ventured in. He had always found them repellent. Beyond the café on the corner of Oudekerksplein, it was as if he passed through a force field into another reality. Gone was any of the light-heartedness, even that tawdry, titillated light-heartedness, of the rest of De Wallen. The lanes were eerily silent. No traffic, no bicycles, only the sound of footfall on hardened snow, and low-voiced negotiations through half-opened doors. Posthumus found he missed the giggles and cheery banter of the tour groups, which had riled him just minutes earlier.

There was only one reason to be in this dank little patch of town. Sex. Two reasons. Sex and money, depending on which side of the window you were on. And, most likely, fear. Posthumus tried not to catch the eyes of any of the women, skimming their features, bodies, for one that might be Tina. A row of black women. He walked on by. A pale, skinny body. He raised his eyes. Blonde hair, but not Tina. He turned away. She rapped the window angrily. An empty room – barstool, washbasin, white bathroom tiles, a hard-looking bed, CD-player and plastic flowers on a shelf. A woman with a tumble of dark curls, hands behind her neck, arching her back, thrusting her hips towards the glass. Another cupping her hands under full, soft breasts; the next, long legs, muscular, posing immobile. A small cluster of men stared in at a window as a girl gyrated, suggestively running her fingers under her thong.

The place made Posthumus feel dirty. But he realised, with a twinge of distaste, that he was getting aroused. He turned into a dead-end alley. At the end, a faded sign painted on the wall advertised MILORD, a bar and porn-show joint. Otherwise, more windows. The women in the first few seemed Hispanic. South American, maybe. It seemed at times as if someone had grouped the women according to type, as if sections of the alleys catered to certain tastes. Posthumus peered into a doorway that led to a darkened passage. He could see rooms barely bigger than the beds inside them. Boxes, lit red, each containing a skinny girl. He hesitated, and walked in. The passage branched into others. At the end of one of them, a muscular man, thirty-something, stood and stared at Posthumus. Most of the boxes had their curtains drawn. In others, stood a few slight, bony women. But no Tina.

Posthumus moved out of sight of the man at the end of the corridor. He felt that he was learning to read this corner of De Wallen, and that this warren of corridors was a notch below even the alleys outside. He could imagine Tina in a place like this. He stopped to look at a girl about her age. Thin, pale, blonde, large eyes. Could he even really remember what Tina looked like? Posthumus was beginning to doubt himself. He caught the girl's eye. She flashed him a little, plastic smile. He took a step towards her, and she opened the flimsy door.

'I . . . I just want to talk to you,' said Posthumus.

'It'll cost,' said the girl.

Posthumus felt oddly shy.

'Um . . . how much?' he asked.

'Just talking?'

'Very quickly. Five minutes,' he said.

'Twenty.'

'Euros?' asked Posthumus.

The girl looked at him as if he were deranged, stood aside, and drew the curtains, as he walked in and shut the door behind him.

'Pay first,' the girl said.

Posthumus took out his wallet, and gave her twenty euros. He noticed his hand was trembling slightly.

'What you want me do?' she said. 'Like this?'

She lay back on the bed.

'I just want to ask you a question,' said Posthumus. 'Do you know someone called Tina, maybe used to work round here?'

The girl sat up.

'What are you? Cop? Immigration? I have papers. Phillip, he have my papers.'

She nodded out to the corridor. Posthumus noticed how heavy her accent was.

'No, no, not police,' he said.

'A fucking journalist?'

It sounded like a quotation.

'No, not a journalist either,' said Posthumus. 'I . . . I'm trying to help a friend of Tina's, and I need to find her.'

Tina, there must be a hundred Tinas. What the hell was he doing here?

'Salvation Army,' said the girl.

It was a statement not a question. Posthumus did not reply.

'No, I no know Tina,' she said.

'She's about your age,' said Posthumus, 'also blonde, thin, with a high voice, like a little kid.'

He remembered something Anna had said.

'And I think maybe she did drugs. Had a fight with someone here,' he said.

'Why you ask?' the girl said.

She stood up and pushed the twenty euros back at Posthumus.

'You go now. Here, take.'

'I told you, I'm trying to help a friend of hers,' said Posthumus.

He did not take the money.

'Please, do you know where I can find her?' he asked.

'You go now, or I call Phillip,' the girl said.

This was pointless. Posthumus made a move towards the door.

'You look good man,' the girl said.

She appeared to be listening for something out in the corridor.

'But really, no Tina here. Not now.'

Posthumus strode swiftly out into the alley. This was ridiculous, the whole thing was absurd. What was he supposed to do? Trawl the streets asking everyone he met? Peer into windows, on the off-chance Tina might be there? It wasn't going to work. 'Not now'. Not ever? Not even Tina? She probably didn't use that name. Pointless. And Merel had had no luck with Marty. He'd see what she had to say, but maybe it was time to take a different tack.

At the top of the alley, he turned towards the Oude Kerk, and headed back to De Dolle Hond.

Anna's taxi pulled up as Posthumus rounded the corner into Nieuwebrugsteeg. He called to her as she climbed out, and hurried from the end of the street to join her. She had on a large, gaudy jersey he had never seen before, probably borrowed from someone at the hospital.

'Didn't expect you quite yet,' said Posthumus.

'I couldn't get to see Paul,' said Anna, 'he was still under sedation.'

'Maybe you can try again, when you go back in for the check-up,' said Posthumus.

Anna didn't answer. They walked in to De Dolle Hond together. Anna stopped in the doorway. She looked around the café.

'Well,' she said. 'I see.'

There was a catch in her voice.

'Let's get on with it,' she said after a while, and walked over to the door to her apartment.

Posthumus followed, with a nod to the forensics men.

Upstairs, he mentioned the Thunderclap, told Anna the police were treating the fire as arson, and that they would probably want a statement. He tried to get her to contact the insurance people, said that he had arranged for the cleaners to come.

'Later. I'm going to get changed. I'll see what I can find; there's some stuff I hardly wear in the guest-room cupboard,' was all she replied.

She seemed dazed, didn't even look in on her bedroom, went straight to the drier, and on to the guest room. Posthumus stayed in the office. Was it shock, some sort of defence mechanism? Was she in denial, perhaps? It was all very well being concerned about Marloes, but Anna didn't seem to be taking in the fire at all.

'Have you found Jelle Smits?' she called from the guest room.

'Working on it,' answered Posthumus. 'Hang on, I'm about to make a call.'

He took out his phone, and dialled his GP. Maybe he could give some advice, and besides, Posthumus had wanted to talk to him about Zig. Posthumus got through to the assistant, and left a message for Dr Bentinck to call back, on a private matter. Bentinck was a crime-story aficionado, who enjoyed nothing more than demolishing medical aspects of TV series. He had relished the fact that information he'd come up with back in the summer helped Posthumus get to the bottom of the murder of Amir Loukili. Bentinck would call.

Merel came in as Posthumus was putting away his phone.

'The guys downstairs let me come straight up this time,' she said. 'I cut the Pia interview short, I couldn't take much more. The *gossip*.'

'Anna's back,' said Posthumus, giving Merel a warning glance. 'She's checked herself out, and is going to court for Marloes.'

'Be with you in a minute,' Anna called from across the landing.

Merel called back a greeting. She looked at Posthumus, questioning silently. He shook his head, gave a slight shrug.

'What happened with Marty?' he asked.

'It was odd,' said Merel. 'First he denied knowing Smits, then when I pushed him, said he didn't know where he was, and was trying to get hold of him himself. He seemed genuinely surprised about the fire, though.'

'What's this about Marty?'

Anna was back in the room. She had on a full-length coat, dark jeans, a different jersey, but the same shoes she had arrived wearing. Merel turned to her.

'We thought he might have something to do with the fire,' Merel said.

'Marty?' said Anna.

Posthumus explained about Marty and Jelle Smits.

'So you think this might have been to scare me off going on with Marloes?' said Anna.

'Or maybe just to distract you,' said Posthumus.

He could see Anna's jaw set firm.

'Though where Marty could have got his hands on a huge firework like that, at this time of year, who knows,' said Merel. 'These things are so strictly controlled.'

Anna stiffened. She stared at Merel, a flush of colour coming to her cheeks.

'Irene,' she said.

Posthumus looked at her, frowning. Her voice was dead, but her eyes were blazing.

'I-*fucking*-rene,' she said. 'That's where he got it. She and her Albert do a nice little line in under-the-counter fireworks every New Year. I'll *kill* the bitch. My phone! Give me my phone!'

She thrust out a hand to Posthumus.

'I don't know,' said Merel. 'I was with her this morning, and she seemed really worried about you.'

'Of *course* she bloody was! She probably thought Marty had done me in!'

Anna bounced her upturned palm up and down in front of Posthumus, like an insistent beggar.

'Phone!'

Posthumus reached out and put his hand gently over the top of hers. With the other hand, he took out his own phone.

'I've already spoken to the police about Marty,' he said. 'I'll call them and tell them this about Irene. They'll be able to take proper action.'

He gave her hand a squeeze, let it drop, and selected the number he had entered earlier in the morning for Flip de Boer. Anna let out a sound something between a growl and a howl, clenched her fists, turned and thumped the base of one hand against the wall. Posthumus walked out on to the landing, phone pressed to one ear, middle finger closing off the other. Merel went over to Anna and put an arm around her shoulders. Anna was leaning bent forward, with both forearms against the wall. Her breathing was jerky. She closed her eyes, and said nothing.

'This is all so awful for you,' said Merel.

'My poor, poor Dolle Hond,' said Anna, her voice barely audible.

'Look, what are you doing about tonight?' said Merel. 'Will you be staying with PP? Or if you prefer, come round after court and stay at my place.'

Anna straightened herself up, smoothed out her coat, and ran her fingers through her hair.

'I'm staying here,' she said. She turned to look at Merel. 'Sorry,' she said, with an attempt at a smile. 'Bit of a scene.' She took a deep breath.

'My God, Anna, it's completely understandable,' said Merel.

'Not that sort of behaviour,' said Anna, with a nod back to where she had been standing against the wall. 'The de Vries temper. It's notorious. PP always was the only one who knew how to deal with it.'

Merel shrugged it off. 'Short and sharp,' she said. 'Sometimes I wish I could do that, blast it out and get it over with, instead of brooding. But, how about it? My place tonight?'

'Thanks, that's really kind, but I'm staying here. I'd prefer to be here.'

'Do you think that's wise?' said Merel. 'Is it even possible? There's no gas, no heating, you can't get into the bedroom, everything reeks of smoke. At least go and stay with PP, that's closer.'

'Taking my name in vain?' said Posthumus, coming back in.

'I'm trying to convince Anna to stay with one of us for the night,' said Merel.

'Well, you certainly can't stay here,' said Posthumus, his voice firm. 'Sorry, Anna, for once, no argument.'

Anna was silent.

'Either it's back to hospital, or, if they give you an OK at the check-up, then it's my place,' Posthumus went on.

'I can stay next door,' said Anna.

'Next door?'

'In Marloes's apartment, she won't mind, I know,' said Anna. 'I have to be here, I'm sorry, I just have to. And in the morning, too, to be on hand.'

'There's gas and electricity at Marloes's?' asked Posthumus. 'Nothing worked when I went in last night.'

'I turned them off, but everything's still connected,' said Anna. 'I'll be fine there, I promise. And it won't feel like I'm deserting the place.'

Posthumus could see that this was as far as Anna would go.

'I'll go across and turn everything on, get the place warmed up,' he said.

He came up to her, and put his arms around her. Anna rested her head on his shoulder.

'Thank you, PP.'

'Good news is, the police are on to it,' said Posthumus. 'They're already on their way to Marty, and they're sending some men round to speak to Irene and Albert now.'

'Let me know what happens,' said Merel. 'But hey, you guys, I must be going, I should get back to the paper.'

'And me to court,' said Anna.

She gave Posthumus a peck on the cheek, as she moved out of his embrace.

'My phone, PP? Please. I need to call a cab.'

Posthumus slid the key into the guest-house door. He had brought some of Anna's own sheets. They smelled faintly smoky, but he thought she'd prefer her own. The key turned with no resistance. Like before. And he was sure he had locked the door when he left last night. He thought for a moment. He remembered the noises he had heard when he came in to collect the box of Zig's newspaper clippings.

'The yards,' he said to himself. 'Of course. The back yards.'

He had been wondering how someone had gained access to De Dolle Hond's kitchen. It was as easy as anything to get between the yards behind the guest-house and De Dolle Hond. Between most of the buildings in the block, come to that, with all the half-walls, tumbledown fences, shared gardens.

Carefully, Posthumus opened the door. He closed it quietly, and hung Anna's sheets over the end of the stairway banister. Again, a slight rustling from upstairs. Enough light filtered through the window above the door to allow him to see dimly in the hall, but the stairs ascended into darkness. For a moment he contemplated going in to Marloes's apartment and switching on the mains, decided against it and, with one hand on the banister railing, began slowly to climb the stairs, wincing as the wood creaked. He turned the corner in the stairway, taking the initial few steps towards the first-floor landing, but stopping when his head was level with the final stair. The landing was in darkness. Faint lines of daylight came through gaps under one or two of the doors. Posthumus went on to the top of the stairs, and looked around. A shadow passed across the line of light under the door at the far end of the landing. Swiftly, hoping the noise his shoes made on the wood sounded as if it came from more than one man, Posthumus crossed the floor and flung open the door. He blinked in the sunlight. A sleeping-bag on the bare bed, a small camping gas cooker with a pot on it, candle-stubs in bottles, and, cowering in the corner, a small figure.

'Tina!' said Posthumus.

14

Posthumus poured more coffee into one of Marloes's big, bright mugs, and pushed it across the table to Tina. He gave the tabletop another wipe with a cloth, setting more specks of dust to rise, swirl and settle again. The old house cracked and creaked as hot water coursed through its radiators. It had taken him some time to persuade Tina to come down into Marloes's apartment. She sat on a wooden chair, legs drawn up tight to her, feet on the seat, arms hugging her knees, one hand cautiously extended to hold the cup.

She had told him how, soon after making her statement to the police, she'd run away to stay with a friend in Rotterdam, frightened that she would be taken in for drugs, or somehow blamed for Zig's death. She said how she had cleaned up, come back a few weeks ago to try for work in Amsterdam, and when she realised that Marloes was no longer there had sneaked in at nights to camp in her old room.

'Please, *please* don't make me go, I don't *have* nowhere to go,' she said. 'And don't tell *her*.'

Tina had nodded towards De Dolle Hond.

'I know she comes here, but hardly never. And I'll pay. *Some* way, any way.'

Posthumus had ignored the implication. He'd said he would speak to Anna. He had not said that Anna would be staying in Marloes's apartment. The part about Tina thinking she'd be blamed for Zig's death – he'd let that pass. And he had not yet mentioned Jelle Smits.

Tina took a long sip, grimaced a little at the milkless, sugar-less brew (coffee was all Posthumus could find in the cupboard), and put the mug back on the table.

'And I didn't have nothing to do with that fire last night, neither, in case you're thinking,' she said. 'It wasn't my candles or whatever.'

'Of course it wasn't,' said Posthumus.

But he *had* been thinking – wondering, at least. Just where did Tina fit in to all this? She looked up at him. Her large, dark eyes seemed somehow at odds with her blonde hair. How old was she? Early twenties, he guessed. About the same age as Zig, though she seemed much younger.

'I was well scared, though,' said Tina.

'You saw it?'

'Couldn't hardly miss it, could I?' she said. 'Thought it would get me.'

'You didn't see anyone going in?'

'Saw *him* running out.'

'Who?'

'The tall one, that pianist geezer what always says "howdy". Completely starkers.'

Tina gave a little giggle.

'Zig would have laughed at that. Zig didn't like him, old poser. Maybe the fire was done special by someone, just to make the old tosser roll starkers in the snow.'

She giggled again, but Posthumus saw that she was blinking hard, on the verge of tears. She unfolded her arms, and leaned forward to put a hand on Zig's Vermeer painting, which Posthumus had taken off the table to make room for them to have coffee, and propped up against one of the other chairs.

'Have you ever lost someone what you really loved?' Tina said.

Posthumus felt that familiar knot in his gut.

'You loved Zig?' he asked.

'He was my friend.'

There was something in the simplicity of that statement, yet in the way Tina gave it such enormous weight that almost moved Posthumus to tears himself. He felt an odd connection with this little waif.

'Once, yes,' he said. 'I did lose someone like that. My brother. And for a long time I blamed myself for his death. Maybe I still do. Sometimes I feel that everything I do is an atonement for that. You know, to make it better somehow.'

There was a silence. Tina looked at him. It felt to Posthumus like a silence *between* them, rather than simply a gap.

'Do you blame yourself? For Zig's death?' he asked.

He spoke very softly. Tina dropped her eyes to Zig's painting. She swung off her chair, picked up the canvas and walked over to stand it against the wall, near the door. She took a step back.

'Didn't finish it, did he?' she said.

Her voice was bright, brittle.

'Started it after New Year, like always, and worked on it all that time, and he didn't even finish it.' She turned to face Posthumus. 'Same with the one before. Months and months. He loved those paintings.'

'What was the one before?'

'Dunno, a family. It had dogs in it.'

'And before that?'

'Can't remember. I didn't know him much before that.'

Tina came back to sit at the table.

'Those paintings was really important to him,' she said. 'But he wouldn't never tell me why. It was the one thing he wouldn't never talk about.'

She gave a sad little smile.

'Always talking, Zig, wasn't he? And tweeting, "I'm doing this, I'm doing that", all day long. But those paintings, that was private. "A story between me and the canvas," he said.' Tina gave a rough imitation of Zig's accent.

'He wouldn't even tell Marloes,' she said.

Posthumus brushed his palm lightly over the tabletop between them.

'Zig loved Marloes, didn't he?' he said.

Tina looked down. 'Marloes was like his mum. And to me.'

Posthumus waited a while, then he leaned forward a little over the table.

'Do you really think Marloes could have killed Zig?' he asked.

Tina drew her legs up tight against her body again, put her arms around her knees. No answer.

Posthumus spoke quietly, and slowly. 'What really happened that day?' he said.

'Dunno. I was wired, wasn't I?'

Tina's answer came quickly. Too quickly. She looked up. This time her eyes were filled with tears.

'I really *was*. I don't fucking *remember*.'

That's not what you told the police,' said Posthumus.

Tina flashed him a look of mistrust.

'You told them that what Jelle Smits said was true,' Posthumus said.

'I don't see him no more!'

The mistrust had turned to fear. Posthumus did not want to lose what he had. Gently, then.

'Tina, I am trying to help Marloes,' he said. 'Me and Anna, and we really need to know what happened that day. *Was* it true, what you told the police?'

She did not answer. Posthumus waited.

'It's all mixed up,' she said, after a while. 'You know, blurry.'

'Perhaps you've been trying to remember?' asked Posthumus.

Again Tina said nothing.

'Maybe I can help you,' said Posthumus.

'You don't get it,' said Tina. 'There's whole loads of stuff I can't remember. Days, weeks sometimes. Old guy like you, you've never been there.'

'Maybe I have,' said Posthumus.

'You wouldn't understand,' said Tina.

But her voice was less certain. She turned away.

'Maybe I can, a bit,' said Posthumus.

Tina breathed out a 'huh'. She looked at him again. Her expression read: You? How?

'My father had a disease, once, soon after my brother died,' said Posthumus, 'which made him forget nearly everything.'

'My nan had that,' said Tina. 'Forgot who we were, then even who she was.'

'It wasn't quite like that,' said Posthumus. 'This was a virus, but one that hit him really badly, in his brain. He *knew* who he was, but he said it was like he had forgotten everything *about* who he was, all his past, the long-ago stuff. He said it was like he didn't exist any more, had lost his place in the world. I helped him get it back.'

'How?'

'We played games,' said Posthumus. 'Memory games. And ever since he was a boy, he had kept a diary. So every day, I read him some of that, bit by bit, up to the present, to help him put the picture back together, reclaim his life.'

'And did he remember everything again?' asked Tina.

'Not everything. But enough.'

'That's a nice story,' said Tina.

'So maybe we can try something like that?'

'I've never kept no diary.'

'Something else, then,' said Posthumus.

'Like a game?'

'A bit like that,' said Posthumus.

He leaned a little further forward, kept his tone gentle, matter-of-fact. 'The day that Zig died, Jelle was with you, wasn't he?'

Tina nodded.

'What time did he leave?'

She shrugged.

'Try something for me,' said Posthumus. 'For the moment don't try to remember anything, just close your eyes.'

'I don't like closing my eyes.'

'OK, then look at something. Just one thing. Zig's painting, maybe.'

Tina turned slightly in her chair.

'I want you to think of that day, of you and Jelle in your room. Nothing else, just you and Jelle.'

'I was wired, I told you.'

'Just you and Jelle, OK?'

'OK. But I *was* out of it.'

'Try. Think of Jelle leaving.'

Tina nodded. 'Goddit,' she said.

'Now think of your room. Your window. Outside – was it light or dark?'

'Dunno. Dark, I think. A bit. Dunno. I told you.'

'And outside your door, quiet, or people?'

'Oh, people, noise, I remember *that*.'

'Are you sure?'

'I've always remembered *that*.' She turned back to Posthumus. 'I don't think much of your game,' she said.

Posthumus shrugged.

'Can I stop looking at Zig's painting now?' Tina asked.

'Sure.'

Posthumus sat back in his chair. So, Jelle Smits had left when he and the others from De Dolle Hond were on the landing, not in the afternoon. The man Anna had seen running down the stairs.

'And before that, before Jelle left, what happened?' he asked. 'Earlier in the day. There was a fight?'

Tina shook her head. 'I don't *know*, I keep telling you, it's all confusing,' she said. 'Someone came in, there was shouting.'

'Someone came *in*? You mean not Marloes? Someone from outside? Who?'

'I dunno. A man, I think. I didn't see.'

'When was that?'

'I dun*no*. Maybe it wasn't then, maybe it was another day. *I* don't know. It could have been Marloes. Even Jelle couldn't remember.'

'Even *Jelle* couldn't remember? What do you mean even Jelle couldn't remember?'

'He couldn't, not properly. Marty helped him.'

'*Marty?*'

'He helped him. Like you're helping me now, only not nicely. In a Marty way.'

'How do you know *Marty*?' asked Posthumus.

Tina had gone back into her knee-hugging position. She would not look at him.

'I used to work in this . . . place,' she said. 'He was a john.' She glanced quickly at Posthumus to make sure he understood. 'Always asked for me,' she went on. 'I *hated* him. Most of all of them. He always wanted to see me cry. And *real* tears.'

Posthumus felt a similar revulsion welling in him as he'd felt earlier that morning, at the Oude Kerk. He felt like going over and putting his arms around her.

'And what do you mean, Marty *helped* Jelle?' he asked instead.

'To remember. Jelle was also confused,' said Tina.

She mumbled something further.

'What was that?' asked Posthumus.

'And maybe he gave Jelle some money,' said Tina, speaking so quietly Posthumus could almost not hear her.

'And that is the story Jelle told to the police?' asked Posthumus. 'The story Marty helped him remember?'

Tina nodded.

'And he said you must say the same?'

Tina nodded again. Posthumus got up, and walked around to the back of Tina's chair. He put his hand lightly on her shoulder.

'Tina, this is very important,' he said.

The front doorbell rang. Posthumus ignored it. He bent over Tina slightly.

'Do you know where Jelle is?' he asked. 'You *do*, don't you?'

Tina nodded. The doorbell rang again.

'Can you bring him to me? Or at least get him to phone?'

'Maybe.'

Posthumus straightened up. He heard his name being called from the street outside. Or rather, he heard: 'Charon! You in there?'

'Wait a moment,' he said to Tina, and walked out into the hall to open the front door.

'Cornelius, I didn't expect you,' he said, as he heard Tina scuttle back upstairs.

'Good God, Charon, what's happened? Cry woe!'

'Come in,' said Posthumus. 'Sorry, I've been meaning to call again, but . . .'

'Of course, of course. Thought I'd drop by. The lot next door said you were here. How's Anna? *You* look like you've hardly slept, *and* as if you need lunch. True? Come on! It's gone two o'clock. Out. My treat.'

Cornelius looked around, up the stairs to the first floor, through the door into Marloes's apartment. 'This place, I'm afraid, does not appeal,' he said.

Posthumus smiled. Lunch on Cornelius was a rarity.

'Anna's been in hospital, but she's checked herself out, and gone to court,' he said. 'She is determined that she's fine. And lunch would be a very good idea indeed. I shall tell you about the fire. And out is an even better idea, thank you. I was about to go down to the Nieuwmarkt, to get some supplies in. Anna's going to be staying here.'

He shepherded Cornelius towards the apartment.

'But there's something I have to do first,' said Posthumus.

He ran up the stairs. Tina was sitting on the end of her bed, huddled against the radiator.

'You *will* bring Jelle to see me, or at least get him to phone?' said Posthumus.

He needed to hear it from Jelle himself. More than that, he'd need somehow to get Jelle to confess before the police or examining magistrate, if he wanted to claim that Jelle was an unreliable witness. That wasn't going to be easy.

'Will you?' he said.

Tina nodded.

'You have a phone?' Posthumus asked.

'Course.'

He wouldn't push it and ask for the number.

'I'll give you my number,' he said, taking out his notebook.

He hesitated a moment, then from the folder inside the back cover took out one of the visiting cards he used for work. He wrote two numbers on the back.

'That's my mobile, and my landline at home,' he said. 'My name's on the other side.'

Tina turned the card over. '*Funeral* Team?' she said.

Posthumus nodded.

'You're a strange one,' said Tina. 'What's this funeral team?'

'We arrange funerals for people who don't have anyone else, or we try to find family,' said Posthumus.

'Like with that Luana girl?' asked Tina.

She named a young prostitute, who had been murdered in the autumn. Posthumus and Sulung had tracked down her mother, and a young son, in Albania, had arranged for her to be buried in her home village. There had been a quite a bit of media coverage.

'Yes, like her,' said Posthumus.

'I heard about her,' said Tina. 'That was a nice thing to do.'

Posthumus went back out on to the landing, closing Tina's door behind him. Work. He hadn't given it a thought. And he hadn't said for sure to Alex that he wanted Friday off. She would be wondering if he was coming in or not, might be wanting to schedule something. Posthumus crossed to the stairs and took out his phone. Alex answered immediately.

'Alex, things are getting complicated here, I don't think I will be able to make it in tomorrow after all. Just wanted to check, is it all clear on the diary front?'

'We've had one in, this morning. I've got you down for the house-visit with Sulung tomorrow, though I can sort that, don't worry. But there is Mrs Henderson later in the afternoon. Cremation.'

'Damn.'

He'd forgotten about that. He'd had long discussions with the old lady's only relative, a great-niece in New Zealand, about what to read at the funeral, had put a few things together, but not finalised it.

'Look, I'm going to be on the Nieuwmarkt later. I'll drop in afterwards and sort something out.'

'I'm afraid Maya's not here this afternoon.'

Alex spoke in a polite telephone voice, but he could picture her grinning. Not having to cope with Maya would make a swift swoop back to the office infinitely easier. He picked up on Alex's tone.

'So kind of you to say so,' he said.

He gave a little laugh, pocketed his phone, and went back into Marloes's apartment. Cornelius was looking at Zig's painting. Posthumus pointed out the dot he had seen, in the figures 201.5 in the lower corner, told him about Tina.

'So, from what Tina said, it seems our surmise that Zig painted one a year was true,' said Posthumus, 'and we can also take it the *Cnoll* painting immediately preceded the Vermeer.'

He took out his notebook, opened it to the list he had now adapted, and laid it on the table.

1) 201.1_{2007} *Still Life*
2) 201.2_{2008} *The Syndics*
3) 201.3_{2009} *Jewish Bride*
4) 201.4_{2010} *Cnolls*
5) 201.5_{2011} *Vermeer*

'I checked the online paintings, and the photo I have of *The Syndics*,' said Posthumus. 'It's hard to see, but they all seem to have those extra dots. Even so, the idea had occurred to me anyway, swimming sets of lengths at the Zuiderbad – you know, ten crawl, ten backstroke, ten breaststroke, then again.'

'I most certainly do *not* know!' said Cornelius, with a look of mock horror. 'That sounds positively exhausting, and the logic escapes me.'

'Think of it as Ten A, Ten B, Ten C, and so on,' Posthumus continued. 'I think what we have with the numbers is not dates, and not solely a series, but a *set* of numbers. Five different lots of 201, whatever 201 is. A set, and in sequence.'

'Impressed by your feat of fitness, baffled by your reasoning,' said Cornelius. He took out a notebook of his own. 'Not a set or sequence, as much as a *story*,' he said, placing the book beside Posthumus's on the table.

Posthumus read what Cornelius had written.

Still Life	*Display? Peak/prime. The moment. (death?)*
Syndics	*Officialdom, Drapers. (mistaken: judgement)*
Jewish Bride	*Love. Romance. (given previous two: reconciliation?)*
Cnolls	*Family. Dogs fighting: conflict. Humour?*
Vermeer/ milkmaid	*Tranquillity, nurturing, peace.*

Posthumus frowned.

'Explain,' he said.

'Lunch,' said Cornelius. 'There's an interesting new place on the Zeedijk.'

The two men walked to the corner of the street, then turned up alongside the guest-house towards the Zeedijk. Posthumus noted a police car parked, half on the pavement, outside Irene and Albert's tobacconist's. He didn't say anything. Cornelius was already in full flow.

'I remain convinced,' Cornelius was saying, 'that the question to ask is why *these* paintings? They are all national treasures, all in the Rijksmuseum. When did you say young Zig acquired Dutch nationality?'

'I'm not sure, I'll have to check the papers we found. Five or six years ago, I think.'

'And five annual paintings,' said Cornelius. 'It is possible that here we have a catalyst, or the trigger, to his beginning the project. Perhaps this is where you should seek the answer to your "set" of 201.'

Posthumus looked sceptical.

'*However*,' said Cornelius, 'my theme for the moment is the five individual choices of work. I believe they tell a *story*, they are not simply a sequence, or a series, or a set, but a *progression*. And here, perhaps, might lie a clue to what happened to the unfortunate youth.'

'Cornelius, get on with it.'

Cornelius bowed his head briefly, and took out his notebook.

'Picture one, a still life,' he said. 'Still lifes were painted for show, very often with produce or flowers at the peak of perfection, before decline and rot. *So*, what do we have here? What was Zig wanting to represent by this particular choice? Beauty? A highpoint? The moment? Death, perhaps? Picture two, *The Syndics*. Officialdom. Put aside for a moment that they are drapers. I can imagine the young man seeing them as judges, officials sitting in judgement.'

Cornelius stopped and looked back at the restaurants along the Zeedijk, then he turned again.

'No, it's further on, I thought we'd passed it,' he said. 'To continue. Picture three, *The Jewish Bride*. Love. Romance. Or, given my reading of *The Syndics*, possible reconciliation. Atonement, even. Picture four, the Cnolls and their pets. A problem for me, I admit. Family? I don't know. The little dogs are fighting. So, conflict? Or release? The dogs' young mistresses have set them free. Humour? Perhaps the atonement of the previous years has released Zig, he can joke again. And so we have Vermeer, the milkmaid, the full bowl of milk. Nurture. Serenity. Tranquillity. Perhaps we can comfort ourselves that young Zig found peace before he was killed.'

It had been a long day, a stressful week, and he'd had very little sleep. Posthumus had to stop himself from bursting out that this was the biggest load of crap he'd heard in a long time.

'I thought you said we had a story,' he said instead.

Even so, Cornelius looked hurt.

'Well, the bones of a story. As I said, it's more of a progression, a line of development, a possible plot.'

This time Posthumus did sigh.

'I'm sorry, Cornelius, but this gets nowhere, especially not anywhere that gives me something I could put before a judge.'

They had reached an Asian snack bar. It was empty.

'This is it,' said Cornelius.

Posthumus had been hoping for a bowl of thick Dutch pea soup. They went in.

'That's not to say I'm not grateful,' Posthumus said. 'It's really helpful to have a different perspective, it's just that I feel the pictures can't take us anywhere; we need to focus on solid material, stuff the police and lawyers can grasp.'

He broke off to order a stir-fry, waited for Cornelius to do the same. They stood in silence for a moment, then Posthumus went on.

'I've decided to forget about Tony Wojciechowski for the time being, and concentrate on Zig,' he said. 'But not on the paintings. Rather, on questions I have about his pathology report, and on proving Jelle Smits to be an unreliable witness. I'm pretty much there with that.'

'Forgive *me*, dear Charon, but I think you are wrong,' said Cornelius.

He appeared a little sulky.

'An unwise decision,' he continued. 'These two stories intertwine; when we find out how, *then* we will be making progress.'

'I need hard facts.'

'You've always been a man for building *up* stories, not a reductionist,' said Cornelius. 'You should follow your natural instinct.'

'We don't have the time,' said Posthumus.

His stir-fry arrived. In a cardboard box. Posthumus suppressed any feelings of distaste, and picked it up. Simultaneously, his phone rang. Typical, he thought and glanced at the screen. He held his hand poised for a moment, then replaced the stir-fry on the counter.

'I'm sorry, Cornelius, I'm going to have to take this,' he said, heading to the door.

15

Posthumus stood beside the old city gate and public weigh-house on the edge of Nieuwmarkt. It seemed appropriate, he thought, to be meeting Dr Bentinck beneath the window where the Guild of Surgeons once had its dissecting room. Doubly so, as the reason the room was there in the first place had been the ready availability of cadavers from public executions on the square below – material for anatomy lessons, as painted by Rembrandt. Corpses, paintings, medical men, were all shifting loosely about Posthumus's tired mind, when he saw Bentinck crossing the square.

It had been good of the doctor to agree to meet up at the start of his rounds. Posthumus had even had time to finish lunch after the call, and pick up groceries for Anna. Like many Amsterdam GPs, Bentinck still did his house calls on foot or by bicycle. To Posthumus's pleasure, he had offered to meet at an exact place and time, a rare arrangement in these days of the vague 'text me'. Posthumus checked his watch. Three thirty precisely. Even more rarely, for a doctor, Bentinck was on time.

Posthumus stepped forward to greet him, but as he did so, a hand grabbed on to his shoulder, and spun him violently around. It was Marty, sweating, despite the cold, and slightly out of breath.

'*Saw* you fucking standing there,' said Marty. 'You're fucking behind all this, I know! The fucking filth round the butcher's, asking all sorts of questions, people looking for Jelle Smits. You fucking back off, you hear? It's got nothing to do with you.'

Marty was almost shouting, but he looked more scared than angry, nearly in tears. He swung around, and lurched off back towards the Zeedijk, turning his head for a parting shot.

'I've got powerful friends, like you don't even know. Back off!'

Posthumus had drawn breath to answer, but hadn't had a chance to say a word. He was suddenly aware that he was standing with his mouth open. What the *hell* was really going on with Marty?

'Life does appear to be exciting. What have you got yourself into this time?' said Bentinck.

He was standing behind Posthumus, looking similarly taken aback.

'I'll fill you in,' said Posthumus.

The two walked south, along Kloveniersburgwal, as Posthumus quickly sketched the background to what was going on. He told Bentinck of the blood in Zig's room, of his surprise at reading in the pathology report that Zig had a subdural haematoma. The term was already familiar to him, from back in the summer, when he'd been tasered and had fallen and hit his head on the side of a lavatory bowl. Concussion, in layman's terms, but a serious form, caused by bleeding under the membrane between the brain and the skull. Sometimes fatal, and frequently hard to detect immediately. Posthumus had assumed that Zig had died of bleeding, had been cut during a fight. This opened up another possibility.

'Could the haematoma have killed him?' Posthumus asked. 'The pathology report didn't draw any conclusions.'

'It wouldn't have, but yes,' said Bentinck, 'an acute, or even a chronic subdural haematoma could be fatal, especially if not detected and treated. It can be hard to spot at first, people don't realise how bad the injury is, sometimes don't even go to a doctor.'

'So, whatever caused Zig's haematoma need not necessarily have happened on the night he died?' said Posthumus.

'Not necessarily.'

'But wouldn't that show up in the pathology report, that the haematoma was from earlier?'

Bentinck thought for a moment. 'It would be hard to pinpoint,' he said. 'There are so many variables. A pathologist would probably simply state the fact of the haematoma, and if pushed by an examining magistrate wouldn't go much further than saying that it occurred anything from three hours to two to three days before death.'

'And an acute or chronic haematoma could have been caused by a fight?' said Posthumus.

'A blow to the skull, yes.'

'With a heavy object then, or someone bashing his head against something,' said Posthumus. 'Or even Zig hitting his head himself, by accident.'

'It would not necessarily even have to be hugely forceful. Subdural haematoma is a classic finding in shaken baby syndrome, though of course that's babies. Even so, one of the chief problems with adults is that people don't realise their injury is so bad.'

Posthumus knew the danger signs from the advice he'd been given in the summer. Headaches, confusion, dizziness, momentary losses of consciousness.

'And dismiss the headaches and dizziness,' he said.

'Absolutely, and if they start taking aspirin, or are on some other sort of anticoagulant like warfarin, that makes the bleeding even worse,' said Bentinck.

Of course. Acetylsalicylic acid. Aspirin. The report noted large traces in Zig's blood. He had been popping aspirins.

'This is it,' said Bentinck, stopping at a house near the corner with Rusland. 'Anything else you'd like to know?'

'That's given me quite enough to think about, for the time being,' said Posthumus. 'Thanks so much for taking the time.'

'Absolute pleasure,' said Bentinck. 'One condition: that you tell me how it all turns out. I wish my life were so exciting.' He nodded towards the door. 'Gammy leg,' he said, pushing the bell.

Posthumus shook his hand, and continued along the Kloveniersburgwal towards the office.

The speech he was preparing for Mrs Henderson's funeral needed only a few finishing touches. Sulung had agreed to stand in at the ceremony if Posthumus couldn't make it, and had left for the day. Maya, thankfully, had not been in. That particular hush characteristic of government offices after four in the afternoon had long since settled over the building. Posthumus leaned back in his chair, and swivelled it to face the window. Some seagulls descended, squabbling, past a patch of pale blue sky.

'Penny for them.'

Posthumus swivelled back. Alex had come in. She was looking particularly vivacious today, in red and black and green, generating a warmth in this winter weather that made him feel he wanted to hold his hands close to her, like a fire. They'd had a long conversation at Reception when he arrived, about De Dolle Hond, Marloes, everything.

'The fire?' asked Alex, perching in her favourite spot when Posthumus was alone in the Funeral Team office, on the corner of his desk.

'Subdural haematomas, actually,' said Posthumus.

'Crikey! Well, I guess I did ask.'

Posthumus grinned. He explained about Zig, and the conversation with Dr Bentinck.

'So the bang on the head could have happened earlier than the wound to his temple?' said Alex. 'Does that help you?'

'That's what I was thinking about.'

'Like William Holden, maybe?' said Alex.

'William Holden?'

'You know, that movie star from the fifties, got drunk and fell in a hotel room, hit his head on the bedside cabinet and bled to death. Or so they said.'

'You and old movies!'

'It's a famous case,' said Alex. 'And it could've been like that. Only with Zig concussed, rather than drunk.'

'Well, something like that might partly let Marloes off the hook, but it wouldn't be enough. No, there was a fight in this case, possibly two,' said Posthumus. 'The question is when, and who . . . and *why*? And unless I can answer that, and show that Marloes wasn't involved, it's not going to help.'

'Well, go for it!' said Alex. 'You were right about Amir when no one else was getting it, remember. And cheer up. You're looking really down, and exhausted.'

'I am pretty tired,' said Posthumus.

'Go home, take a bath, treat yourself to something nice, go to bed,' said Alex.

Posthumus gave a weary mock salute. 'Ma'am,' he said.

'Anyway,' said Alex, 'that's what I'm about to do, it's nearly five. I'm closing up downstairs, and then I'm off. See you on the way out.'

She swung off his desk, and was gone.

Posthumus turned back towards the window. Truth was, that encounter with Marty earlier had shaken him. And it was unsettling that Marty had apparently not been arrested in connection with the fire. Were he and Anna wrong about that? Maybe Marty had been taken in, and released? He'd like to know what was going on there. Posthumus wondered what office hours detectives kept. De Boer had said, when Posthumus had rung him with the information about Irene and the Thunderclap, to call him if anything else came to light. And he had just been threatened. With a witness.

Posthumus reached for his mobile. The call was answered after three rings.

'De Boer.'

'Pieter Posthumus here.'

'Ah, Mr Posthumus! I was just about to leave, but I'm glad you caught me. So I can do this in person. I owe you one.'

Posthumus heard himself splutter a little. What was all this about?

'I have just made the quickest arrest of my career,' de Boer went on. Posthumus could hear the beaming smile in his voice. 'I was going to send one of the team around to tell Ms de Vries in the morning. We have had a full confession regarding the fire at De Dolle Hond.'

'*Confession?* Marty Jacobs?'

'No, not Jacobs,' said de Boer. 'Irene Kester.'

'Irene!'

'Apparently when the boys, when my team, went around, Mrs Kester burst into tears the moment she saw them. It took a while to calm her, I believe.'

De Boer was warming to this, Posthumus could tell.

'Swift, smooth, perfect, and I have to admit great for the statistics, too.'

'But *why*? Irene?' said Posthumus.

'Apparently, she bore a grudge against Ms de Vries for excluding her from the café,' said de Boer. 'She says she had been drinking, set the firework only to scare Ms de Vries, with what turned out to be an extremely dangerous home-made extended fuse, and maintains she never meant to start a fire.'

'I see, I see. Thank you,' said Posthumus.

He realised he ought to be sounding more pleased, but he couldn't pick up on de Boer's cheeriness. What had all that been with Marty, then?

'We will also be charging Albert Kester with dealing in illegal fireworks,' de Boer went on. 'Ms de Vries will be receiving official notification of all this shortly. Victim Support will also be in touch, should she wish to talk to them.'

De Boer paused.

'And not Marty Jacobs?' said Posthumus.

'He would appear to have had nothing to do with the crime.'

Posthumus started to speak, stopped, then began again.

'My original reason for phoning was that earlier this afternoon Marty Jacobs threatened me in the street, told me to back off, warned me that he had powerful friends.'

There was a brief silence.

'Would you like to make a formal charge?' said de Boer, his voice serious again.

'No . . . no.'

Posthumus faltered.

'No, not yet,' Posthumus said.

The conversation ran aground. De Boer offered nothing more. Posthumus awkwardly wished him a pleasant evening, and rang off.

De Boer walked over to the window. He looked out over the IJ Tunnel bureau car park, towards the rush-hour traffic streaming in and out of the tunnel. Marty Jacobs *had* acted extremely suspiciously, the lads said. They wanted to keep an eye on him. Something was up here. He was not sure what it was, but it made him uneasy. The man Posthumus was on to some-thing, and he was clearly good at this sort of thing. De Boer's gut told him there was a connection here with the Vermolen case, and that Posthumus seemed to be grasping at it. And he had to admit, the root of his own unease lay in the discomfort he felt about Marloes Vermolen never having made a confession.

De Boer acted on a decision he had made earlier in the morning, after his first call with Posthumus about the fire. He picked up his phone and pressed the button to ring back the last incoming call. He didn't bother with a greeting, but launched straight in.

'Mr Posthumus,' he said, 'you mentioned when we spoke this morning that you had reason to doubt the reliability of one or more of the witness statements in the Vermolen case. I wonder if you would care to elaborate.'

De Boer listened carefully. Posthumus was pretty much blowing out the evidence of that junkie, Jelle Smits. De Boer had never set much store by that. There were aspects of the case that bothered him more. Like how Vermolen had managed to administer the drug to Wojciechowski. He hesi-tated. Was this wise? If it got out. Rationality, self-interest, told him to put on the brakes, at least go through formal channels. But he liked Posthumus, respected what he had heard about him. And, what the hell, the man was a colleague. Of sorts.

'Mr Posthumus,' said de Boer, realising with a twinge of awkwardness that he had interrupted him. He turned from the window, glanced out to the corridor, and, as he was talk-ing, walked over to close the door.

'I'm sorry. I wanted to ask you a question,' he said. 'You were the first to draw our attention to the connection between the Zagorodnii and Wojciechowski cases. I was wondering whether you had looked further into that? Into other connections between the two.'

Posthumus was surprised when de Boer immediately called back, even more so when the detective himself brought up Marloes's case, and mentioned Zig and Tony. He seemed to be offering an opening.

'You're aware of other connections between Zagorodnii and Wojciechowski?' Posthumus asked.

'Wojciechowski was known to the police,' said de Boer. 'I'm sure you realise that. Investigators at the time were certain he was a *loverboy*.'

'I had gathered as much. What was the connection?'

'I've been reviewing the files. It appears to have been through a pimp, one László Kiss. The name is familiar to you?'

'It is,' said Posthumus, after a fraction of a hesitation.

'Kiss was also a frequenter of the FitFast gym, as was Zagorodnii,' said de Boer.

He paused, took an audible breath and went on.

'One line of thought,' he said, 'might be to look into how the drug that killed Wojciechowski was administered to him.'

'The pathology report says the drug was ingested.'

'You've been doing your homework. Yes. Traces were found in a sports drink,' said de Boer. 'It was known to police that such drugs were present at the guest-house, and the line taken was that the suspect had doctored the drink during Wojciechowski's second visit that afternoon, on the occasion after he and the suspect had had an altercation, witnessed in the street.'

De Boer paused momentarily. Posthumus sensed a 'but' coming.

'The drink was one of those protein shakes mixed at FitFast gym,' de Boer went on, 'in Wojciechowski's own container, a steel water bottle found in his sports bag.'

There was a short silence at the other end of the line.

'Thank you,' said Posthumus.

'I hear from the prosecutor that Ms Vermolen continues to protest her innocence,' said de Boer.

'That is part of the problem. As far as the psychological report goes,' said Posthumus.

'Yes,' said de Boer. 'A large woman, I recall?'

He seemed to make light of it.

'And not the sort I can imagine working out at a gym,' he continued.

'Again, thank you,' said Posthumus.

'Of course, I'm not quotable on any of this,' said de Boer.

'Of course.'

De Boer ended the call, and replaced the handset. Well, he'd done it. No use regretting that now. But had he simply shifted responsibility to Pieter Posthumus? De Boer walked over to the hat-stand in the corner to fetch his coat. There had been a time when justice meant all to him. It was the reason he had joined the force. Before career, reaching targets, getting results got in the way.

On the walk back to De Dolle Hond, Posthumus was deep in thought. He went to the guest-house first, knocked softly on Tina's door.

'May I come in?'

Tina was sitting, as before, on the end of her bed, huddled against the radiator.

'Did you manage to get hold of Jelle?' Posthumus asked.

Tina nodded.

'And? Can I get to speak to him? Do you know where I can find him?'

Tina shrugged. 'He won't come,' she said, 'but I give him your number, didn't I. He said he might phone.'

Might. Well, better than nothing, thought Posthumus.

'Thank you, Tina,' he said. 'Anna should be back soon. I'll speak to her, and try to get her to let you stay.'

'Promise?'

'I promise that I will speak to Anna. She's not back yet, is she? Has she been over?'

Tina shook her head. '*He*'s been, though,' she said.

'He?'

'Fat Man. Marty. Bashing the door, yelling. I didn't go down.'

'How did he know you were here?' asked Posthumus.

Again Tina shrugged. 'Jelle, I guess,' she said.

Posthumus came further into the room. Still wearing his outdoor coat, he stood beside Tina, facing the radiator, warming his hands.

'Could it have been Marty who fought with Zig, do you think?' he asked.

'Didn't hardly know him, did he?' said Tina.

Her face brightened. 'It was a bloke though, what fought. I been thinking about it for you. Dunno how I know that, but I do. Voices maybe,' she said.

'And that day, or some other day?'

Tina shrugged. 'Could of been another day,' she said. 'Dunno. The day that Zig died is a bit of a blur.'

'How was Zig the last time you saw him, do you remember?'

Tina thought for a bit.

'He was acting funny,' she said. 'I thought he was pissed or something.'

So ... dizzy, concussed, taking aspirin. And quite possibly the day before.

'And you're sure Marty didn't fight with him?'

'Not with Zig, with Marloes,' said Tina. 'And not fighting or nothing, just yelling.'

Posthumus turned to stare at her. She gave a little giggle.

'She was going to tell his mother! Tell his *mother*!'

'Tell Marty's mother what?' asked Posthumus.

'What he did to me, innit?'

Tina chuckled. She seemed to relish the idea of the bully brought down to size in such an absurdly elementary way. Then she looked up at Posthumus.

'You will bring her back, won't you?' she asked. 'Marloes?'

'I hope so, Tina, I hope so,' said Posthumus.

Back downstairs he picked up the groceries he had bought for Anna, and the junk mail off the mat. Junk mail and an official-looking envelope. He turned it over. From a company of valuators and surveyors. He slipped it into his pocket to give to Anna, let himself in to the apartment, and gave the place a quick spruce-up to make it more hospitable for her. It was after six o'clock when he went across to De Dolle Hond. Outside, Simon was tacking a notice on to the wooden hoarding that boarded up the window.

'Quite a few customers been round already,' he said. 'I got tired of telling the same story to everyone.'

He stood back to admire his work.

'Anna back yet?' asked Posthumus.

'Couple of minutes ago,' said Simon. 'She's upstairs.'

'Good,' said Posthumus. 'There'll be something to add to your story, but I want to tell her first. Good news. For some.'

'Tomorrow, then. I'm off, I'm already late again.'

Posthumus walked towards the door.

'Mind your step in there,' called Simon. 'The cleaners have just been. Dumped a whole lot of stuff ready for tomorrow morning.'

Anna was upstairs at her computer, filling in an insurance assessment form. At least she's taking the fire on board a little more, thought Posthumus. He'd been worried by the way that she seemed simply to be blocking it out. But Anna met the news of Irene's arrest with total silence, and shrugged off the idea that Victim Support would be in touch. She turned back to the screen. Posthumus changed the subject. He'd have a quiet word with Victim Support about Anna himself.

'Paul any better?' he asked. 'You've been back to the hospital?'

Anna swivelled her chair round to face him.

'A bit. He's still partially under sedation, though out of danger. They won't have to transfer him to Rotterdam, but he'll be in the AMC for a while yet,' she said.

'And you? The check-up OK?'

Posthumus had already googled 'smoke inhalation', and knew what danger signs he should be looking out for.

'I'm fine,' said Anna. 'And glad that I was there for Marloes today. It was the right thing to do.'

Her voice didn't sound as rough as it had done earlier, but she seemed subdued.

'How was it?' asked Posthumus.

Anna shook her head. 'Awful. Everything that I'd hoped wouldn't happen, did. Marloes was all over the place, kept going off on her tangents. I mean, you were right, I know, if you don't *know* her, it does sound potty, the way she talks. And of course she denied everything, but got agitated about it, so that the denials seemed too much.'

Anna pushed her fingers into her thick hair and closed her eyes.

'She looked so frightened,' she said. 'Kept saying, "I'm not mad, I'm not mad, am I? I'm not mad."'

Anna's voice was soft.

'It all seems so hopeless,' she said, 'and . . . all this.' She gestured weakly with one hand towards the café below, then opened her eyes to look up at Posthumus.

'What are we doing, PP?' she said. 'Where's it all going? Is it doing *anything* for Marloes?' She slumped back in her chair. 'I think I've had enough.'

Posthumus had rarely seen her like this, not even when her father died. He moved over, sat behind her on her desk, reached out and rested a hand on her shoulder. He told her what he'd been doing, how much he'd found out, mentioned how he'd been focusing on Zig. It all seemed pathetically little.

'The judge was really pushing her on her relationship with both of them,' said Anna. 'On whether she had fought with Zig, and why she'd fought with Tony. And of course she plays straight into their hands, going on about how upset she was that Zig was leaving for Berlin, and how Tony laughed at her when she said she wanted to help him get out of the life he was in. So then the judge asks if she felt abandoned by Zig, so she says no, she's always been alone, so then he asks if it disturbed her, if she felt a man was getting too close to her. It was like he was ticking boxes on the psychiatric report. And she gave all the wrong answers, well, I mean she gave the right answers, the honest answers, but the right answers are the wrong answers, except they're not wrong, not like that. Oh God, I don't know, you know what I mean.'

'The right answers in the wrong ears, maybe. Taken in the wrong way,' said Posthumus.

But the thought had occurred to him, he had to admit, when he read the psychiatrist's comments on Marloes's simultaneous fear of abandonment and of commitment, that maybe there was something in it.

'Oh, PP,' said Anna. 'What to do?'

Posthumus kept his hand on Anna's shoulder. Did he go so far as to agree with the analysis that there was a paranoid element to Marloes's anxieties? A 'deeply disturbed relationship with men that found outlet in psychotic episodes'? He thought not. He hoped not. Besides, his commitment at this point was to Anna, to the promise he had given to her. And – if it didn't sound too self-aggrandising – to the truth. Posthumus was beginning to feel even more strongly that pieces of this story did not fit. And he knew of old that once that niggling feeling started, he could not rest until he had set the pieces right.

'Look,' he said to Anna, 'you must be exhausted. Why don't you call it a day, and go next door? I've made the bed, Marloes has a microwave, and I've left some ready meals for you in the fridge.'

It was the first time Posthumus had ever bought a ready meal.

'PP, you're a saint,' said Anna. 'Thank you.'

She took the hand that was on her shoulder and squeezed it.

'But there's one more thing I need to ask you,' she said, getting out of the chair. 'Could you do me a huge favour?'

She opened a desk drawer, took out a key ring with a large silver P dangling from it.

'Paul's spare keys,' she said. 'Could you go round to his place tomorrow morning, and get him some clothes? Pyjamas, toiletries, underwear and stuff? He's in a hospital shift at the moment; he's got absolutely nothing, not a stitch. He was, you know . . .' Anna stopped, slightly embarrassed.

'Yes, I'd heard. Where's he live?'

'Diemen.'

'*Diemen?*'

Posthumus felt his saintliness slip a notch. That was miles out east.

'I'm sorry,' said Anna. 'But I have to be here to talk things through with the cleaners in the morning, there's someone coming from the insurance, and an equipment rep, stuff Simon can't do.'

'I'll take a tram,' said Posthumus.

'Tomorrow's fine,' Anna went on, 'he'll be OK till then, but if you wouldn't mind dropping it off at the hospital after? A big ask, I know, but if there's any spark left in me at all, I should go to court. Even if it's only so's Marloes can see I'm there, that I've not deserted her. It's the prosecutor's closing arguments.'

The momentary flash of energy Anna had shown seemed to die. Of course he'd do it, but sometimes, Posthumus felt, he was a bit of a pushover.

'Come on,' he said, 'let's go, I'm also knackered.'

He pulled his scarf tighter, began to button up his coat.

'Oh, I almost forgot,' he said, reaching into his coat pocket. 'There was a letter for Marloes. You're dealing with all that, aren't you?'

Anna looked at the back of the envelope, opened it and scanned the letter, frowning slightly.

'Some idiot seems to think she wants to sell the guest-house,' she said. 'Chancer. I'll deal with it tomorrow.'

She placed the letter on her desk.

'Come on,' she said to Posthumus. 'Let's get out of here.'

Posthumus put a hand on her arm.

'There's just one thing,' he said. 'I didn't let on earlier, it didn't seem the right moment. I'm afraid you have a housemate.'

He told Anna about how he'd found Tina hiding next door. 'I promised I'd ask if she can stay.'

'Oh, what the hell, why not?' said Anna, with a laugh. 'Things can hardly get any worse, can they? Now, home!'

The two of them went down the stairs, through the darkened café, acrid with the stink of the fire, and out into the street.

16

No post, only his newspaper on the mat inside the street door. Posthumus picked it up, and began to make his way up the steep stairs to his apartment. A glass of wine, something quick to eat, and an early night. Especially that. He tensed slightly as he passed Gusta's door on the first floor. Not tonight. He could do without Gusta tonight. She had surely heard him rush out in the early hours, and wouldn't relent until she'd drained every detail out of him. But the door remained shut.

Posthumus let himself in to his apartment, and leaned back against the door. It felt as if a week had passed since he'd last been home. He ran his eyes over the long room. Bart Hooft's poems and last night's paper on the dining table, the ponder-box beside the armchair, the bowl of chickpeas soaking in the kitchen. So much for lamb couscous. That idea seemed to belong to an even more distant past. Posthumus dropped the newspaper he was carrying on to the dining table, and began to take off his coat. A small report on the front page of the paper caught his eye, one of those tasters for a longer article within. He stopped, one arm in a sleeve of his coat, one arm free, and flicked to the relevant page. Immediately, he phoned Merel. Voicemail. Shaking off his coat, Posthumus left a message.

'Merel. You've seen the papers? Of course, silly question. But there's a report here about the police recovering a backpack belonging to a Najib T. And a gun. An anonymous tip-off, apparently, and there's something about a duffel bag and scooter, too. That just has to be our Najib. They're saying that he . . . well, have a look for yourself. Ring me. But not after nine. I'm having an early night.'

Forty minutes later, the chickpeas were simmering on the cooker, Posthumus had eaten a meal of reheated leftovers, and had the best part of a bottle of wine still in front of him. Jelle Smits had not yet contacted him, but, he realised, Jelle was not going to be enough. Posthumus might never hear from him, and even if Jelle could be persuaded to admit to the police that Marty had 'helped' him with his story and that he hadn't seen Marloes on the stairs, that alone would not let Marloes off the hook. He'd have to find who it was who had fought with Zig, would have to prove that it wasn't Marloes. Posthumus needed more than Jelle Smits. Zig himself, then. His subdural haematoma might have occurred a day, or even two days, earlier than the cut to his temple. Zig concussed, confused, dizzy, and falling to hit his head, like that actor William Holden? A possibility. Tina's recollection seemed to back that up. That would mean culpable homicide, rather than murder, but didn't exonerate Marloes. There was still Tony.

Posthumus sat spinning Bart Hooft's Namiki pen on the polished surface of the dining table. Spinning, then stopping it with his middle finger. Spinning and stopping. Yesterday's paper with its 'Witch of De Wallen' headline lay neatly folded in front of him, beside the one he had just brought upstairs, unread apart from the short Najib T. report. Merel had still not rung, but there was no mistaking it, despite the regulation abbreviation of his surname, Najib T. had to be Najib. So, he'd been right after all, in what he'd reasoned out back in the summer. Posthumus stopped the pen in mid-spin. He'd been right about Bart, too. Both stories built up after working at pieces of a puzzle, until he was satisfied that they fitted. He thought again about Zig and Tony Wojciechowski.

Cornelius had told him to trust his instincts. Zig's and Tony's stories intertwined, Cornelius said, and that was where the answer lay. Posthumus had always known that, it had gone against the grain to focus only on Zig, yet somehow he had lost confidence in his own capabilities. In his instincts. But he had been right about Bart and Najib. And, Alex had reminded him, about poor drowned Amir, long before anyone else suspected a thing. And all from following an instinct when he sensed something was wrong. He ought to be doing what he was best at, not analysing, but composing; considering the flotsam and jetsam of a life, and forming from it a story, reassembling it into a valid whole. Posthumus got up and began pacing the space between the dining table and the window overlooking the canal. After a while he stopped, picked up his phone off the table, and texted Cornelius.

Apols about earlier. You are right. Zig and Tony cases shld be seen as one.

Then he went back to pacing, this time the full length of the apartment, all the way to the kitchen and back to the front window.

The pieces, he needed to set out the pieces. What were the links between Zig and Tony?

The paintings. Tony had one, though Posthumus did not know why. *The past.* They had possibly worked together in the sex trade, Tony had testified against Zig's pimp. *Marloes.* She loved Zig and disliked Tony, she had possibly argued with Zig about his going to Berlin, and had certainly thrown Tony out into the street – on the day he was killed. Tony, who had been wanting to make up with Zig after falling out some time before. Again, Posthumus did not know when or why. *The pimp.* László K., whom he now knew as László Kiss. Habitué of FitFast gym. The man that Pogo at the gym said had killed Tony, the man who had been arrested and released, who had an alibi, even though gym attendant Robbie said he was at FitFast the night of Tony's death. Robbie, who had since disappeared, but could not himself be ruled out as a suspect. László Kiss was in jail when Zig was killed, but, Pogo said, managed to run his little racket by phone.

Posthumus stopped at the window, and stood looking at a young couple crossing the bridge outside. The girl slipped, let out a squeal, grabbed on to her partner's arm and cuddled up tight. A little group of kids ran about on the iced-over canal, stopping and skidding on their soles, this way and that, playing human dodgems. Posthumus's breath steamed the window slightly. He traced a pattern with his finger. Two circles overlapping. Just where did Marty come in to things? Even if he had nothing to do with the fire (and was Irene's confession for real?), what was he up to, getting Jelle Smits to change his story? Had he fought with Zig himself? Tina seemed to think not. Did he even know Tony? Tony, perhaps the trickiest piece of all. A *loverboy*, a groomer of young girls, luring them into prostitution. De Boer had as much as confirmed that on the phone this afternoon, but the inspector had not told Posthumus much else that he did not already know. Except that the drug was administered to Tony in a protein shake, mixed in his own drinking bottle, and probably at FastFit. Who had the opportunity to do that? Not Marloes, surely. Back to László Kiss again, and Robbie. Any of the others? Marty? Jelle Smits? Posthumus couldn't picture either of them getting by unnoticed at the gym. And a motive? Zig himself, maybe. Perhaps it was Tony who had originally recruited him, and he bore a grudge. Marloes had told Anna she thought they once worked together. Was that what their falling out was about? And how come Tony, then, had one of Zig's paintings? It was back to the paintings. What was 201? Did that idea hold any water? And Cornelius's odd scenario for them all, was there anything in that? What had he said? A story of death, judgement, reconciliation, finding peace.

Posthumus's thoughts were beginning to slide all over the place. Like the kids on the ice outside. He turned from the window. This was no good, he was exhausted. The timer on the cooker beeped. Wearily, Posthumus walked over to the kitchen. He drained the chickpeas. He'd bag and freeze them in the morning; he was about to drop. Enough. Posthumus climbed the spiral staircase, and went straight to bed.

The dream. He hadn't had the dream in weeks. Posthumus lay awake in the dark, the images still raw of the nightmare that had begun to trouble him in the days after he'd discovered Zig's body, the dream that somehow confused his brother and Zig: Zig, the cherub crashed to the floor in a pool of blood; Willem, the broken angel twitching on tarmac. All that blood. Posthumus glanced at the dimly lit face of his bedside clock: 3.03. He closed his eyes, turned his head back, and sank into the pillow. That blood. A scenario: Zig has a fight, one or two days before he dies. One day, say. Thursday, the thirtieth of June. He's concussed, has a headache, feels dizzy and confused, but like so many others, he doesn't go to the doctor. Takes aspirin. Tina notices his odd behaviour. Jelle, and possibly also Tina, overhears the fight. Next day, Friday. The first of July. Zig's haematoma worsens. Perhaps he is passing out from time to time. Anyway, he falls, hits his head, severs his temporal artery. The pathology report noted that. It's close to the surface. There would be a lot of blood. Aspirin, a decoagulant, would make it worse. Zig staggers about the room, tries to staunch the flow with his duvet. All that blood. The picture that confronted Posthumus from the landing was still burned into his brain.

But who had Zig fought with? There were other pieces that had to fit. Posthumus lay perfectly still, enveloped by darkness. What of Marty? Was he making too much of Marty? Why would Marty get Jelle to lie about the fight? Tina said that Marty had a fight not with Zig, but with Marloes. Was the Jelle story simply Marty getting back at Marloes, and nothing more than that? Nasty opportunism, getting Marloes discredited or out of the way, so that she wouldn't let on to his mother about Tina. Teaching her a lesson. It was a pathetic story that did rather fit Marty. Possible, but there had to be more to it than that. Different images were entering and leaving Posthumus's mind. Pogo, Merel. Strands flitting by. He tried to grab at them. Straws in the wind, an apt expression. Merel in De Dolle Hond after interviewing Marty. What had she said? That he was sulky, and he had it in for his mother. Not that, there was something else. That he had a big plan, a business venture, that he'd been smug and pleased with himself. Marty, looking smug and pleased with himself, walking on the Zeedijk with Jelle Smits. It was there, somewhere, but Posthumus felt himself slipping back into sleep. He could not quite grasp it. Then, suddenly, Pogo. Pogo and Marty, but not Marty on the Zeedijk. Near the Zeedijk, Marty threatening him on Nieuwmarkt, walking away. A phrase that hung unattached, then floated by, another strand in the wind – 'powerful friends'. Pogo. Pogo had said that about László Kiss, that he had powerful friends. And that was Marty's threat on the Nieuwmarkt. A common enough phrase, but . . .

Posthumus knew he had to make some notes. He was awake enough to be aware, but not to move. He tried to force himself on to a level of consciousness that gave him control over his body, but a stronger force was sucking him back. His body did not move. Quickly, in the few seconds he knew he had left before sleep sucked him in, Posthumus began to visualise his room, attach thoughts to familiar objects: 'powerful friends' draped as a banner over the bedpost, smug Marty beaming on the wardrobe door, holding a rolled contract, Zig attached by the side of his head to the radiator, blood all over it, Pogo at the door, Marty, Pia Jacobs, Marloes, arms linked, dancing a weird dance across the foot of the bed. Posthumus attempted to hold it all in a single picture that he might carry with him, hoping it would still be there in the morning.

17

Before he showered, Posthumus slipped on a dressing gown and spiralled down the metal staircase to make some notes. The image he had tried to fix in his mind in the middle of the night was still there. Just. Downstairs, his phone was blinking, still on the dining table. Posthumus cursed softly. He'd been so tired, he'd forgotten to take it up to the bedroom. If he'd missed Jelle Smits . . . but for the moment he resisted, ignored the phone, and made hasty notes on a sheet of A4 in his workspace, before any other thoughts intervened. He went across to the dining table to see who had called. Three voicemail messages. Merel and two unidentified numbers. It must have been Smits. He'd missed him. Posthumus accessed voicemail and drummed his fingers impatiently on the table. Merel was first in line.

'Hello, PP. Nine thirty. I know you said not after nine, but I thought I'd try. Hope I haven't woken you up.'

Merel spoke in a half whisper, almost as if Posthumus were sleeping somewhere inside the voicemail and she might disturb him. Crazy girl. He gave a little smile. His fingers stopped drumming.

'I've just spoken to Aissa,' the message went on, 'it's true. That is Najib. The police have already been round. And apparently, in that first letter Najib wrote, he told them that he wouldn't be able to come home any more. Now they know why. He must have found out about Khaled. So you were right. Speak tomorrow.'

Merel ended with a double kiss. Second message: 23.03. It sounded like one of those duds, when someone's phone has rung you from their bag or pocket by mistake. Muffled voices, a man's and a child's, scuffling sounds. Then, clearer, but still in the background: 'Just say. Tell him.'

The child. Or could it be Tina? Her voice was so tiny. Another scuffle, then a short silence and the male voice spoke: 'This is Jelle Smits. It's true. What Tina said. I couldn't remember right, about the fight and that. Hey, I can't help that, man!'

Again, Tina saying something, muffled in the background. Then Jelle again.

'And Marty, he helped me get it straight, didn't he? But, hey, I'm not going to no cops or nothing. That's it.'

End of message. Third message, 23.47. Tina.

'I'm sorry, 'bout Jelle and that. I did try make him come, but he wouldn't. Later he said maybe. But to you, not the cops. He don't like cops. Marty had to make him go.'

Her voice brightened. 'But I done what you said, with your games and that. I wanna help Marloes. So I thought of Zig, and the last few times I saw him and all, and where, and what we was doing exactly, bit by bit, like you done with me. And it *was* a man, what came, not Marloes! Dunno when 'xactly, but it was before Zig was acting funny or drunk or whatever, I know, 'cos we'd had a bit of a giggle on the stairs, and the front door rang, and Zig said it was for him and went back down, and I went to my room, but I heard him, didn't I? I heard him say hello to Zig at the door, 'cept he didn't say hello, he said "howdy pardner". It was howdy-man! An' I remember thinking, Zig doesn't even *like* the old tosser.'

The message went on for a few seconds, but Posthumus had stopped listening. Howdy-man? *Paul?* What would Paul have to do with visiting Zig? Posthumus put down the phone, and went back upstairs to shower. Surely not. It was his own fault, playing tricks with Tina's mind, putting ideas in her head. She'd been talking about Paul, had seen him rolling in the snow during the fire, and was making associations that didn't exist. And he had been encouraging her with his memory exercises. Was that any different from what Marty had done with Jelle? Or maybe Tina was simply saying this to please him, because Jelle wouldn't come forward, and she thought it would help Marloes. *Paul?* What would Paul fight with Zig about? That piece did not fit at all.

Posthumus tried to dismiss the idea, but he could not blow it out completely. Tina's message was still troubling him as he walked to FitFast. There was a tram stop just across from the gym, where he could catch a Number 9 to Diemen. He had Paul's spare key in his pocket, there'd be time enough later to put together some things for him and take them to the hospital. He'd ask Paul about Zig then. First he wanted to look in at the gym, to see if Pogo was there. He paused outside the door and looked in through the glass. FitFast was busy with the pre-work crowd. Someone else was at the counter, but as Posthumus watched Pogo came from a room at the back and handed something to the other attendant, who went towards the fitness rooms. Posthumus went in. Pogo was busy with clients at the computer.

Posthumus walked over and sat at the far end of the juice bar. The second attendant returned, and poured Posthumus a freshly squeezed orange juice. Posthumus watched as other clients came up to order at the bar. Cans of sports drink, mostly. One protein shake, which the attendant prepared in a lidded polystyrene cup, the sort takeaway coffee came in. A couple more men buying the protein powder, and taking it with them to the fitness room.

'They mix it up themselves?' said Posthumus to the attendant, trying to sound chatty.

'Mostly. Best you have it after you've worked out.'

So, whoever drugged Tony's drinking bottle would have had to do it where? The police had grilled Marloes about drugs in the guest-house, and Tony's second visit that afternoon. But on the phone, Flip de Boer had sounded uneasy about that, had as much as urged Posthumus to have another look. So, where? 'After you've worked out,' the attendant said. In the locker room, then? Somewhere that Tony had left his bag unattended while he was in the fitness room. Posthumus remembered, from his first visit, that there were bags left under the benches in the locker room. And if it happened in the locker room, that would mean that whoever did it had to be a man.

The attendant moved away, putting an end to small talk. Posthumus pulled across one of the newspapers lying on the counter. Another Witch of De Wallen headline. Pogo bounced up, scrubbed, shiny, almost obscenely energetic for the hour of day.

'Pieter Posthumus, isn't it?' he said. 'Come back for your free trial?'

'Later, maybe,' said Posthumus, indicating his orange juice. 'I was passing, and felt like a juice. I enjoyed our chat the other day.'

Posthumus held Pogo's gaze. Pogo's eyes hardened.

'It's OK, mate,' said Pogo to the other attendant. 'I can sort this. You go finish up in there, if you like.'

He waited until his colleague was back in the fitness room.

'So you *are* a journalist. Or a cop,' he said.

'Neither,' said Posthumus, 'but I will come clean. I'm not here for a free workout.'

He tapped the newspaper beside him, with its artist's sketch of the courtroom, Marloes viewed from behind, but large and eccentrically dressed, identifiably Marloes.

'I'm trying to get to the bottom of this,' he said.

'Private dick?'

'Nothing so grand,' said Posthumus. 'I just think they've got the wrong person.'

Pogo said nothing, he seemed to be sizing Posthumus up.

'I mean,' said Posthumus, tapping the picture of Marloes. 'Has she ever been in here? Did you or Robbie ever see her?'

Pogo shrugged. 'Picture looks familiar, but then it would, wouldn't it?' he said. 'If she's been all over the news 'n' stuff.'

Posthumus plunged straight in. 'László Kiss,' he said.

Pogo didn't react. His face remained quite still.

'You said he was running his operation from jail,' said Posthumus, 'that he had powerful friends. Who did you mean?'

Nothing. Pogo's eyes flicked upwards, to a CCTV camera directed over the bar.

'Boss of this place,' he said eventually. 'Got his fingers in all sorts of pies.'

'What sorts of pies?' asked Posthumus.

'Told you last time. Escort. Boys, girls, places in De Wallen, who knows what else.'

'Name?'

'Henk de Kok. But you don't want to go there. You really don't want to go there,' said Pogo.

He took a step closer.

'You can't get at him,' he said. 'No one can get at him. Police have tried, tax boys have tried, everyone. But he's well protected, isn't he? A nice thick cushion of fall-guys all round, and him sitting pretty in the middle. Just a rich property tycoon, isn't he? You'll come off second. *Very* second.'

Pogo stepped back, and turned towards the other end of the counter.

'I hate the fucker,' he said, his voice low. 'Reasons of my own. But you heard *none* of this from me. If anyone asks me, the topic never came up. Ever.'

He walked back to the computer. Posthumus drained the remainder of his orange juice, and got up to leave.

'Good morning, Mr Posthumus, next time your free training session I hope!' said Pogo, as Posthumus passed him on his way to the door.

His voice was bright, public.

'Good luck!' he called, as Posthumus left.

Anna sat at Marloes's big, wooden table, nursing a mug of coffee. Another mug stood ready beside her, and a large coffee pot. The door to the apartment was open. Beside it, Zig's painting leaned against the wall. Anna stared at it as she sipped her coffee. It felt odd to be sitting at Marloes's table, having slept in her bed, and to be drinking coffee from one of her chunky mugs, looking at Zig's painting. A bit creepy, to tell the truth. Like she was stepping into Marloes's shoes. Anna sighed. Enough of all that. The cleaners would be next door in a minute. She needed to be getting on with it. She took a last sip, and got up from the table.

'Tina!' she shouted up the stairwell, for the third time that morning.

Tina appeared at the top of the stairs, looking sulky and a little crumpled. Getting up before eight o'clock was clearly not a regular Tina activity.

'I'm here, innit?' she said, coming down the stairs.

'There's some bread on the table, I'm going next door. Grab yourself a sandwich and some coffee, and bring it straight over. Make sure Marloes's door locks behind you.'

The girl could do a bit of work for her keep, thought Anna. It certainly wouldn't do her any harm. Anna went out into the street and along to De Dolle Hond. She let herself in, and switched on one of the lamps that had been rigged up to run off power from upstairs.

Anna looked around her. She felt a pain, a tightening at the top of the stomach just below her breastbone, and at the same time nausea and a sense she was about to cry. Years ago, decades ago, she had gone on her first holiday without her parents, a school camping trip, and had been desperately homesick. She had never forgotten that feeling, and she was experiencing something like it now. Her dear, dear Dolle Hond. Christ, but she hoped that Irene would suffer! Just thank God it wasn't any worse. Most of the panelling was still intact, the old bar looked undamaged. The mirrors were gone, though, and one of those big Delft vases. She heard Tina come in behind her.

'It's freezing in here,' said Tina. 'And it stinks, something horrible.'

'Well, that's what we're here for,' said Anna. 'To clean things up a bit.'

A van pulled up outside. Doors banged.

'Finish up your breakfast, then let's get cracking,' said Anna. 'You can sit at the bar, but watch where you're walking, there's glass around.'

The cleaners came in, and went through to the kitchen. They'd see to the fire damage and heavy stuff. She'd get Tina, and Simon when he arrived, started on the rest. Anna heard a knock on the café door. She turned as the door was cautiously pushed open. Mrs Ting!

'I'm sorry we're closed, as you see there's been a bit of an accident,' said Anna.

She had to stop herself saying 'Mrs Ting'. After all these years of Mrs Ting playing the fruit machine, Anna still knew her only by the nickname they'd given her. Mrs Ting walked on into the café.

'I'm sorry,' said Anna again, indicating the destruction behind her with one hand, but Mrs Ting simply smiled and nodded her head slightly to one side. She had a canvas shopping bag over one arm, and was carrying what looked like a bundled-up blanket. She walked over, placed the bundle on the bar, loosened the wrappings a little and lifted a metal lid, releasing an aromatic cloud of steam.

'Wow!' said Tina, leaning over the bundle. 'Hot soup! It smells *amazing*. Soup for breakfast, cool!'

Mrs Ting reached into the canvas bag, pulled out plastic bowls and spoons, and began dishing up. She handed Anna a bowl.

'Oh my! Thank you. *Thank* you,' said Anna.

Now she really was going to cry. The soup seemed to have perked Tina up no end. She was chattering away to Mrs Ting, telling her all about the fire, or what she knew of it at least. And then, for some reason, she started talking about Zig. Mrs Ting seemed to understand her. Simon arrived.

'Soup!' said Simon. 'Awesome. Just the thing in this weather.'

He greeted Mrs Ting. He always did. She nodded back, as she always did, and gave him a bowl.

'Thanks for coming in early,' said Anna to Simon. 'As soon as I've spoken to the insurance assessor, I'm off to court. The cleaners will be in the kitchen, mostly, if you could start on the café. Tina here is going to help you.'

Mrs Ting put on a pair of rubber gloves, and walked over to the fireplace, where she carefully began collecting pieces of the shattered Delft vase that lay on the floor. Simon glanced at Anna. She shrugged. Simon took his soup behind the bar, and began picking up intact bottles from among broken glass.

'Anybody home?'

The café door swung open again.

'Heavens! Quite a party.'

Anna turned around to see who had come in.

'Cornelius! This is a surprise.'

'I thought I would bend my feet thither, to see if you were up and about, and that all was well. But you would appear to have things under consummate control.'

'That's so kind of you,' said Anna, 'and so unexpected.'

She looked Cornelius in the eye.

'PP sent you, didn't he?' she said, smiling.

'I cannot tell a lie,' said Cornelius. 'But I should have come anyway, dear Anna. I'm often at a loose end after dropping Lukas off at school.'

'It was you what came next door yesterday, wasn't it?' said Tina.

'Who came, yes indeed,' said Cornelius. 'So you must be Tina.'

'Tina is going to help with the clean-up, just as soon as she has finished her breakfast,' said Anna.

She looked at Tina pointedly. Tina ignored her.

'You was talking about Zig's painting,' said Tina to Cornelius.

It sounded almost like an accusation.

'We *were,* indeed,' said Cornelius. 'And how might you know that?'

'I come down again, didn't I? I was listening outside.'

'A very singular thing to do,' said Cornelius.

'Know your enemy, innit? That's what Zig always used to say,' said Tina.

'And *am* I the enemy?' said Cornelius.

Tina scowled at him. 'I wanted to know what you was about, didn't I?' she said.

'And what we were "about" met with your approval, I trust?'

The insurance assessor had arrived. Anna excused herself from Cornelius and went to meet him.

'You was talking about Zig's painting,' said Tina. 'It's good, isn't it?'

The question sounded like a test.

'I like that one in particular,' said Cornelius. 'I gather you are familiar with some of the others, too.'

'"Familiar with some of the others too".'

Tina gave a passable imitation of Cornelius's accent.

'Yeah,' she said. 'I know 'em.'

'And do *you* think that Zig is telling a story with them?'

'Dunno, do I?' she said. 'They was private, "a story between me and the canvas", Zig always said.'

'Ah, but you see there *is* a story there,' said Cornelius. 'Zig's paintings all come from paintings in the Rijksmuseum, but he paints his ones as if they happened just a few minutes later. He got the idea from a version of *The Nightwatch* at Schiphol.'

Cornelius looked at Tina, but there wasn't a flicker of recognition.

'It's a painting of a whole lot of people standing in a group,' said Cornelius, 'but in the airport version, it's as if you've arrived a few minutes late, and they've all stopped posing and are doing something else completely.'

'Zig hated being late,' said Tina. '"The whole world can change in five minutes," he always used to say.'

'Oi! Tina! Get your arse in gear, I need some help here,' called Simon from the other end of the bar.

'Haven't finished my coffee yet, have I?' said Tina. 'Besides, I'm talking with mister swallowed-a-dictionary here.'

'Don't tell me,' said Cornelius, 'another of Zig's inimitable expressions.'

Anna came back from the kitchen.

'I'm so sorry, Cornelius,' she said. 'It's really sweet of you to come, and thank you, but I have to be off. I need to get to court in time.'

She turned to Simon at the bar.

'The assessor will be here a while,' she said, 'but I can't wait any longer for the kitchen equipment rep. If he doesn't want my custom I can take it elsewhere.'

'Well, that's five minutes late what'll change *his* world,' said Tina, with a chuckle.

Anna gave Cornelius three quick pecks on the cheeks, and left.

'Missie! Enough, now,' said Simon to Tina.

Tina eased herself off the stool and walked around to the other side of the bar. Mrs Ting took a roll of tissue paper from her canvas bag, and began carefully to wrap the pieces of the Delft vase she had collected. Cornelius stood deep in thought, then he took out his phone to call Posthumus.

A Number 9 arrived as Posthumus was putting his phone back into his pocket. He sat on the tram, staring out of the window as it passed the zoo, thinking about what Cornelius had said. So, Cornelius thought that Zig had had some sort of life-changing experience, which triggered the paintings. Something that had transformed the world for him in a few minutes, and not necessarily for the better. That's what drew him to the Schiphol painting. A few minutes later, and all was different. Or a few minutes *late*. Zig hated being late. Posthumus focused on the knitted woollen hat of the woman in front of him. He placed the tips of his finger together. The tram rocked as it twisted through the dog's-leg past the Tropenmuseum. Perhaps Cornelius had a point. And, given his reading of Zig's first choice of painting, the still life, as having to do with a peak, or with death, Cornelius was convinced that Zig's transforming experience was either a love that peaked and decayed, or a death. Posthumus mulled this over for a while, then he took out his phone. Or a death. In which case, there was a chance Zig's transforming moment might have been public. It took him a few seconds to remember Zig's proper first name. Then he googled: Stefan Zagorodnii.

The first page comprised the usual 'people with the name of' and genealogy sites. Then a skater, a politician, a few more sports reports. After page six, Posthumus gave up. He'd been hoping for a newspaper report. Something. Anything. But Stefan Zagorodnii had clearly never made headlines. Posthumus was about to put away his phone, then checked himself. Not headlines, perhaps, but . . . He made a call.

'Merel?'

'PP! I'm just about to go into an interview.'

'I'll be quick. Do you have access to a wire service?'

'ANP, yes.'

'Any chance of me checking its archive?'

'My wicked, wicked uncle.'

Merel hung up, but a few seconds later a text beeped in.

Login NwePost
Password Redac26
mxx

It took him a while to find it, and there wasn't very much of it, a small strand that probably hadn't been picked up by many papers. But it was there. A death in De Wallen. Overdose. The victim, known as Mel C, had been involved with a *loverboy*. A distraught Stefan Zagorodnii (19) said he had been drinking late with friends, and arrived to discover the victim in a state of collapse. He tried resuscitation until the ambulance arrived, but to no avail. Zagorodnii himself had eventually to be sedated.

Posthumus looked up. The tram passed the familiar gates of the Nieuwe Ooster cemetery. Zig, nineteen? He checked the date of the archived report: 2006; 21 January 2006. Posthumus scanned the piece again. The incident had occurred the previous day. Posthumus closed his hands over his phone, and moved them gently back and forth, as if he were shaking dice: 20 January. He stood up. One of the standing passengers immediately took his seat.

'Twentieth of January,' said Posthumus, half aloud.

He stroked the hair on his temple, where it was beginning to grey.

'Twenty, one.'

The passenger who had taken his seat glanced at him. Posthumus put away his phone. The twentieth of the first: 20.1. Or, 201. If the first painting was done in 2007, that would be numbered 201.1. Then one a year until the Vermeer, the last one, 201.5. That would correspond perfectly with the dates on the paintings, the Vermeer dated before it was finished. Dated when it was *started*. A painting begun each year, on the anniversary of that death in De Wallen, dated and numbered in succession. Posthumus had to stop himself from exclaiming aloud. He had found Cornelius's trigger.

He looked up at the information screen. Paul's stop was next. Posthumus went over to stand by the door. So, he'd discovered what lay behind the paintings. But how did that help Marloes?

18

'I've said all along that Irene Kester was an odd one.'

'Knocks it back, too, you can smell it on her.'

Marty ignored the two gossiping customers. He had worries of his own.

'A pound of mince, please, and four of those chops,' said the skinny gossiper.

Sullenly, Marty weighed and packaged the meat, avoiding eye contact. It was all fucked up. Everything was going wrong. He couldn't get hold of Marloes's lawyer, she was in court all day, wasn't she? How was he supposed to have known that? And she didn't return his calls. So how the fuck was he going to get Marloes to sign? And it didn't help, having Henk de Kok down his throat the whole time. *And* he couldn't find Jelle Smits. He thumped the meat down on the counter.

'Got out of bed the wrong side this morning, did we?'

Marty ignored the remark. 'Seven euros forty,' he said.

The two customers exchanged glances. Marty held out his hand for the money, and shifted his weight from foot to foot. That little bitch Tina knew where Jelle was, but there was no getting at her, especially now that Anna from De Dolle Hond was in the guest-house. He took the notes, and handed the customer back her change. What was *that* all about? She'd put a stop to Marloes selling the moment she got a whiff of anything. Marty could feel it all slipping away from him: Martin Jacobs Management, the money, getting at his mother, the lot.

What made it worse was that he'd told his mother that he had set up a company, that he was going to make it big. And she'd just laughed. *Laughed.* But he'd had to do *something* after the police came. She'd gone ballistic, yelling on at him about the disgrace, and what a useless lump of nothing he was. He'd wanted to show her.

'For me, a piece of that pâté, and four fillets of pork.'

Marty turned to cut the pork. He had nearly crapped himself when the police came in, thinking it was about Marloes and Jelle and all that. Indignation came easy when they questioned him, partly from the relief that it wasn't about Marloes, partly from real shock. He'd had fuck-all to do with the fire! That meddling Pieter Posthumus was behind him being landed with that one. Marty heard another customer come in. Posthumus needed to be taught a lesson, him and that Anna de Vries both. They would see what he was about. He turned back and reached into the vitrine for the pâté.

'Do me some of your *pekelvlees*, as well,' the customer went on.

'And I'll have your neck.'

It was a man's voice. Marty glanced up. He noticed the black leather jacket first. Marty lifted his head completely. Henk de Kok was standing in the shop.

Paul de Vos. The label was handwritten, slipped under a clear plastic cover on the doorpost. Out of habit, Posthumus pressed the bell, as he would have done on a house-visit for work. A ground-floor apartment, probably because Paul had a piano, he thought. He let himself in, wrinkling his nose at the sour citrusy smell that met him. Unwashed dishes, garbage. That was familiar enough, too.

The sink in the kitchen was cluttered with plates. Empty plastic takeaway cartons overflowed from a half-open bin, a pile of pizza boxes lay stacked beside it. Posthumus opened the back door to let in some air. He might bag the rubbish later, and take it out. But that was it. There were limits. The fridge was a collage of paper: flyers, invoices, concert tickets, old postcards, a tax demand, a letter from the council, all held on with magnets in the shape of musical notes. Posthumus scanned the collection. Habit again, partly – it was what he did week in and week out, scouring apartments. But partly, it was that he could not get Tina's phone message out of his head. He flipped through the postcards and old birthday cards: Rob & Willie, Mxx, three more from a Margriet. No Zig.

Posthumus walked through to the sitting room. For a moment he half-expected to see one of Zig's paintings on the walls, but of course not. Piano, a large television, a sofa with beer bottles and a full ashtray on the floor beside it. A good few hundred CDs. Posthumus walked over for a look. A couple of albums by Paul's ex, Sarah Lindberg, quite a bit of country and western, but apart from that an eclectic mix. Posthumus would have been hard put to it to pinpoint Paul's musical taste. He checked what was in the player. Soft Cell. Paul doing his homework so that he could impress Anna. Nothing anywhere that might link Paul to Zig. But what would there be? He'd ask Paul straight out, when he got to the hospital.

In the bedroom, Posthumus investigated the wardrobe and pulled open drawers. No sign of any pyjamas. He put together a pile of underwear and T-shirts, none of them that new, but it was all he could find. A pair of Paul's cowboy boots stood beside the bed. He was not going to carry those all the way to the hospital, he'd find something more suitable. Another full ashtray on the bedside table. And a laptop. Would Paul want that? Posthumus shrugged. Anna hadn't asked for it. A photo:

Paul, Sarah Lindberg and a young girl, must be a daughter. The girl looked familiar, perhaps she'd come to De Dolle Hond. That, perhaps? Posthumus left it. Paul might see that sort of thing as a step too far. He'd stick to clothes. Posthumus added a shirt, a pair of jeans and a thick jumper, for when Paul was discharged. He packed everything into a carry-all off the top of the wardrobe, dropped in a pair of shoes and toiletries that he'd gathered in the bathroom.

Back in the kitchen, he bagged the rubbish, put it outside in a scrappy yard, and left the apartment. He slipped Paul's keys, with the annoyingly heavy P dangling from the ring, into his trouser pocket, and turned south towards the metro station. It was a longer walk than the tram stop, but the quickest way to the hospital.

When she heard why he'd come, the nurse at the ward reception desk let him go in.

'Just a few minutes, because we're outside visiting hours,' she said. 'Mornings are busy, and the patient is still undergoing procedures. So please, keep it short, his wife's already here.'

Wife? Posthumus tried not to look surprised. Maybe Anna had come after all, and had blagged her way in. He followed the signs to Paul's ward.

Posthumus glanced along the row of beds. No sign of Anna, the nurse must have been mistaken. Paul was lying on his back, half propped up against the pillows, with his arms outside the bedclothes, both bandaged with gauze. He looked as though he were asleep. His hair had been drawn back from his face, and his lips were bright red, as if he were wearing lipstick. Carbon monoxide poisoning, thought Posthumus. It was one of the signs he'd learned he should look out for in Anna; it took twenty-four hours or so to kick in. Paul's smoke-inhalation damage must be bad. Posthumus walked over to the bed, put the bag down on the floor, and spoke softly.

'Paul? You awake?'

Paul half opened his eyes. He seemed to take a while to register who Posthumus was.

'Hard to talk, man,' he said.

A nurse walked by and looked at Posthumus enquiringly. He indicated the bag on the floor.

'Mr de Vos is about to go for hyperbaric therapy,' she said.

That meant nothing to Posthumus.

'Oxygen,' said the nurse. 'He should be keeping conversation to a minimum.'

Posthumus nodded. 'I won't be a minute,' he said, more to Paul than the nurse. 'I'll just unpack these.'

He pushed the bag with one foot towards Paul's bedside cabinet.

'Anna asked me to bring you some stuff,' said Posthumus. 'I'll put the basics here, and the rest over there in the cupboard.'

Paul nodded, his eyes shut again. 'Thanks, dude.'

His voice was hoarse, there was a rasping as he breathed in. Posthumus squatted beside the bag and unzipped it. His face was level with Paul's, close up. Tina's phone message kept replaying in his head. 'Howdy-man.' He had to ask. If he said nothing else.

'Paul,' said Posthumus. 'I need to ask you something. You never told us that you visited Zig the day before he died. Why? What's going on?'

Paul struggled, as if to sit up, and gave a short yelp of pain.

'Didn't do that, man,' he said. 'Not me, not the blood.'

He sank back into the pillow, coughing. A deep, bubbling cough.

'But you did visit Zig?' said Posthumus.

Paul nodded, then shook his head. His eyes were closed.

'Not then. Not that,' he said.

'The day before?' asked Posthumus. 'Did you go there the day before Zig died?'

Paul shrugged his shoulders, and winced.

'And there was a disagreement?' said Posthumus.

Paul mumbled something. Posthumus leaned closer to catch what he was saying.

'Knocked him about a bit. Lost it. He said vile shit.'

'But you saw the post-mortem report?' said Posthumus. 'That night I was reading it in De Dolle Hond?'

'Not the blood,' said Paul.

There was another fit of coughing. Posthumus heard voices behind him. He glanced up. The nurse was back. She looked at him accusingly. Paul was hacking badly, and there were beads of sweat on his forehead.

'Mr de Vos is going for his treatment,' said the nurse.

There was an edge of anger to her voice. Two porters moved in to lift Paul from the bed. Posthumus turned to the woman who had come in with the nurse, recognising her as she walked up to him. Sarah Lindberg, Paul's ex. He introduced himself.

'I've been with the doctor,' said Sarah, as Paul was wheeled from the room. 'It doesn't sound good. There's quite a bit of internal tissue damage. Are those Paul's? How kind of you. Let me help you unpack, you look a little flustered.'

Posthumus put the bag up on the bed.

'The nurse said Paul's wife was with him,' said Posthumus. 'I didn't expect . . . I thought it might be someone else.'

He felt his toes curl at his own ineptness.

'I dropped the "ex" when I asked at Reception,' said Sarah. 'I thought it would help. I knew visiting wasn't until the afternoon and I could only come this morning. Hope I'm not usurping anyone's position.'

She looked at him, lightly teasing. She seemed poised, entirely in control. Her confidence made him feel discomfortingly bashful.

'No, no you're not, not at all,' he said. 'I'm sorry, it's just that I thought you and Paul didn't see much of each other.'

Sarah looked at him as if she knew better than that 'no you're not, not at all'.

'I thought Paul might need me,' she said. 'Sometimes even an ex has a role. When you've travelled rough roads together. Listen to me! I sound like a cheesy lyric.'

She began unpacking clothes from the bag.

'Paul's been having a bad time of it lately, I thought he'd appreciate an old friend,' she said.

She held up a pair of boxer shorts, with a little laugh of recognition. 'God, *these* go back,' she said.

'It's all I could find,' said Posthumus, a little on the defensive.

'Don't remind me!' Sarah smiled. 'You know Paul well?' she asked.

She folded the boxers, and put them with the other underwear. Posthumus opened the bedside cabinet, and put Paul's spongebag on the top shelf. He was about to add the bulky ring with the keys to Paul's apartment, but thought better of it and replaced it in his trouser pocket.

'Not really, only from the café, De Dolle Hond, where the fire was,' he said.

'You're from De Dolle Hond?'

'In a manner of speaking.'

'Are things OK there?' said Sarah.

'It's not as badly damaged as we thought,' said Posthumus, 'but Anna, the owner, is pretty cut up.'

He felt himself skidding towards tricky territory again, and groped for safer ground.

'It must be awful for her,' said Sarah. 'I mean it's bad enough for us, but I guess she's been there all her life.'

'I'm sure it's quite as upsetting for the two of you,' said Posthumus, 'with Paul so badly hurt.'

'The two of us?'

'I'm sorry, I meant your daughter . . .'

Sarah froze. She looked hard at Posthumus, the T-shirts she was about to hand him held in mid-air.

'Our daughter is dead,' she said.

Posthumus felt his guts knot.

'I'm sorry, I'm *so* sorry, I didn't know. As I said, I didn't really know Paul well. In his room. I was getting the clothes. I saw a photo.'

Posthumus could hear himself stammering; he collected himself a little.

'It is the worst thing that can happen to a parent, the worst,' he said. He skipped a beat. 'I know,' he said, his voice quiet.

Sarah looked at him a long time. Posthumus took the T-shirts.

'Paul and I reacted in different ways,' said Sarah at last. 'That was part of the reason we split up. I'm told that often happens. Paul never really got over it. Still hasn't. He can't let go.'

Posthumus closed the bedside cabinet.

'He idolised her, idealised her,' Sarah went on. 'For years he spoke about her in the present tense, he still lights candles on her birthday, the right number each year.'

Posthumus nodded. His mother had done that, for Willem.

'He even used to wait outside her school,' said Sarah, 'as if she were going to come out with the others. You know about last year?'

Posthumus shook his head.

'There were hate-tweets against him on Twitter, saying he was a paedophile and all sorts of dreadful lies. Some kid had photographed him outside the school. It all blew over, but that's what I meant when I said he'd been having a bad time. And now this, poor sod, I thought he could do with a familiar face.'

Posthumus noticed Sarah was blinking.

'Well, that's that! Unpacked,' she said, her voice unconvincingly bright.

Posthumus realised she was speaking literally, about Paul's clothing.

'I'll put the shoes and jumper and stuff in the big cupboard, with the bag,' said Sarah, running her fingers through its side pockets. 'Does someone need this, do you think? It's not Paul's.'

Posthumus glanced at the sheet of bright yellow A4 that she'd pulled out and unfolded. He felt the blood drain from his face. He almost snatched the paper from her.

'It's mine,' he said. 'I'm sorry, I mean . . . I'll see to it. I need this.'

19

On the metro, Posthumus sat staring at the sheet of yellow A4, as if he were a slow reader.

Personalised Welcome and Price List
Welcome to FitFast
JAN JANSEN

He knew the rest. He'd got one himself on his first visit to FitFast. Posthumus let his hand drop, and stared out of the window. What the hell was this doing in Paul's bag? And who was Jan Jansen? An alias? Surely not, it was such an obvious choice for a false name. But Paul with FitFast connections? Posthumus glanced at the sheet again. There was a date on the bottom, as happened when you printed out an email. And a time: 20/08/10 21.32. Posthumus frowned, folded the paper, and put it in a jacket pocket. When was Tony killed exactly? It was certainly around that date. He thought for a moment then reached for his phone, realising with a flash of irritation that Alex was off at university on Friday mornings. Still, perhaps that was a good thing; he'd speak to the temp. With any luck, Maya and Sulung would already be off on the house-visit.

The station announcement crackled faintly, barely audible. Bijlmer. The train was one of the old, corrugated tin-can types, its interior daubed with a garish design that Posthumus presumed was an ironic reference to graffiti. A pre-emptive strike, on behalf of the rail company. He waited till the doors had pinged shut and the oncoming passengers settled down, then he made the call.

'Rebecca,' he said, as the temp answered. 'Pieter Posthumus here. I'm working from home, and I need a quick look at a file. No need to bother Sulung or Maya, just attach the whole thing and send it to my personal email, you'll have that. The file's under Archive, Closed Cases, 2010. The name's Wojciechowski.'

He had to spell it for her three times, and hung up just as the speaker crackled weakly into life with the next station announcement.

Posthumus got up, and paced to one end of the carriage. He felt uneasy with the way his mind was moving. He didn't particularly like Paul, or at least felt the man was not right for Anna. OK, admit it, he was jealous. But if he were to go embroiling Paul in all this, he had to be pretty sure of his ground – or it would be even worse than with Marloes. He couldn't simply go grabbing at passing straws, here. If he was wrong, or if he was letting some absurd sort of jealousy warp the way he thought, that would be the end of things with Anna. He paced the length of the carriage again.

Paul had had a fight with Zig, the day before Zig died. What about? Because of 'vile shit', Paul said. What was that about? And what was the connection between him and Zig, or with Tony for that matter? Posthumus thought Paul was a bit of a sleazebag, but he couldn't see him in Zig's or Tony's world. But then, there were the rumours that Sarah Lindberg mentioned. Posthumus turned to pace again. No, he couldn't see it, not little girls. Or boys. He noticed he was getting looks from the other passengers, and sat down. The train stopped. Duivendrecht. Road, rail, metro, criss-crossing in stacked concrete overpasses. People walking in all directions. It seemed a world away from Posthumus's

Amsterdam, of canals, bicycles, hump-backed bridges. And of gruesome death. Of girls like Tina, of a courtroom where Marloes was, this very moment, most likely heading for a 'guilty' verdict. Of him and Anna. Posthumus closed his eyes for a moment.

How could he simply dump all this on her? Fragments, odd suspicions, pieces he couldn't quite connect. He had all the parts of the puzzle, he felt, but was not quite managing to put them together. He needed somehow to throw all the pieces in the air, let them fall in a different formation, look at them freshly. The link was there, but he wasn't seeing it. And something was gnawing at the back of his brain. A half-memory, something from the past few days, something he had noticed but not noted. Oddly, Merel's text kept coming to mind. Insistent, involuntarily, like thinking of an elephant when you have been told not to think of an elephant. But what that was about, Posthumus couldn't work out. The password she had sent? The act of logging on to a website?

The train passed the gaunt, grey towers of the Bijlmerbajes, Amsterdam's chief jail. He needed to talk this through with someone, and certainly not Anna. A sounding board. And he needed to talk *about* Anna, about him and Anna and what to do if Paul was involved, how to handle it. He reached for his phone. Cornelius answered immediately, out in the street somewhere, by the sounds of things.

'Charon!'

'Cornelius, I really need to talk with you. As soon as. Can we meet up somewhere?'

'I'm up your end of town, just about to ascend to my agent on the Rokin. Mere poets do not get lunch, so shall we say in an hour? There's an Italian coffee place across the road, Bar Italia.'

'I'll wait for you there,' said Posthumus. 'By the way, I think I've got to the bottom of the paintings. You were right, there is a story behind them.'

'All the more reason then; *à bientôt.*'

The email from Rebecca arrived as the train went underground. Posthumus saved the attachment and opened Tony's file. The small phone screen wasn't ideal, but he could manage. He located the Case Report details. Yes. Date of death, 20 August 2010. He took out the yellow A4 again, to double-check. Then he went back to the Case Report. Posthumus was so preoccupied with the Wojciechowski file that he missed his stop.

Central Station. No matter. Posthumus glanced up at the station clock. There was still the best part of an hour before Cornelius would be out of his meeting, but there wasn't much point now in going home. He'd walk straight on down to the Rokin, find that Italian café and wait. Better still, he'd drop by the guest-house first, it was pretty much on the way, see if Tina was there and maybe sound her out a little more on what it was that Zig didn't like about Paul. As he walked, Posthumus listened again to the 'howdy-man' message that Tina had left on his voicemail earlier. 'We'd had a bit of a giggle on the stairs, and the front door rang, and Zig said it was for him and went back down.' *Zig said it was for him.* So, Zig knew that Paul was coming, it was an appointment of some sort. And it ended in a fight.

There was no answer when Posthumus rang the guest-house bell. He walked next door to De Dolle Hond. Anna had said she might get Tina to help Simon clean up, while she was in court, but neither Simon nor Tina was there. They'd probably gone somewhere for lunch, Posthumus reasoned, and ran up the stairs to Anna's office to drop off Paul's apartment keys.

Anna sat with her back to the office door, working on the computer. Or not working, but looking at some sort of video, of a party downstairs in the café. The last person Posthumus wanted to see. He stopped dead on the landing, and almost retreated down the stairs, but Anna turned to greet him.

'I thought you were in court,' said Posthumus.

'There was a problem with the mikes in the courtroom,' said Anna. 'It all ground to a halt as the prosecutor was starting his closing argument.'

'So we've got more time?'

'Till Monday, probably, unless the PA system is fixed in time and the judge decides to reconvene. One of the clerks is going to call me. I thought I'd be more useful here, *and* . . .'

Anna held up a letter.

'This letter that you brought across from Marloes's yesterday, the one from the surveyor? I checked up on it. It's bloody *Marty*, or "Martin Jacobs Management" to be exact. The slimy bastard was trying to buy Marloes's place behind our backs. And she was so confused and beaten down by things, I think she probably would have gone along with it. But I've put a stop to *that*, at least. That puts a different light on things, don't you think?'

That was it, then. Marty's 'business venture'. And maybe the thought that had come to him in the middle of the night – that the set-up with Jelle was just nasty opportunism, Marty getting Marloes out of the way – wasn't far off the mark. Posthumus felt his mind beginning to race.

'It's worth following up, anyway,' said Anna. 'How are you getting on? We haven't had much chance to catch up.'

Paul. Paul was on the computer screen, standing beside the piano on the podium downstairs, saying something. Anna followed Posthumus's gaze.

'Oh this,' she said. 'I was just taking some time out, looking at the place how it was. This was Paul's first gig, summer two years ago, remember? The first live music in the bar for decades. Simon made a video.'

She swivelled back to the computer and turned up the sound.

'It was Zig who introduced us, you know,' she said. 'I'd forgotten that.'

But Posthumus was listening to Paul.

'Dudes and dudesses,' Paul was saying, 'this first number is for a very special girl. It's not what you're going to hear for the rest of the night, but it's a tradition for me whenever I have a new gig. It was her favourite song, she even took her nickname from one of the band. This one's for Melanie. My Mel.'

For the second time that day, Posthumus felt the blood drain from him, his guts knot. Paul sat at the piano, and began a pop tune that had so pervaded the media that it had come into even Posthumus's radar. Anna grimaced.

'The Spice Girls,' she said, 'on a *piano*, and with Paul singing. I thought I'd made a *big* mistake.'

Posthumus took a step back from the door.

'Mel,' he said. 'Mel. Mel C! I've got to go. I'm sorry, I've *really* got to go.'

He turned, and ran down the stairs.

Posthumus walked fast along the Damrak towards the Rokin, dodging on-comers, weaving past groups of tourists. Paul's daughter's name was Melanie, her nickname that of a girl in her favourite pop group, Mel C, the name of the girl who had died of an overdose, who had made Zig so distraught, the death that had triggered his paintings. Mel C, who the wire report said had been involved with a *loverboy*. Quite probably Tony. Posthumus stopped dead in the middle of the Dam, and said it out aloud: 'The photos.'

He took out his phone and stood, coat flapping in the wind, people pushing past him, pigeons pecking at the cobbles about his feet, as he accessed the Wojciechowski file. Not the Case Report this time, but the photographs. He almost flashed past the one of the CDs – close up, with the Spice Girl album that had struck him as out of place at the time. Posthumus felt a little shudder run down his spine. He scrolled on swiftly. The bedroom. He wanted the picture he had taken of the drawer with a batch of photos, each showing Tony with his arm around a different girl. And there she was, on the top of the pile. Melanie. Was *that* why he felt he'd maybe seen her before, when he looked at the photo of Sarah, Paul and their daughter in Paul's apartment?

Across the bottom right-hand corner, Melanie had signed Mxx. Posthumus remembered now that he'd jotted that down in his handwritten notes at the time, in case it helped with tracing a relative – though when he'd looked at the notes again a few days ago, he hadn't made the connection, he thought he might have mis-written Mexx. And suddenly it occurred to him why Merel's text had been niggling him all day. She always signed her texts mxx. And he'd seen it somewhere else in the past few hours. Posthumus started walking again, rerunning his visit to Paul's apartment in his head. The fridge. The postcards on the fridge, one of them was signed Mxx, he was sure of it. Not that that mattered. He'd had the shake-up he needed, the pieces of the puzzle now lay in a different pattern, and it was clearer, *much* clearer, how they might all fit together.

★ ★ ★

At Bar Italia he ordered a coffee, took out his notebook, and began jotting down points, drawing curved lines and arrows of connection. By the time Cornelius walked in, he had it. Almost.

'It's Paul,' Posthumus said, even before Cornelius sat down.

Cornelius stopped, coat halfway down his back, and looked at Posthumus over the top of his glasses. He said nothing, shook off the coat, folded it over the back of an empty chair, took the seat opposite, and leaned back, his eyes fixed on Posthumus all the while.

'Tell me,' he said.

'Zig first,' said Posthumus. 'That I think was a mistake, an accident.'

He explained to Cornelius about Zig's subdural haematoma, about how he'd had a fight of some sort with Paul the day before he died, and that Zig, confused and concussed, could well have fallen and cut his temporal artery.

'The bleeding from his temple would have been profuse, quite enough to kill him, especially if he was already faint, not quite in control of himself,' he said, 'and it doesn't take much of a blow to cause a haematoma.'

'And no one picked up on this?' said Cornelius.

'The haematoma is mentioned in the pathology report,' said Posthumus, 'but the pathologist is not supposed to draw conclusions, and, according to my GP, it's hard to pinpoint, anyway, when a haematoma could have occurred, and reasonable for the police to assume that it was all part of the same fight. It might have been different if Marloes's lawyer had questioned the pathologist before the examining magistrate, but that didn't happen.'

'Motive?' said Cornelius.

'I'm not sure we need one, if all we are talking about is a fight,' said Posthumus. 'But there were rumours going round on Twitter about Paul, and he said to me that Zig had said "vile shit" about him, so it's possibly something to do with that, I don't know.'

'Rumours about?'

'I'll get to that in a minute.'

A waitress came up to the table. They ordered coffee and panini. For once, Posthumus barely gave the menu a thought.

'And you're certain it was the fight with Paul that did the damage?' said Cornelius. 'What about that witness who said he saw Marloes running down the stairs?'

Posthumus explained how he had discredited Jelle's statement, about Marty and his 'business venture', about Marty and Tina.

'Marty's got some very shady connections,' said Posthumus. 'Whether it was for them, or off his own bat, I think he jumped at an opportunity when he saw it, to get hold of the guest-house, and to get Marloes out of the way, to stop her broadcasting his sexual tastes.'

'And you're saying Paul was similarly opportunistic?' said Cornelius. 'Why on earth would Paul let Marloes take the blame for Zig's murder?'

'Because he really thought she had done it,' said Posthumus. Cornelius frowned.

'Doesn't everyone?' asked Posthumus.

Their coffees arrived.

'Like everyone else, Paul assumed whoever had inflicted the wound that led to all that blood had killed Zig,' said Posthumus. 'I don't think he gave a thought to the possibility that it was a fight they'd had the day before. A pretty minor blow could have done it, pushing Zig violently against a wall, no blood. I don't think Paul had the slightest idea that he might have been responsible until he saw the pathology report, when I was reading it at De Dolle Hond the other night. And by then he was in it too deeply already.'

'Surely not. If he came clean about Zig, even now, that would help Marloes, wouldn't it? Why shouldn't he say something?' said Cornelius.

Posthumus leaned closer, over the table. 'Because he killed Tony Wojciechowski,' he said. 'He's letting Marloes take the rap for both.'

'Whoa, whoa, whoa, sharp Charon,' said Cornelius. 'Are you not perhaps overstretching yourself here?'

Posthumus told Cornelius about Paul's dead daughter Melanie, about Zig and Mel C.

'I think you were pretty close in your reading of the paintings, about their representing a *story*, a progression – from sin, through judgement to atonement,' he said. 'But perhaps you weren't quite there. I think Mel's death was the trigger for them, they were a way of Zig expiating his guilt, of getting it out in the open. He convinced himself that if he'd arrived just a few minutes earlier, if he'd not had that extra drink with his friends, he could have saved her. Seeing that painting at Schiphol gave him the idea. One painting a year, begun each January on the anniversary of Mel's death, focused on the idea that a few minutes can change things completely. They tell a story. You were right.'

Cornelius gave a nod of acknowledgement, but he looked sceptical. 'And you think Paul's daughter was working as an underage prostitute?'

'She was an addict,' said Posthumus. 'That's the way men like Tony work – the handsome boyfriend, a few years older, with lots of money, offering glamour, excitement, drugs. And before the kid knows it, she's not only having sex with him, but with his "mates", too. Then, because she needs the drugs, or wants the money, or doesn't want to lose the glamour, or the boyfriend, she does what he says.'

Posthumus pushed his coffee cup away from him.

'If I had a daughter who died like that, I could quite easily do what Paul did,' he said. 'Think if it were Lukas.'

Cornelius turned away.

'As a general motive, it is understandable,' he said, glancing back at Posthumus, 'but that report about the girl dying was from five or six years ago, you say. Tony was killed when?'

'In 2010.'

'Two years ago,' said Cornelius. 'So, what happened? Why didn't Paul do it right away? There has to be some more immediate motive.'

'I'm not there yet,' said Posthumus. 'A trigger perhaps, finding Tony again, something else that happened. I don't know.'

'I'm sorry, Charon, I need to play devil's advocate here. It's what a lawyer might ask. Or Anna. And that, I imagine, is your problem. Anna.'

Posthumus straightened his back, sitting taut, upright in his chair, staring out of the window. Bar Italia was a little below street level, all he could see were the hips and legs of passers-by. The waitress brought their panini. He didn't touch his.

'And how does it come to be that Paul's trio has a regular night working at De Dolle Hond?' Cornelius went on. 'Coincidence? Or some masterplan of revenge he's been working on for years?'

'Neither coincidence, nor masterplan,' said Posthumus. He spoke slowly, still looking distractedly out of the window. 'Summer, two years ago,' he said.

He turned back to Cornelius to explain.

'Anna's just been watching a video of Paul's first gig at De Dolle Hond, in the summer of 2010,' he said. 'I wasn't listening to her properly, but I'm sure she said it was Zig had got Paul the job. Zig wasn't in that world any more, Marloes had rescued him. Maybe Mel's death played a part in that. He'd been a close friend of Mel's, tried to save her. He and Paul were friends enough for Zig to get Paul a job. I think they were friendly enough with each other till a few months ago, when there was Twitter gossip about Paul. Tina told me once that Zig was always tweeting. That, I feel sure, is somewhere behind the fight with Paul.'

Cornelius kept his eyes on Posthumus, and began eating.

'But when it comes to Tony, something else is going on,' Posthumus continued. 'Something that happened around the summer of 2010. The question is, what?'

'What, indeed?'

Posthumus went on, quietly, almost as if talking to himself. 'Tony and Zig had fallen out, but in the summer of 2010 Tony was back on the scene. Zig didn't like it, Marloes didn't like it, she tried to throw Tony out, but Tony seemed to have some sort of power over Zig. The same, perhaps, that he'd had over Mel. Perhaps Tony stopped his game after Mel's death; he did once testify against Zig's pimps, and originally the police thought that was the reason he was killed. But maybe he was back at it again, trying to draw Zig back in.'

Cornelius wiped away a smear of goat's cheese from the side of his mouth.

'And this has something to do with triggering Paul to kill him?' he said.

Posthumus nodded. 'If he was grooming young girls again, yes,' he said. 'Paul's wife – ex-wife – says he never got over Mel's death. If Paul had finally tracked Tony down, if Zig had been hiding Tony's whereabouts, but now that Tony was back on the scene had revealed it. Or if Paul found out that Tony was back at his old tricks, with other young girls, that could be the spark we need.'

'Even if we are to accept that,' said Cornelius, 'you're telling me that Paul, with cool premeditation, killed him?'

'By giving him an overdose, don't forget,' said Posthumus. 'The same way that Melanie died.'

He told Posthumus about the sports drink, about FitFast, and the yellow welcome leaflet.

'There is a dramatic justice there, I grant you,' said Cornelius. 'But Jan Janssen? Do come on, my dear Charon, who would give such an obvious *nom de guerre*?'

'You don't expect to be asked your name,' said Posthumus. 'It was the same when I went. I didn't want to take out membership or anything, simply to slip in, but I was given this free-trial hard sell. And when Pogo caught me on the back foot, with the little story I'd invented, and asked me my son's name, I said *Willem* – of all the names I could have chosen, naming my lie after my dead brother! You don't think. You say the first thing that comes into your head.'

'And you're saying that Paul is so deeply unpleasant, so cynical, that he is prepared to let Marloes take the rap, as you put it, for a murder that he committed,' said Cornelius. 'I know you have a problem with the man, but that, surely, is a step too far.'

'I'm saying that he *was* thinking along those lines,' said Posthumus. 'Don't forget that the re-emergence of Tony's murder, and its link to Marloes, came out of the blue. I think Paul panicked a bit, and reasoned that if Marloes was going to go down for one killing, she might as well go down for two – till he realised that it was he, and not Marloes, who was responsible for Zig's death. Until then he was prepared to let his original crime piggyback on what he thought was hers.'

'And now he has changed his mind?'

'It's troubling him, I know,' said Posthumus. 'He saw the pathology report only on Wednesday. Since then, there's been the fire, and he came close to losing his life. There's not a lot he's been able to do about Marloes these past few hours, except lie there and think about it; about life, too, I imagine.'

'So you think he might, given a little impetus, be ripe for a confession?' said Cornelius. 'That's as well. Even if your scenario is correct, you're going to need a confession, I surmise, for it to hold up. But do you think that you are the man for the job?'

'Go to the police, you mean?' said Posthumus. 'That's what I did about Marloes, and see where that got me. No, before I do that, I must be certain. I'm going to have to confront him – but behind Anna's back? That's my problem.'

'Ah, Anna. Anna is the real reason you wanted to talk with me, *n'est-ce pas*?'

'Part of me wants to be certain about Paul's guilt before I even speak to Anna,' said Posthumus. 'And part of me just wants to drop the whole thing.'

Posthumus laid both hands over his closed notebook on the table.

'How can I tell her?' he said. 'And what if I am wrong?'

'How can you *not* tell her?' said Cornelius. 'And what if you *are* wrong?'

Posthumus said nothing.

'If you are wrong, you have no other candidate, and Marloes will most likely be convicted,' said Cornelius. 'Even if you are only half right, about Zig, that may not help her much. If you are right, it becomes a question of favouring Marloes, or Paul. Which in turn becomes a question of your own conscience. Do you speak up, or for ever hold your peace? It is a question which, for you, brings other considerations into play.'

'Anna.'

'Can you go through the remainder of your life not having told her what you think?' said Cornelius. 'Especially if the remainder of *her* life could, in some way or another, involve Paul.'

Cornelius leaned over, and folded his hand over Posthumus's forearm.

'The choice, unenvied Charon, is yours. Or perhaps it is Anna's. Or given the strength, the duration, and the value of your friendship, perhaps it is one you should make together.'

Posthumus sat in Bar Italia for a long while after Cornelius had gone. When he left, he walked slowly, up the Rokin, across the Dam, and up the Damrak towards De Dolle Hond. At the café door he stood a moment, breathed in deeply, exhaled for what seemed an interminable time, and went inside.

Anna was still in her office, working again at the computer. Posthumus pulled up a chair and sat beside her.

'So? What was the rush, just then? Where've you been? You're on to something, I can see,' said Anna.

She swivelled her chair towards him, eyes shining, a half-smile edging up the corners of her lips. Her expression clouded a little when she saw Posthumus's face.

'What's up?' she asked.

'Anna. This isn't going to be easy, and there are parts of it I'm still not clear about,' said Posthumus. 'But I can't go any further without telling you. Interrupt me, ask any questions you like, but please hear me to the end.'

Posthumus outlined for Anna the scenario he had talked through with Cornelius. Anna asked a few questions at first, then grew quieter and quieter. When Posthumus had finished, she sat in silence. Posthumus reached over, and took her hand. She flinched a little, but did not move away.

'You and your always wanting to get to the bottom of things,' she said.

Her voice was flat. She sat immobile.

'I suppose I did ask,' she said.

'I don't want to make the same mistake twice,' said Posthumus. 'Not after what happened with Marloes. I *know* that I can never let go until I feel that I've got things right, only this time there's more to it than that. It's not like at work, I realise that now, not with living people as part of the story. Not with you at the heart of it.'

Posthumus leaned forward, and took Anna's other hand.

'Truth matters to me,' he said, 'more than anything. More than *almost* anything.'

Anna looked at him, her face still blank.

'I am sure that I am right about all this,' said Posthumus, 'but there are still gaps that need to be filled. I think if we wanted to get Marloes acquitted, we would need an admission from Paul. I could go ahead, and probably get that, but . . .'

Posthumus stopped mid-sentence. His mouth and throat felt completely dry.

'For me, there are three people involved here. Paul, Marloes and you, and one way or the other there are losers. I think I've discovered the truth, but I can take a step back.'

He did not go on.

'It's me who has to speak to Paul, isn't it?' said Anna, at last.

'I'm here, you know that, whichever way things go,' said Posthumus.

Anna stood up. She brushed her palms down the side of her skirt.

'And I said only yesterday that things could hardly get any worse,' she said, her voice bright, a little shaky. 'Come on, visiting hours have already started, I'll call a cab.'

The journey to the hospital passed almost in silence. Anna sat staring out of the taxi window. She spoke twice.

'I thought it was concern,' she said, as they passed the Stadhuis and joined the traffic on Wibautstraat, heading out of town.

'Concern?' said Posthumus.

'On Wednesday night, after I'd closed the café and we were upstairs. He kept asking me about the day, about what I'd learned from the lawyer, about Zig. I thought he was helping me to get it all off my chest.'

As they pulled into the hospital car park she spoke again.

'But there are gaps,' she said, 'you admit that. So, yes, maybe Zig's death was the result of their fight, but then it's an accident, isn't it? And if Marloes isn't responsible for that, maybe that's enough to get her off?'

Posthumus looked at her across the expanse of the rear seat. Her cheeks were flushed. In the hard winter light, he noticed how exhausted she looked, the crow's feet that had begun to form around the corners of her eyes.

'I think, if we're going to do this at all, we should be looking for truths, not half-truths,' he said. 'We need Paul to come completely clean, about everything.'

The central atrium at the AMC felt like the food court at a shopping mall. Plastic chairs, indoor plants, a florist, food counters. Posthumus sat at one of the tables and waited. Beside him, a father shared a pizza with his two children. A man in a wheelchair edged past. Another, wearing a dressing gown, sat alone, making a call on his mobile, beside him a noisy group of girls, around a table piled with presents. People passed in all directions, walking fast, intent on this ward, or that. He checked the time. Anna had been gone over half an hour. He sipped the mineral water he'd bought, watched as someone walked over to the cash machine, punched in her PIN, then retrieved her card, and walked away empty-handed, disconsolate. He picked up a couple of empty drinks cans and discarded paper napkins from the table alongside, walked over to a bin and threw them away, returned to his table, checked his watch again. Forty minutes. He looked up.

Anna was coming back down the corridor from Paul's ward. Posthumus got up, and walked towards her. She held her chin high. He noticed her eyes were red. Anna stopped as she got to the edge of the atrium. She looked at Posthumus steadily, and nodded.

Posthumus turned to one side. He took out his phone, and called Flip de Boer.

EPILOGUE

A Sunday afternoon at De Dolle Hond

'But *backpacking*! Can you believe it, I mean, *Marloes*?'

The day that Marloes was released, she had announced she could no longer bear to live in the building where Zig had died, and that she was – for the first time in her life – going travelling. She'd been determined to do it alone, wouldn't even let anyone come to the airport to see her off. Her only concession, after the farewell drink at De Dolle Hond, was that Anna could walk her up to Central Station. They had just left.

'People do it, who are older than her,' said Simon, from behind the bar. 'And anyway, one of the lot who used to live next door has a guest-house or something now in Nepal, so I guess that will be a sort of a base. Mother Hen coming to roost with the chicks.'

'Well, all speed to her,' said John, the Englishman, raising his glass. 'And to De Dolle Hond, and to the man of the moment: Pieter.'

Posthumus nodded to acknowledge the toast. He shifted his weight slightly on the stool at the corner of the bar, and leaned back against the wall. It was the first Sunday De Dolle Hond had been open since the fire, and they were all here, the usual Sunday afternoon crowd. Not the Kesters, of course. Irene remained *non grata* in the café, and probably faced jail for arson, anyway. Posthumus could still detect the acrid, burned

287

smell hanging in the air; it could linger for a year or more, he'd been told. But the damage hadn't been as bad as they'd thought, not in the main body of the café, at least. The brand-new kitchen out the back was nearly finished, Anna's bedroom above it was habitable again, the water and smoke damage had been cleaned up, and though there was still thick plastic covering the destroyed panelling near the kitchen door, Cornelius had rustled up an English master woodcarver who could reproduce it. The piano had gone.

'Funny old moo, Marloes, but she'll manage,' said Tina, her voice quiet, the remark intended for Posthumus alone. She was sitting on the stool beside him sipping a Coke, in companionable silence mostly.

'And you?' said Posthumus. 'You're managing all right?'

'Now, yes, thanks to you,' said Tina. 'She pays OK.'

Tina nodded in the direction of Central Station to indicate Anna. Posthumus had persuaded Anna to keep Tina on as a cleaner-cum-concierge, after Anna had decided to rent the guest-house from Marloes – a move that seemed part of Anna's strategy of coping, a new venture. And, God, what she'd been going through . . . one moment her lover risking his life trying to save her, the next she finds he's killed two people, and he's wrenched out of her life anyway. As always, Anna had shown very little to the world, even to him, but she had thrown herself into rebuilding De Dolle Hond, and into her new scheme for Marloes's place.

'You've been very quiet since Mr Walking Dictionary left,' said Tina. 'Where did he get off to all of a sudden?'

'Cornelius has gone to pick up his son from a violin lesson; he'd lost track of the time,' said Posthumus. 'They'll be back later.'

He'd been hoping Merel would be in, too. Even Mrs Ting was in position, at her usual place at the fruit machine. Mrs

Ting, who had carefully gathered the pieces of a Delft vase shattered by the blast of Irene's Thunderclap, and returned two weeks later with it put back together: beautifully, with professional skill. She hadn't said a word, simply handed it to Anna, smiled, and gone over to the fruit machine.

John came up to the corner of the bar to order another round. 'Same again thanks, Simon.'

He turned to Posthumus. 'Good to see the place open again,' he said. 'But no more Fox Trio, eh? Who'd have thought?'

'He got out of hospital a couple of days ago,' said Simon as he poured the beers, 'straight into the nick.'

'Where he belongs,' said John.

Tina drained her Coke, slipped off the barstool, and without a word walked towards the street door, her shoulders slightly hunched, crunching an ice-block in her mouth.

'You know it was him who suggested we put the TV in here,' said Simon. 'That night with *Crimebusters*, remember? He helped me get the set down from the attic, and all. It's funny how you suddenly remember things like that, and see it all differently.'

Posthumus was silent. He had also been rerunning so much, in a new light: Paul pressing him to talk Anna out of her bid to free Marloes, or probing her for details of Zig's pathology report, both times feigning concern. That betrayal had hurt Anna more than anything.

'What do you mean?' said John. 'What do you think he was up to?'

'Trying to turn us all against Marloes, wasn't he? Make sure she got the blame for Zig's death. Evil bastard.'

'Paul didn't know then that the fight he'd had with Zig was what killed him. Not till much later. He really thought Marloes had done it,' said Posthumus.

His voice was quiet. He held back from adding: 'And didn't we all?'

'But he was still happy for her to take the cop for the one he *had* done, the *loverboy* he topped,' said Simon. 'Why are you suddenly defending the bastard?'

Posthumus shrugged. At least people had the decency to hold back on talk about Paul when Anna was around, even though it always crackled below the surface.

'I'm sure the whole story will come out in the trial,' he said.

But he knew the story. More than the papers had got hold of, anyway. Paul's confession to Anna had matched piece for piece the sequence of events and explanations that Posthumus had put together. And it had provided the missing elements: Paul's trigger for killing Tony, years after Melanie's death, and what lay behind the fight with Zig.

'Yeah, fair trial, like Marloes was getting,' said Simon, noting the price of the round on John's tab.

'As long as it's not another trial by gossip,' said Posthumus. It was extraordinary how swiftly the arrow of blame, in the media especially, had swung round.

'*Crimebusters* has been very quiet on the subject, I see,' said John, reading Posthumus's expression. He stretched his fingers around four glasses, and carried them carefully back across the café.

Posthumus rested his elbows on the bar and brushed some stray crumbs from the Sunday afternoon apple pie into a small pile. That was true, yet it was just the sort of story *Crimebusters* would relish. Especially the part about Paul and Mel. It seemed that Zig had met up with an old friend of Mel's, and she had told him that Paul abused Mel, and that was why she had run away. Posthumus flattened the pile of crumbs with his forefinger, then slowly built it up again. So Zig had begun to blame Paul for Mel's death, had started with the vicious tweets, and the whole situation had spiralled out of control, in a sad mess of mischances and unintended consequences.

Posthumus shifted his position slightly on the bar stool. Apart from the statements he and Anna had made to the police, and a quiet word to Cornelius and Merel, they had not spoken to anyone about what they knew. Posthumus didn't believe that Paul had abused Mel. He'd always thought the man a bit of a sleazebag, but not *that*. Anna had just clammed up on the subject, and refused to have anything more to do with him. Either way, Posthumus felt, it was up to Paul to tell his own story. That was important. The truth had to come out, and from the source. A confession. As expiation for Paul's sins? Posthumus's Catholic upbringing sometimes caught him by surprise. As an excuse for his own sins, perhaps? He was still having dreams in which Zig's and Willem's bodies somehow melded. Posthumus flicked the pile of crumbs apart, then began to gather them up again. He had never liked Paul, especially when Paul started coming on to Anna, but the man had saved her life, for God's sake. And, if anything, Posthumus had sympathy for the way in which Paul blamed Tony for Mel's overdose, and for his frustration that Tony could never be punished. He could even understand Paul's trigger to murder: how Paul could just about cope with that situation when Tony appeared to have reformed, when he had even testified against the pimps – until he had seen Tony at work again, in the same place as he would have first met Mel, with a girl her age. 'He had to be *stopped*,' Paul had said to Anna. There was an irony there, that something connected Paul's impetus to kill Tony, and Marloes's to protect Zig . . .

'PP! Sorry I'm late. Work, work, work, even on a Sunday. It looks like I've missed Marloes?'

Posthumus felt a hand on his shoulder and turned, beaming: Merel!

'She left about half an hour ago,' he said. 'Anna's walking her up to the station. Let me get you something to drink.'

'Just a coffee thanks. So she's really doing it, going backpacking?'

Posthumus nodded.

'And Anna's taken over the guest-house? That's definite?' said Merel.

'Yep. She's giving it a makeover, and is going to run it as an affordable B&B.'

'A *makeover*?'

Posthumus smiled. Anna's feeling for interior design, if her apartment upstairs was anything to go by, was rudimentary. He lowered his voice.

'I've asked Marie to give her some advice, you know, the woman who runs that new boutique around the corner,' he said.

Merel glanced towards the fireplace, where Marie was sitting.

'Oh, the vase! Mrs Ting's vase. It looks amazing,' said Merel, as she caught sight of it. 'Anna told me about that.'

She turned back to Posthumus. 'And the others,' she said.

Posthumus gave her a warning glance. 'For your ears only, the others,' he said.

For years he had nagged Anna to have the Delft pieces, which had been in the café since before her grandparents' time, valued. She had finally done so after the fire, and the amount ran into tens of thousands of euros, but Anna wanted them to remain where they were, in the café. So their worth was not information to be broadcast.

'Of course, of course,' said Merel, as Posthumus indicated to Simon to bring her a coffee. 'By the way, what on earth happened to Marty? Have you *seen* what he looks like?'

'Not seen, but I heard about it,' said Posthumus. 'Tina told me. He got beaten up. Badly, I hear.'

'He looks *dreadful*. I've just seen him coming out of the butcher's: black eye, bruises on his face, one arm in a sling, both hands bandaged.'

'It's got something to do with next door, and whatever he was up to there, I am sure,' said Posthumus. 'But I find it hard to feel any sympathy for him, not after all Tina has told me.'

'Oh, that reminds me, I've got something for you,' said Merel. She fished in her bag, and pulled out a newspaper clipping. 'Yesterday's paper,' she said. 'Have a look.'

Posthumus read the clipping and frowned. The name only faintly rang a bell.

'Onno Veldhuizen?' he asked.

'Lisette's letter, remember?' said Merel. 'He's the guy from InSec, the one she blew the whistle on, the one who had to do with Khaled and all that.'

Posthumus read the clipping again. Veldhuizen found garrotted, on the outskirts of Amsterdam. He folded it, and put it into the inside pocket of his jacket, just as the café door swung open and Anna and Cornelius arrived back together, with Lukas in tow carrying a tiny violin case.

'Well, that's it, she's off, safe and sound,' said Anna to the café at large.

She walked up and pecked Merel on the cheeks. 'Good to see you,' she said.

Merel greeted Cornelius, and gave Lukas a big smile.

'PP's been telling me that you're definitely taking over next door,' she said to Anna.

'Marloes's apartment will stay the same. It's always there, as long as she needs it, but, yes, the rest is going to change,' said Anna. 'Quite the beginning of a new era, I think.'

She turned to the rest of the café. 'And that calls for drinks all round!'

Appreciative noises rippled through the room. Anna went round to help Simon; Cornelius and Merel took seats alongside Posthumus, at the corner of the bar. Lukas walked over to watch Mrs Ting. When everyone had a fresh drink, Anna raised her glass.

'To the future,' she said. 'To many more Sundays at De Dolle Hond, and to those who have helped put the café back together.'

She nodded to Cornelius, and gave a particular glance to Mrs Ting, who had accepted a cup of tea. Then she walked over to the place behind the bar where she so often stood, across the counter from where Posthumus was sitting. She said nothing, but gently rested one hand on his forearm. Pale sunlight filtered in through the café window, conversations settled back into individual burbles.

Posthumus leaned back against the wall, relaxing into the gentle rhythm of it all. Cornelius was telling a story, about one of their Lonely Funerals, but as Posthumus listened he felt a familiar sensation. A niggle. A scratching at the back of his brain. Something he had seen or heard in the last half-hour had struck an odd note. It was something he knew would dog him, that he would not be able to let go of until he had placed it correctly. But not now. Not for the moment. Posthumus leaned forward, took a sip from his drink, and prepared to be entertained by Cornelius.

Pieter Posthumus will return in

DEADLY SECRETS

MAY 2016

Personal gain or political principle? That's the question
Pieter Posthumus must answer in the third of the Amsterdam
Lonely Funerals series, when a controversial delegate at an
environmental conference is attacked and left for dead . . .

The whole world seems to have descended on
Amsterdam for the Earth 2050 conference. As the city
gets busier, Posthumus is thankful that work is quiet.

But then one of his friend's former colleagues is left for dead
under a bypass. Ever curious, Posthumus agrees to look into
the case, sparking memories of his own time as a student
radical. Amsterdam has always attracted people with fierce
views . . . but is someone willing to kill for their principles?
Or did the attack have a much more personal motive?

Forced to contend with family secrets, political
machinations and international conspiracies, Posthumus
finds himself in ever deeper, darker waters as he
tries to uncover what really happened, and why.

Read on for an exclusive extract . . .

I

Ben Olssen checked the wall clocks for a third time. TOKYO, NEW YORK, AMSTERDAM. After eight o'clock on that one. She wasn't coming. He reached for his phone, hesitated. He wouldn't text. Not again. He'd corner her at the conference. Ben put the phone back on the table, and grimaced at the last sip of bitter coffee. The cup rattled as he replaced it on the saucer. His eyes flicked around the room. High ceilings, burnished mahogany, potted palms, dimly lit. More like a movie set than a station café. You half expected an Edwardian touring party to come in through the door; a shiny black locomotive to be steaming alongside the platform, rather than the grimy yellow and blue Dutch Rail train he could see through the window, filling with stragglers from the evening rush hour. He would wait until that pulled out, and then he would leave.

A waiter – black tie, full apron – passed the table. Ben signalled for the bill. He flipped his laptop closed, rested his fingers on the lid for a moment, then re-opened it and shut the computer down completely. It was running slowly again. He didn't like that. Maybe that firm the concierge recommended would be able to find out what was up, better than the Helsinki IT guys could.

The train pulled out. Ben dropped a couple of coins on to the bill in the saucer, and got up to go. As he put on his coat, he caught a man in a black leather jacket, two tables away, watching him. But no, that was ridiculous, Ben thought.

Nothing wrong with that. People in cafés always glanced up as you came or went. He was getting paranoid: the feeling somebody had been watching him at the hotel, and now this. All the same . . . he was glad he'd been able to get out to the houseboat that afternoon, even if there hadn't really been time to talk things through.

Ben left the café, taking the escalator that ran down from the platform to the station arcade. At the foot of the escalator he turned right, towards the rear entrance. For a look at the old Shell building across the IJ, he told himself. For old times' sake. He knew, though, that he was waiting for a call or a text, that he might even double back and check out the café again, to see if she was there.

The back of the station was a mess, an obstacle course of holes, hoardings and scaffolding. Pedestrians and bicycles tangled with building works; ferries pushed up against each other at the piers. Across the water, the former Shell HQ thrust up, floodlit, covered in some sort of artsy cladding. It had been the scene of the start of his glittering career. Ben gave a little smile. And of many another conquest. Ben the Bedder, they'd called him. But there were still people who hadn't forgiven him for hopping from an internship at Greenpeace to a job with the enemy, people who didn't buy his 'I'd rather be inside the tent, and fight from behind the lines' argument. If they only knew . . . His phone chirruped an incoming message. He glanced at the screen. At last.

Sorry sorry sorry. Problem this end.
Only got away just now. Forgive me?
Lunch tomorrow maybe?
xoxo
PS You still so gorgeous?

Ben replied with a single 'yes', in answer to all three questions, and pushed the vivid image of her that the text had sparked, the smell of her, to the back of his mind. Lunch would work, just. Yes, he could wait that long. He frowned, crossed a bicycle path without looking, nearly colliding with a cyclist, and walked along the waterfront, eyes still down on the pavement. He shrugged off his overcoat. Camelhair. Heavy. Too much with the sweater he was wearing. He hated travelling in shoulder seasons. April was always like this. The weather had been cold, blustery and raining when he set out earlier in the evening, but now the night seemed almost balmy. He felt uncomfortably hot. He decided to go straight back to the hotel, cutting through the subway that ran under the tracks a little further up, rather than doubling back to the station arcade. Ben let out an irritated curse at the 'No Pedestrians. Use Other Side' sign at the entrance to the subway. He was buggered if he was going to cross through the arches then over four lanes of traffic just to have to repeat the performance in reverse at the other end of the tunnel. The walkway here was quite wide enough, the sodium orange light that criss-crossed through the shadows of the arches more than ample. Besides, there was already someone coming towards him from the other end. And someone following him in.

It was only when he was halfway along that Ben began to feel uneasy.

The junkie slipped into an alley off the Warmoesstraat, on the edge of De Wallen. Behind him, the stream of tourists surged, clotted momentarily, flowed again. People out for a festive night in the red-light district. But the alley was quiet: a single, smart restaurant at the far end, the rest back doors and blank walls, leading to a waterfront dead-end. The junkie took a few unsteady steps down the deserted street. Stopped. Listened.

He swayed slightly, as if to music no one else could hear, stared a long while at a cigarette butt lying on the paving stones, moved on. He was wearing a T-shirt and a thin blue jersey, with a rip down one side; a black woollen hat. And a heavy camelhair overcoat. He'd had a stroke of luck earlier. And not only with the coat. There had been a thin leather fold-over with a credit card and some cash buttoned in a small inside pocket. Rich toffs often did that: hid away a little something to be safe. He'd traded the card, and a wad of the cash had gone straight away, too. On more than he'd been able to score in a long time. He'd already spiked. Pure. Like kissing the creator.

The junkie headed to the darkened alcove of a fire exit where he often took shelter, warmed by the kitchen on the other side of the door. He leaned against the doorpost, slid down to the ground, and began to fumble in his backpack for his gear.

The restaurant door opened and momentarily cast a pale, trapezoid shaft of light across the alley as a couple came out: blond, well-dressed, arm-in-arm. They glanced down at the junkie, lying inert in a doorway, then at each other. She arched her eyebrows slightly; he released one of those secret, comforted smiles upright onlookers in De Wallen give as they step by the fallen – in affirmation of their own self-control. The couple continued, joining the flow of the Warmoesstraat, and then turning left into the Nieuwebrugsteeg. They hesitated a little outside a café, looking in at the warm, wood-panelled interior. 'De Dolle Hond,' she read aloud, and cocked her head to the lit window, suggesting a nightcap. He bent towards her, whispered something, and pulled her in closer. She giggled, and they walked on.

At about the time the junkie in the alley around the corner was becoming the next case for the municipal Funeral Team, Pieter Posthumus was comfortably positioned on his customary stool at De Dolle Hond, where the bar met the wall, beneath a collection of old medals and badges. From the other side of the counter, Anna nodded towards his empty glass.

'Better not. School night,' said Posthumus.

'Go on,' said Anna. 'On the house. The place will be dismal if you go, too.'

The last of the regulars had left a few minutes earlier. De Dolle Hond was quiet, even for a Tuesday, with only a handful of other drinkers. A couple, arm-in-arm, paused in the street outside. For a moment it looked as if they were about to come in, but they turned and walked on. Anna dangled a bottle of Posthumus's favourite wine at him.

'All right, but just a drop,' he said, tapping his glass below the halfway mark.

Anna poured him some wine, then moved away to serve a customer at the other end of the bar. Posthumus watched her go. He didn't like that 'dismal'. Since the business with Paul, Anna had put up the barriers. She had made no contact with the man, no longer had musicians in the bar, and never spoke of him. That was her way: total, 100 per cent. After all these years – decades – Posthumus knew that, but he was used to being admitted to her side of the wall. Not this time. That hurt. It made him feel left out, powerless. He'd always been able to help before. He knew not to push it, though. He also knew how to respond to Anna's subtle signals. Like that 'dismal'.

Posthumus got up off his stool, and began to collect glasses around the café. A late night wouldn't hurt, his work for what people had come to call the Lonely Funerals Team – the munic-ipal department that arranged burials for anonymous corpses found within the city limits, or for those who died without friends or family – was quiet at the moment. There had been only one funeral in the past few days: a woman who had died alone, on the sofa, in front of the TV, surrounded by mounds of fag-ends and empty wine bottles. He neatened some scattered beer-mats back into a pile. The only outgoings on her bank statement were payments to the supermarket, tobacconist and off-licence: a sad succession that told a lonely tale. Cornelius, who from time to time now came with him on house-visits, had used that in his poem for the funeral. Posthumus put the empty glasses he had collected on the corner of the bar, and sat down again. The elegy had been one of the poet's best so far. Posthumus had been telling Anna about it.

'Thanks, PP.'

Anna moved the glasses he had gathered to the washing area, and picked up the conversation again.

'So, did anyone come?' she said. 'To her funeral.'

'Two ex-colleagues, from before she retired,' said Posthumus. 'More out of guilt than anything else, I suspect. But she had some beautiful embroidered pashminas in the apartment, and we draped one over the coffin, so there was at least some sort of personal touch.'

'I hope that didn't go up in smoke with the rest of her!' said Anna.

Posthumus smiled. That was more like the Anna he knew.

'And what is this, anyway?' Anna went on. 'A parable? You trying to tell me something? "Reclusive old woman dies alone, and gets eaten by her cats"?'

Posthumus shot her a quick glance to reassure himself she was joking. Perhaps this was the moment to attempt a step behind the wall, to get her to talk a little – but a cascade of laughter came from the small entrance area at the outside door. Anna looked over in immediate recognition.

'Gabi!' she said, even before Cornelius's wife had come through the inner door. 'I'd recognise that laugh anywhere,' Anna said to Gabi as she walked up to the bar.

Posthumus smiled and nodded a greeting. Gabrielle was with a sharply dressed woman, tanned, fit-looking, younger than she was.

'And it hasn't changed in *years*,' said the woman. 'Teachers used to say she was doing it on purpose, and threaten dark punishments.'

'I don't know if you've met Christina,' said Gabi. 'Christina Walraven?'

Posthumus shook his head, and Anna murmured something about not quite being able to place her. Gabi did the introductions.

'You were at school together?' said Posthumus to Christina.

'You needn't sound *quite* so disbelieving,' said Gabi, with just a ripple of that cascade again. 'She's not as young as she looks, there're only two years between us. And yes, we were. In London.'

'Daddy was posted to the embassy while Gabi's father was ambassador, and she had instructions to look after the new arrival,' said Christina. 'Slumming it with the daughter of a lowly attaché.'

'Oh, nonsense,' said Gabi, turning to Anna. 'She was always going on like that. Not *true*, don't believe her!'

'Either way, two years was a *big* age gap back then, to a sassy teenager with an innocent of fourteen in tow,' said Christina. 'Good Catholic girl that I was.'

'It wasn't like that for long,' said Gabi, with a grin. 'By the way, has anyone been asking for me, or left anything behind the bar? Tall young guy with glasses.'

'No one's given anything to me,' said Anna. 'You expecting someone?'

'My new assistant. He was supposed to be with us tonight, but the sweet kid's been working late to put together some material I need for tomorrow. Never mind, he'll probably be along in a tick. Meantime, drinks! Piet, come and join us.'

'Is Cornelius coming in?' said Posthumus. He moved over to a table near the fireplace, the one he knew Anna liked friends to sit at because it was within conversation distance of the bar.

'No, he's at home with Lukas,' said Gabi.

Posthumus nodded. Lukas was a serious little lad, and quite responsible, but probably not yet old enough to be left alone in the evening. The others joined him at the table, as Anna went about getting their order.

'Gabi told me about this place,' said Christina, looking around at the heads carved along the top of the wainscot, the old tiles in the fireplace and big Delft vases. 'I didn't know bars like this still existed so near De Wallen. This part of town's so *tacky* usually.'

She took out her phone, clicked a rapid succession of photographs, and dropped it back into her handbag. (A Hester van Eeghen, Posthumus noticed, and not only that but in a colour that proclaimed it didn't have to serve for every day, that there were more designer thoroughbreds awaiting outings in the home stable.)

Christina read his glance. 'Your shirt's not too bad, either,' she said. 'Zegna? It's an unusual shade.'

Posthumus coloured slightly. The shirt had been in a half-price sale but even he had winced as he bought it.

'*Touché*,' he said, and Christina laughed. Posthumus let the moment go, and lighted again on De Dolle Hond.

'The building is 1620s, probably,' he said. 'It's been in Anna's family a hundred years or so, hence all the stuff.' He waved a hand at the constellations of old prints, brasses and Toby jugs that rose above the wainscot.

'Anna's done wonders. You'd hardly know,' said Gabi *sotto voce* to Posthumus, as Anna came over with the drinks.

It was true. The damage caused by the fire a few months earlier had been seamlessly repaired. All that remained was a faint, lingering burned smell. That could stay for a year or so, the cleaners had said. Otherwise De Dolle Hond looked pretty much as it had before. Apart from no longer having a piano.

Anna placed the drinks on the table, and took a seat. 'It's a bit dead tonight, so I can join you for a while,' she said.

She turned to Christina, who had her phone out again, and was skimming through incoming emails. 'You live in Amsterdam?' she asked. 'I know your face, we've met somewhere with Gabrielle before, I think.'

'Greenpeace, maybe? I did a short stint there with Gabi in the nineties. But, no, I live in London. I stayed on for university after Daddy was posted to Brussels, and I've been there ever since,' said Christina. 'It's odd, I guess these days I feel more a Londoner than anything. It's home.'

Posthumus detected a slight creakiness in the way she spoke, an occasional hesitancy or lapse into English that indicated she didn't exercise her mother tongue very much. It was oddly alluring, a bit like a husky voice.

'I'm over for Earth 2050, you know, the big economics conference that starts tomorrow?' said Christina, still multitasking with her telephone.

'Know about it!' said Anna. 'Our finance minister has been trumpeting the "Summit for the Future" and "growth and sustainability" for weeks. Today's early registration, isn't it? The trams are packed already, and you can hardly move in town. Still, I can't complain. I've been taking in a bit of the overflow in the guest-house.'

She nodded back over her shoulder to four men sitting at a table in the corner, Earth 2050 tote bags hanging from chair backs, or propped against the wall beside them.

'I've just hung up my first ever "No Vacancies" sign next door!' she said.

'Cornelius said you'd taken over Marloes's old place,' said Gabi. 'He says you've done it up marvellously.'

'The "marvellously" bit is more PP's doing,' said Anna.

'Just a lick of paint, some new furniture, and a tactful retreat behind the screen of "Dutch minimalism",' said Posthumus.

Christina laughed.

'Haven't you got enough to do as it is, with this place?' said Gabi.

Posthumus shot her a quick glance. Giving Anna a focus, a project, after the whole to-do with Paul was part of the point.

'PP persuaded me to keep on the last of Marloes's found-lings to work as a sort of cleaner-cum-caretaker,' said Anna. 'You've probably seen her. She was around quite a bit during that whole . . . time.' It was just a beat. Within a second, the tough, tousle-haired, can-do Anna was back. 'Little Tina,' she said. 'Just the sort Marloes always took under her wing.'

'That skinny little thing, just out of her teens, who'd been on the game?' said Gabi. 'She looked like she was still a user.'

'Heavens, that's a risk,' said Christina. 'And you're OK with that? She's not turning the place into a drug den or a bordello or anything?'

'Tina is *blossoming*,' said Posthumus. And she was. Timid, damaged Tina seemed inches taller, moved with a new energy, and cared for the place with proprietorial pride.

'Well, we must be doing something right, we're already averaging four stars on TripAdvisor,' said Anna. 'So spread the word if you know anyone coming to town who needs a room for the night.'

As if on cue, three guests from the B&B came in for an after-dinner drink, and Anna got up to serve them.

'So, you're still involved with Greenpeace? Or do you work with Gabrielle in Green Alliance?' said Posthumus to

Christina, claiming a spot of undivided attention before she returned to her phone.

He knew from Cornelius that Gabrielle's organisation was swimming against the tide, but deeply involved in Earth 2050: part of a vociferous environmental lobby determined to make itself heard among the conservative economists and mainstream bigwigs who formed the majority of delegates.

'No, these days I'm tigers,' said Christina.

'Tigers?' Posthumus's brow furrowed. Perhaps it was an acronym. 'Real, live tigers?'

'They're arguably the world's most endangered species, after rhinos,' said Christina, 'so, yes, and the Amur in particular, which you'd probably know as the Siberian tiger.'

She tapped a few times on her phone.

'Here, they're beautiful creatures, have a look. There are probably only about 500 left in the wild, in the far east of Russia, near the Korean and Chinese borders. That's the problem. Medicine and body parts, you know, and the hides of course. At one time they were being poached at the rate of one a day, and the only reason that is dropping is that they're becoming harder to find. Well, not the only reason. We are having some effect, but what with poaching, and logging eating away at their habitat . . .'

'Don't get her started!' said Gabi.

'No, I'm intrigued,' said Posthumus, leaning over for a closer look at the picture on the phone: a female playing with her cubs, a magnificent, glossy animal glowing soft orange against a backdrop of black tree-trunks and snow. 'What a beautiful creature!'

'The world's largest cat,' said Christina. 'In the 1930s there were only forty or so left in the world. That was mainly because of hunting for the skins. Things improved a bit after they were made a protected species, but now there's this other onslaught, as people in China are getting richer and paying over the odds. It's the same with rhino horn.'

'And this is why you're here for the conference?' said Posthumus.

'It might seem peripheral to you, but we need to make our voice heard,' said Christina, with an edge of defensiveness. 'Issues like this shouldn't be allowed to disappear in the general discussion of economics and resources. Our profile has been much higher since we've had Leo onside—'

'DiCaprio,' said Gabi, for Posthumus's benefit.

'And we have other major players and payers, but we still have to work hard to make sure the issue remains part of the powwow. Not just the Amur tiger, but the Asian too, and rhinos and all sorts of other animals that are in danger of being drowned out in the clamour of all the other discussions. But for me, here, now, it's about networking, mainly. I mean *everyone's* here.'

'We've just been to this amazing riverside cocktail party out along the Vecht,' said Gabi. 'Christina's helping me land a celebrity for Green Alliance.'

There was a clatter of bicycle handlebars against the window. A tall young man wearing heavy-rimmed designer glasses came striding into the café, walked straight up to Gabi and handed her a box file.

'Sorry I'm late, it's all there,' he said.

'Niels!' said Gabi. 'That is *so* good of you, staying in late. Thank you! And you've missed an incredible party, too. Come on, sit down, have a drink. Let me introduce you. *Love* the new glasses by the way.'

She moved her chair to one side to make room for him.

'Sorry, guys, I've got to get on,' said Niels. 'And the bike's not locked.' He took a few steps back towards the door. 'But thanks anyway. Cheers, and good luck for tomorrow, Gabrielle,' he said.

He had mounted his bike and was gone before anyone could edge in a syllable about how daring it was to leave it unlocked, even for a few seconds, in this part of Amsterdam.

'Quite a whirlwind!' said Posthumus.

'He's only been with us three months, and already I don't know what I'd do without him,' said Gabi.

'Big day tomorrow?'

'Sort of. I'm on a discussion panel before lunch, and I need to be well briefed.' Gabi tapped the box file. 'I suppose I shouldn't be partying, really, but I've been on such a high all evening,' she said.

'You've landed yourself that celebrity?' asked Posthumus.

Gabi caught Christina's eye and smiled. '*Possibly*. No names for the moment. Let's just say Christina managed to fast-talk us into the VIP enclosure, and that went very well. She's an amazing operator, and she's been a complete star. She even sacrificed a hot date when we ended up staying longer than we thought we would.'

'Well, if it pans out how we're hoping, it will have been worth it,' said Christina. 'Besides, it looks like it's all sorted with Ben. We're having lunch tomorrow instead.'

'Well done you!' said Gabi. 'Glad to hear it!' She turned to give Posthumus a playful glance. 'The tiger lady is having a cougar moment,' she said.

Christina laughed. 'Jealousy! Jealousy!' she said. 'He's not *that* much younger than me.'

'That sounds exciting, who's this?' said Anna, coming back to sit at the table again.

'Did you ever know Ben Olssen?' said Gabi. 'Drop-dead-gorgeous Ben, my intern back when I was at Greenpeace? He and Christina have a bit of history.'

'It was only a little fling!' said Christina, pretending to kick Gabi under the table.

Posthumus ran his fingers back through his hair, over temples beginning to fleck with grey.

Anna shook her head. 'I don't think I remember a Ben,' she said.

'Oh, you'd remember him if you'd met him!' said Gabi. 'He's clever, too. A bright young economist with his head screwed on right. It seems he's over for the conference, and desperate to pick up where he left off.'

'Or so we hope,' said Christina, once again checking her phone. 'Maybe he's gone off the boil, after all. I've been trying all evening to pin him down to time and place for tomorrow, but he hasn't replied.'

Posthumus shifted back slightly in his chair, and suggested another drink. As they were all on wine, he proposed that they get a bottle.

You've turned the last page.

But it doesn't have to end there . . .

If you're looking for more first-class, action-packed, nail-biting suspense, join us at **Facebook.com/MulhollandUncovered** for news, competitions, and behind-the-scenes access to Mulholland Books.

For regular updates about our books and authors as well as what's going on in the world of crime and thrillers, follow us on **Twitter@MulhollandUK**.

There are many more twists to come.

MULHOLLAND:
You never know what's coming around the curve.

HODD